PRAISE FOR *OPERATION WORMWOOD*

"At the heart of this gut-wrenching, savagely realistic novel is a deep theological struggle: why does evil against the most vulnerable go unpunished by a loving, all-powerful God? Escott combines first-hand police experience, superb storytelling, and deep faith in this Dan Brown–style epic."

REV. ROBERT COOKE, RECTOR OF THE PARISH OF ST. MARK THE EVANGELIST AND ADJUNCT PROFESSOR, QUEEN'S COLLEGE FACULTY OF THEOLOGY

"Brilliant! Absolutely brilliant! With skilled, detective-like precision, Escott kept me at the edge of my seat throughout this well-told story of hurt and faith. Filled with a ton of well-researched facts and figures regarding Newfoundland and Labrador's history, criminal investigative processes, and relevant political complications, this novel fills the reader's need for action, suspense, and emotion. This book will make every Newfoundlander and Labradorian reflect on their complicated history and fully intrigue those who come from away. *Operation Wormwood* is wicked . . . simply wicked . . . in every definition of the word."

E. B. MERRILL, S/SGT. (RTD.)
ROYAL CANADIAN MOUNTED POLICE

Operation Wormwood

A Newfoundland and Labrador Crime Thriller

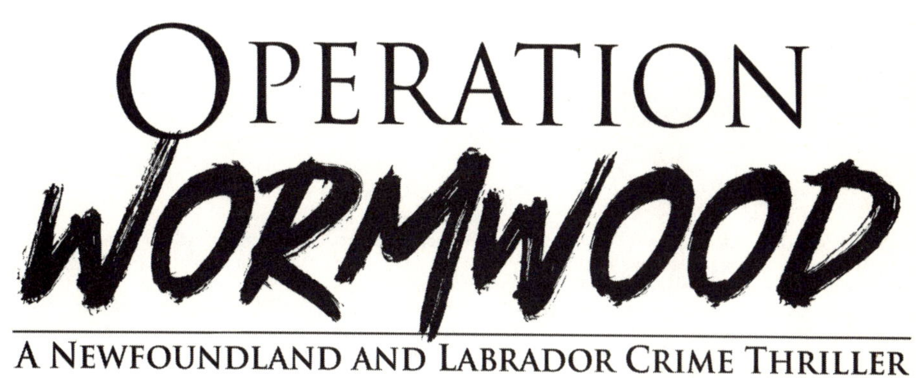

OPERATION WORMWOOD

A NEWFOUNDLAND AND LABRADOR CRIME THRILLER

HELEN C. ESCOTT

FLANKER PRESS LIMITED
ST. JOHN'S

Library and Archives Canada Cataloguing in Publication

Escott, Helen C., 1963-, author
Operation Wormwood : a Newfoundland and Labrador crime thriller / Helen C. Escott.

Issued also in electronic formats.
ISBN 978-1-77117-707-8 (softcover).--ISBN 978-1-77117-708-5 (EPUB).--ISBN 978-1-77117-709-2 (Kindle).--ISBN 978-1-77117-710-8 (PDF)

I. Title.

PS8609.S36 O64 2018 C813'.6 C2018-903512-9
C2018-903513-7

PRINTED IN CANADA

MIX
Paper from responsible sources
FSC® C016245

This paper has been certified to meet the environmental and social standards of the Forest Stewardship Council® (FSC®) and comes from responsibly managed forests, and verified recycled sources.

Cover design by Graham Blair

FLANKER PRESS LTD.
PO BOX 2522, STATION C
ST. JOHN'S, NL
CANADA

TELEPHONE: (709) 739-4477 FAX: (709) 739-4420 TOLL-FREE: 1-866-739-4420

WWW.FLANKERPRESS.COM

9 8 7 6 5 4 3 2

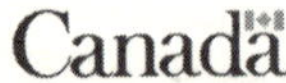

Canada Council for the Arts Conseil des Arts du Canada

We acknowledge the financial support of the Government of Canada through the Canada Book Fund (CBF) and the Government of Newfoundland and Labrador, Department of Tourism, Culture, Industry and Innovation for our publishing activities. We acknowledge the support of the Canada Council for the Arts, which last year invested $157 million to bring the arts to Canadians throughout the country. *Nous remercions le Conseil des arts du Canada de son soutien. L'an dernier, le Conseil a investi 157 millions de dollars pour mettre de l'art dans la vie des Canadiennes et des Canadiens de tout le pays.*

I would never have written this book without the love and support of my husband, Robert—my hero and the real Sgt. Nicholas Myra. Thank you for believing in me long before I believed in myself. I love you forever and always.

It took ten years to write this book, and I always tell our children—Sabrina, Daniel, and Colin: Don't give up on your dreams. My love for our children, and all children, was the reason I wrote this book. You three amazing kids have inspired me to keep going. Thanks for letting me be your mom.

I could not have worked through the issues in this book without the long walks and deep discussions I had with my best friend and faithful companion, Minnie. I saved you . . . then you saved me

It may only be a matter of time before God unleashes a plague upon the earth. — Sister Mary Pius

1

A thick fog hugged the streets of St. John's, the oldest city in North America. The seaport had been surrounded by a bank of fog for three days. The cold, damp air crept into a person's bones, causing a chill that not even a hot cup of tea could thaw. This type of spring weather could last for weeks, causing even the hardiest of Newfoundlanders to curse the damp cold and wonder why they didn't move down south to a warmer climate. It wasn't unusual for a person to develop anything from a common cold to pneumonia this time of year.

The emergency department at the Health Sciences Centre was alive with activity. Charles Horan struggled to carry Patrick Keating through the front doors of the hospital. The elderly Keating was barely able to stand and continuously passed in and out of consciousness. Horan wanted to call an ambulance, but Keating did not want the attention the lights and sirens would bring. The two men could have easily been mistaken for father and son.

The waiting room was standing room only. The thirty-year-old hospital had hardly kept up with the growing population of the province. The once state-of-the-art emergency department was in dire need of simple things like an updated seating area, a lick of paint, and more space. The sniffles and groans of sick people filled the area. The sign on the wall said ESTIMATED WAIT TIME: 4 HOURS. There were three wickets at the front of the room, each with clerks taking basic medical information from patients and determining their level of priority.

Keating's right arm was draped across Horan's shoulders. Horan held the elderly man tight around the waist to keep him from falling as he carefully helped him sit in front of a wicket. Keating's body melted into the chair. The perspiration on his brow was visible, and his mouth sagged as if he was having a stroke. Horan quickly explained that Keating had been sick on and off for over a year. He had a flu that he could not get rid of. He told the nurse he begged the elderly man to go to the doctor, but Keating refused. His symptoms became worse over the past few months. He had an unquenchable thirst but found water bitter and turned his stomach. The thirst was followed by unstoppable nosebleeds. He had lost a considerable amount of weight but attributed this to stress and being overworked. He also had torturous pain throughout his body.

The nurse noted the symptoms and placed a hospital bracelet around Keating's wrist. She prioritized him as urgent but not life-threatening. She brought out a wheelchair and, with Horan's help, lifted Keating onto the padded seat. By this time, Keating was starting to come to and began talking nonsensically. He was unaware of his surroundings, and his speech slurred as he grabbed Horan by the collar and pulled him closer, whispering, "Don't tell them who I am. I don't want the media to get wind of this. I don't want any rumours or panic." Keating was winded and couldn't focus his eyes.

"No, Patrick, don't worry about things like that now. You'll see a doctor soon, and you'll be fine."

Keating's head fell forward, and he passed out again.

Agatha Catania, the emergency department nursing supervisor, didn't care who he was. She was more interested in getting him into triage and assessed. With expert precision from years of crisis medical experience, she took Keating's vital signs. His temperature was 101, his pulse was racing, his respiratory rate was laboured, and his blood pressure was 180 over 95.

She wheeled him into an examination room, and two more nurses assisted her, lifting him onto a bed. "We have to get him into a gown to be examined," she said, and started to unbutton his shirt.

"No, I'll do it." Horan pushed her hands away from Keating's chest. She shoved his hands back.

"I am a nurse, sir."

Horan decided to divulge their secret. "He's the Roman Catholic archbishop for the province, and I'm his assistant. We're both priests. Please, let me do it."

Agatha felt like he was expecting her to bow her head and genuflect at the mention of his title. She was the first person in her Conception Bay family to get a university degree. Her father, a weathered fisherman, broke his back to ensure his only daughter received a good education. He never wanted her to work on the water. Her family had Italian and English roots, but centuries of blending their accent with the local Irish dialect, spoken throughout this island in the cold North Atlantic, left them with a distinctly townie or bayman accent. She was a bayman and a proud Protestant raised in the Church of England but often mistaken for Irish Catholic due to her thick bayman pronunciation of certain words. Four years of university and ten years of working at the biggest hospital in the province could not take the bay out of the girl. Father Horan's assumption that she was a good Catholic girl was more than justified by her words and actions.

Putting this old man into a johnny coat was one less thing she had to do during this busy shift. She moved back to allow Horan to unbutton the shirt. "I'm sorry. Go ahead. The doctor will be in shortly." She walked out of the room, allowing the two men their privacy. By the time Dr. Luke Gillespie entered the examination room, Horan had the archbishop in his hospital gown and a blanket pulled up to his chest. He was mopping his supervisor's brow with a cold face cloth.

"Your friend has a nasty flu, from the looks of this," the doctor surmised while reading the vitals from a clipboard.

"For some time now," Horan informed him.

"Let's have a look." Gillespie took his stethoscope from around his neck and began to listen to Keating's heart and lungs. "How long has he been sick?" he asked as he took the stethoscope out of his ears.

"He's had the flu on and off for a little over a year. He just can't shake it," Horan said. "It started getting worse a couple of months ago. He was tired all the time, and he has lost a considerable amount of weight, maybe twenty to twenty-five pounds, in a short period. He has fevers on and off, and diarrhea."

Gillespie folded his arms and pondered his patient's predicament. "How old is he?"

"He'll be sixty in a month. One more thing," Horan added.

"He has this incredible thirst for water, but every time he drinks it, he throws it up, saying it's bitter and vile." Horan's face showed concern and fear. "He also has uncontrollable nosebleeds. He can bleed for hours. I've never seen anything like it, and he complains of constantly being in pain. Sometimes the pain is so bad he cries, which is unlike him."

The doctor could sense his attachment to this man.

Gillespie tilted the archbishop's head back until his mouth opened and placed a tongue depressor inside. He shone a small penlight into his patient's mouth. He was alarmed to see white spots and a thick coating on his tongue. The doctor threw the tongue depressor in the garbage and felt Keating's lymph nodes in his neck and armpits. They were enlarged.

The archbishop began to come to and broke into a heavy cough. His throat was dry. He could not catch his breath, and his head fell forward. Horan put his arm under the archbishop's shoulders and lifted him to open his airways. Without notice, he broke into a harder cough that came from the pit of his belly. Suddenly, blood spewed from his nose, splattering his chest. He coughed again, and the blood flew through the air. Gillespie instinctively jumped back, but the projectile blood splatter reached him, dotting the top of his scrubs. Keating slid back into a trance. The front of his hospital gown was soaked in his blood. Horan propped up the pillows as the doctor laid him back down.

"I keep him elevated when he is like this so he doesn't choke on his own blood." Horan stared at the doctor as if hoping for an answer.

Nurse Catania, followed by two other nurses, ran into the room, ready to take direction. "I want everyone who comes in here to be wearing latex gloves, masks, and gowns," ordered Dr. Gillespie. "He is quarantined as of right now." The three nurses left and headed toward the supply cabinet to get suited up.

Father Horan was shaking. "Does he really need to be quarantined?"

"It's standard procedure when staff is exposed to blood. You'll have to go to the waiting area." The doctor pointed toward the door.

"Is he going to be all right? I have to notify some people of his situation." Horan took note of the concern on Gillespie's face.

"Call whoever you need. We're going to run some tests now."

Dr. Gillespie felt a sense of panic come over him. He quickly scrubbed the blood off his hands and checked in the mirror to see if any had landed on his face. It was clean. "Thank God for that," he whispered to himself.

Nurse Catania returned, covered in a mask and gown. "Are you all right? What is it?" The look on the doctor's face stopped her in her tracks.

Gillespie hesitated. "I'm okay. I'm thinking of a few possible causes. I can't be sure till I get the tests back." He looked at his patient, who was unconscious in the bed. "I'll write up a requisition for blood and urinalysis. Make sure no one else comes into this room, and keep yourself covered."

"Do you think it's another wave of something like SARS?" Agatha knew she'd have a mountain of paperwork if it was.

Several causes were running through his head. "I'm not sure, but I think it's more serious than the flu." Gillespie looked at the chart again "Who is he? His name and face are familiar."

"Are you Catholic?" Agatha asked.

He looked at her like he didn't understand what language

she was speaking. "I was born Catholic, but I haven't practised in a long time."

"He is the Catholic archbishop for the province. The other gentleman is his assistant."

"I haven't been to church in a long time. He wouldn't be familiar to me. Maybe to my mother," he added as an afterthought. Gillespie shrugged. "I don't care who he is. He's a patient to me. Money and power are no good to anyone in a hospital bed."

* * * * *

It took a few hours to get the X-rays back. Dr. Gillespie stood in the emergency room office examining the test results and looking at the archbishop's results displayed upon the wall when Nurse Catania approached him.

"What does it show?" She stood next to him looking at the screen.

Gillespie shook his head. "I don't know. I've never seen anything like this before."

Nurse Catania picked up the paperwork from his desk and read the results. "He has an infection. That's obvious."

"My gut told me to test for AIDS or HIV," he confessed.

Agatha looked at him with a smirk on her face. "Really?"

He looked away from the X-rays. "The white spots on his tongue and the swollen lymph nodes in his neck and armpits give me concern. I have to go with my gut."

Agatha laid the paperwork down on the desk. "What about a disease similar to SARS?"

"No. Tests are clean for that, too. As a matter of fact, according to all these tests, he is as healthy as a horse. I thought for sure it was going to be tuberculosis, but his lungs are clear." Luke was thinking out loud. "I'm at a loss. I'm really at a loss."

"I just checked on him before coming in here. He's still unconscious, and he hasn't had another bleeding episode yet. So, what now?"

Gillespie was running symptoms and diseases through this mind like a computer searching for information. "He's not fitting into any one disease. It seems like he has bits and pieces of several diseases." A thought popped into his head. "Does his chart say anything about him being a hemophiliac?"

"I don't think so. I'll check." Catania left the room and returned a few minutes later with the archbishop's chart. "No. Nothing about any type of bleeding disorder. Do you want me to test him?"

"Yes. Maybe we'll find a clue there."

Agatha returned to the main nursing station and retrieved the needle and rubber tourniquet to take blood from the archbishop. The nurse at the counter informed her that Father Charles Horan was in the waiting room and wanted to speak to someone.

She put her supplies in her uniform pocket and headed to the waiting area. Horan was pacing in the hallway with a cellphone to his ear, speaking to someone about the archbishop's situation. He said goodbye when he saw Nurse Catania coming toward him.

"Any news?" He was anxious, and his hands were shaking as he tried to put the cellphone into the holster on his belt.

"Not yet. We're running tests. Can you think of anything that may be causing this?"

Horan shook his head. "He was always healthy and active

up until a little over a year ago. He caught the flu and couldn't shake it. He would often complain of pain, saying he thought every nerve in his body was on fire." He shoved his hands in his pants pocket and looked worriedly toward the ceiling.

Nurse Catania wasn't sure if he was looking for answers or divine intervention. She noticed how young this priest was—he couldn't be more than twenty-five. Yet the lines around his eyes made him look much older. He seemed too young to have the responsibility of caring for the head of the church in this province.

"I have seen similar symptoms in a few other priests, but not as severe as the archbishop's," Horan confessed.

"You told us when you came in that no one else around him had these symptoms," the nurse reminded him.

"Not as severe as his. The rectory is old. It's not unusual to hear people complaining about the cold and damp in the rooms. It's easy to catch a flu there, but no one has been as violently ill as the archbishop."

Father Horan loved the historical structure of the rectory but knew it had to be brought up to code in many areas. The rectory was built behind the Basilica of St. John the Baptist. Its construction began after the basilica was finished around 1855. The entire Catholic compound was constructed using limestone and granite imported from Galway and Dublin, Ireland, as well as bricks from Hamburg, and local sandstone quarried from St. John's and Kelly's Island in Conception Bay, giving the buildings their characteristic grey colour. They are located on the highest ridge overlooking the city of St. John's facing toward the Narrows surrounding St. John's harbour. They were purposely built that way to greet fishing vessels entering through the Narrows. The first things the sailors would see were the largest church buildings in North America at that time. Much of the church and rectory remained the same as when it was built, except for the wiring. The cost of upkeep was staggering. The heat alone cost a king's ransom. Declared heritage buildings, they had to stay true to their history, thus drafty windows and cold stone walls kept their residents in a constant state of freezing temperatures, even when it was hot outside.

"What about you? Do you spend a lot of time with him?" Agatha queried.

"I've known him forever. He was the priest at my orphanage when I was a boy." Horan turned to face her. "He's the reason I became a priest. After I was ordained, I transferred back to his office to work with him. When he became archbishop, he chose me as his assistant," he ended proudly.

"So, you're like father and son?" The question came out of her mouth before she could stop it. She never understood the Catholic hierarchy but knew it was inappropriate as soon as she asked it.

Father Charles Horan's face took on a look of smug authority. "I am his assistant. This is not a father-son relationship. We are priests."

Nurse Catania had a feeling that he had answered this question before, maybe many times. She tried to cover her embarrassment by saying, "I need to know his next of kin for his record. He has your name listed, but does he have family who should be making decisions for him?"

"He doesn't have family other than the church." Agatha knew he was lying but didn't know why.

"Okay, well, he has you listed, so I will let you know if anything changes."

Agatha turned and walked back into the emergency unit. She never looked back at Father Horan but could feel he was watching her. She felt like a schoolgirl who had just been disciplined for talking back. Suddenly, the hair on the back of her neck stood up, and goosebumps formed on her arms. She felt cold and decided that, although Father Horan may be a man of God, he gave her the creeps.

* * * * *

Archbishop Patrick Keating was peaceful in his bed when she entered his room. Agatha turned his arm over, tied the rubber tourniquet around his forearm, inserted a needle into his vein, and proceeded to draw blood. She had just finished when he opened his eyes and looked up at her. "I'm taking your blood so we can run some tests to find out what is wrong with you." Her voice was soothing. She was used to calming people down in the emergency area.

"I am so thirsty." His lips were pasty and stuck together. He could barely get the words out.

"I can't give you any water just yet, but I'll get some ice chips. They will give you some relief." Agatha called out to a nurse who was walking by and asked her to bring ice chips for the archbishop. She returned with a Styrofoam cup full and a small stick with a sponge on the end to help wet his lips.

Agatha wet the sponge and rubbed it along the archbishop's lips until they were moistened. At first he seemed relieved, then he licked his lips and began to gag.

"You've put vinegar on my lips!" He tried to spit the water out and wiped his lips with his sleeve. "You cursed woman, where is Charles?" He changed from peaceful to difficult in a matter of seconds. Agatha felt the same air of superiority that Horan had exuded.

They're certainly cut from the same cloth, she thought. "It's ice chips. They'll make you feel better." She tried to calm him down.

"It tastes bitter, like vinegar."

She felt like a servant who had done wrong. "Here, try the sponge yourself. It's soaked in cold water. You can suck on it like a lollipop." She took the sponge out of the cup and handed it to him.

The archbishop put it between his lips and spat it out, coughing and sputtering. "It's vile, woman. Get me some water," he ordered her.

"This is water." Agatha wasn't afraid to talk back to him

He hit her hand, and the cup full of ice landed on the floor. "Get me Charles."

She stood back from the bed, collected her blood vials, and turned to walk away. When she got to the door, she turned toward him. "You're quarantined. No visitors." She placed the vials in the collection tray and thought to herself, *I'm not Catholic. He can go to hell, for all I care.*

2

The radio alarm clock went off at 5:00 a.m. Music blared through the condo, but Dr. Luke Gillespie was already in the shower, warm water rushing over his body. He stood there for a long time, thinking.

His mind was running through every possible disease known to man. He started at A and ran through to Z, then started over again. He couldn't connect the archbishop's symptoms to anything he had dealt with before. He tilted his head back to feel the water on his face, thinking, *What am I missing? Help me find an answer.*

His eyes flashed open when he realized that he was praying.

"Praying," he exclaimed. "I haven't prayed in years. Doctors don't pray, they investigate and find answers," he told himself.

Gillespie was a man of science, not prayer.

Over the years, he had watched families pray and cry, and cry and pray for diseases to be cured, hearts to grow stronger, and life to last longer. Sometimes it worked, sometimes it didn't. It was a crapshoot, really, he finally concluded. Did the dedicated prayers of one family bring an eighty-five-year-old woman back from a massive heart attack? Or did the eight-year-old girl he had once treated for childhood leukemia die because her parents didn't pray enough?

He didn't believe in things he couldn't see. Science made sense to him. God didn't. He wouldn't pray for an answer. He would find one on his own. By the time he arrived at the hospital, the archbishop had been moved to the intensive care unit on the fifth floor. Nurse Agatha Catania had just started her shift.

"They moved him to the ICU just before I ended my shift last night." She saw him searching through the charts on the front desk in the emergency department and knew instantly what he was looking for. "The test came back negative for hemophilia, too," she told him.

Dr. Gillespie was a good doctor. She had worked with him for years. He was dedicated to his patients, but more importantly, he respected the nurses and often asked for their opinion. Not many doctors were willing to take advice from a nurse. Some would rather be wrong than ask for help. Gillespie knew nurses practised medicine on the front line. He understood that some knew more than doctors. He also understood that Agatha Catania was one of those nurses.

"Did he get worse?" He turned around to face her.

"He's lost a lot of blood. I've never seen anything like it. I thought we had him calmed down for the night, then he started bleeding from the nose like a geyser. We couldn't stop it. Luke . . ." She came closer to him and whispered, "It was quite scary. I walked into the room and he was lying there like he was dead, and the blood was just flowing. His gown was covered. I had to feel his pulse to see if he was still alive." She shivered as the picture came back into her mind. "While I was standing over him, it felt like someone was breathing cold air down my neck."

"You're an Anglican, that's all," he joked. "It gives you the willies to stand next to a Catholic archbishop." But Dr. Gillespie knew what she was talking about. There was something about this guy that gave him the same feeling.

* * * * *

Dr. Gillespie took the elevator to the ICU on the fifth floor and used his security pass to let himself in. Three nurses were gathered around the main desk talking and looking through files. They all looked up when the doctor walked in.

"Good morning, everyone," he greeted them.

They all smiled back and exchanged greetings, followed by a rundown of every patient in the unit.

He picked up Archbishop Keating's file and began to look through it.

"He had a blood transfusion this morning," the supervising nurse said as she brought him up to speed. "The doctor who was on last night ordered it. The archbishop was losing so much blood he had no choice."

"Thank you." Gillespie walked over to Keating's room. There was a man standing outside looking at the archbishop through the observation window. He was a big man. His arms were folded, and he was wearing hospital greens. As Gillespie got closer, he could see the man's eyes were red and tears were rolling down his cheeks. He looked like he was deep in thought. When he saw the doctor, the visitor quickly wiped his face with his hands and began to walk away.

"Do you know him?" asked Gillespie.

The man turned around, embarrassed by his emotional state. He nodded yes, took a deep breath, and exhaled in a broken sigh.

"Well, we're trying to find out what is making him so sick and why he has these nosebleeds. Does he have a history of them?"

"I don't know," the big man stammered. "I don't know him that well." He stuttered as he corrected himself. "I knew him years ago. He was a priest at my school." He was shuffling his feet like a trapped rat trying to get away.

Gillespie's interest was piqued. "What unit do you work on? What's your name?"

"Jermaine. Jermaine Cousin. I work in the radiology department. I heard he was here." He hung his head and whispered, "I just wanted to see him."

The doctor had dealt with religious devotees before and knew he had to wear kid gloves when handling them. "I understand. He's your archbishop. I'll make sure he gets the best care." As an afterthought, he added, "Maybe you can say a prayer for him." Luke didn't know where that last sentence came from. He had never uttered those words before.

Jermaine turned to leave. "I've said a lot of prayers for him over the years." Then he disappeared down the hallway.

What an odd thing to say, Gillespie thought as he pushed open the door to the archbishop's room and walked in.

The archbishop was resting peacefully. Someone had put prayer beads in his hands. The nurses had cleaned him up, and he was wearing a fresh hospital gown. There was no trace of blood. Gillespie continued to read through the archbishop's overnight report while standing over his bed. He caught something moving out of the corner of his eye and turned in fright to see a nun sitting on a chair in the corner of the room. She was deep in prayer with her own rosary beads and slowly rocked back and forth while she prayed.

Dr. Gillespie hadn't noticed her when he first walked in the room. She was dressed in the old-fashioned, black and white religious habit that hung to the floor and had the full veil over the back of her head. He had not seen a nun wear the old-fashioned garb in years. He guessed from the tuft of white hair that formed a bang over her forehead that she was in her seventies. He didn't disturb her, because he had dealt with nuns before.

Luke had gone to an all-boy Catholic school run by Christian Brothers. Nuns would visit from time to time to help with Mass or around the office. The boys would jokingly say they looked like penguins and didn't have any feet. The boys would poke their heads out around the classroom door to watch the nuns walk through the school halls. Nuns never walked, they believed—they glided through the halls. No one ever saw their feet. Luke thought they always looked mad, and this nun was no different.

She probably still has a three-foot wooden ruler under that tunic, he thought. *One false move and I could get whipped across the hands*, he thought, then laughed to himself.

Dr. Gillespie tried to leave the room as quietly as possible. He didn't want to disturb her.

"Are you his doctor?"

Her deep voice startled him. He almost dropped the file.

"I am Dr. Luke Gillespie." He reached his hand out to shake hers. She stood up, extending her thin cold hand toward him. Her black tunic reached down to the floor. He was right. Nuns did not have feet. "I treated the archbishop when he came in last night. I'll be his doctor today." Nuns still made him nervous, he discovered.

"I am Sister Pius. I work in the rectory for the archbishop."

Something told Gillespie she was more than a worker in the rectory. She had an air of authority about her, and she was no stranger to giving orders.

"Do you know why his nose bleeds like that?" she asked, like she already knew the answer and was testing him. He felt like a ten-year-old schoolboy being put on the spot by the teacher.

"No, I don't. I'm trying to find out." He studied her face, waiting for the answer.

"He has these bleeds daily, sometimes hourly," she said, approaching the bed and smoothing out the hospital gown over the archbishop's chest.

She is probably like a maid to him or something, Luke thought. Remembering he was the head of the church, she would expect the utmost respect. He added, "If he bleeds again, the nurses will take care of changing the gown as soon as possible. They'll make sure he's kept clean."

"They have washed their robes and made them white in the blood of the lamb." Her statement was loud, direct, and confusing. "His blood is a stain upon the Church." She walked toward the window facing the busy street.

Not knowing what she was talking about, but suspecting the Church wouldn't want its parishioners to know the medical details of their archbishop, the doctor said, "The hospital does not give out any patient's medical information without consent from the patient."

The archbishop began to groan in pain, but his eyes didn't open.

"I'll ask the nurse to give him some more morphine. His chart says he was in a lot of pain all night. He must be feeling it again." Gillespie felt the lymph nodes in the archbishop's neck.

"He has been through great tribulation, but only he has the answer to stop the pain," the nun added. Gillespie wasn't sure why, but he sensed she didn't like the archbishop and suspected she was enjoying his pain.

The man's nose began to bleed like someone had turned on a tap. The thick red blood ran over his lips and down his neck, pooling at the top of his chest on his blue hospital gown. It happened so quickly they were both startled. The archbishop moaned again in pain.

Gillespie grabbed a towel that was hung by the sink in the room. He tilted the archbishop's head back and placed the towel over his nose, squeezing his nostrils together to stop the bleeding. The nun took a step back from the bed like she had seen something that frightened her to the core. Her eyes were wide, and both her hands covered her mouth.

The blood stopped flowing, and Archbishop Keating slumped over in the bed. Gillespie pressed the button on the side to tilt the bed up and keep the patient's head elevated. He didn't want him to choke on his own blood.

"Well, I guess he is washed in the blood of the lamb now," Gillespie said, smirking at Sister Pius, but she didn't react. *Maybe that comment was inappropriate*, he thought.

He was surprised when she didn't try to clean the blood off the archbishop's face. Maybe Luke touching him was making her irritable. He picked up another clean towel and handed it to her, but she put her hands behind her back.

"I don't want to touch him now," she said. "Let the nurses clean him."

He must be hard to work for, Gillespie thought. He tried to make peace with her. "Maybe his time in hospital will make him easier to get along with. Being close to death sometimes makes a person a better human being."

"Sickness and death seldom change a man's heart. They don't change a man's desires."

Gillespie suspected they were both talking about different subjects, and he had no idea what she was talking about.

"Why does his nose bleed like that?" he asked her with great interest.

"Whatever a man sows, he shall also reap."

This woman was like the riddle of the sphinx, Luke thought. "You know what's wrong with him, don't you?" He became accusatory toward Sister Pius. He knew she was holding something back.

"Jesus said He would wash us from our sins in His own blood. The blood of the lamb."

"If you think he has sinned, why were you praying for his recovery when I came in?" He was surprised at how angry his question sounded.

"I wasn't praying for his recovery. I was praying for his soul." Sister Pius let the words slip from her tongue before she could stop them.

* * * * *

What had she done? Sister Pius knew why the archbishop's nose bled like it did. The same reason several other priests in that rectory had nosebleeds. It had nothing to do with the cold dampness in the air of the building. It had everything to do with the cold dampness in the hearts and souls of these men. *Keating and his private club*, she thought to herself. She knew what went on now. Years ago, she'd had no idea. She knew the boys feared him, but he was known for his use of the leather strap. All she could do was help the boys after their visits with him when they cried or turned to aggressive behaviour in the classroom. Sister Pius never understood why so many parents allowed their children to go on camping trips with these grown men. On Monday morning she could tell who had been victimized from the looks on their faces and their demeanour. Well, she didn't know then, but it wasn't long until she figured it out.

Why does his nose bleed? she thought to herself. *Because he will be washed in the blood of the lamb until he confesses his sins.*

"I get the feeling you don't like him," Dr. Gillespie stated. "You know it's not easy being at the top," he said, trying to joke with her again. Maybe she was jealous of the archbishop's power. Women had no power in the Catholic Church.

"Every man thinks he is tried more than his neighbour," she shot back. "Some deserve it."

3

Quidi Vidi Lake is located at the east end of the city of St. John's and is home to the longest-running sporting event in North America: the annual Royal St. John's Regatta. It is a fixed-seat rowing race that draws thousands to the banks of the pond on the first Wednesday in August. This holiday is unique to St. John's and the only one of its kind in the world.

On the north side of the lake stands the historic former American Pepperrell Air Force Base. Its name had been changed some time ago to Canadian Forces Station St. John's. Few people in the city call it by its new name. From the air, you can see that the outline of the base forms the shape of a cowboy hat. It was designed by an engineer from Texas. During World War II, the base housed and employed thousands of American service-men and their families. Today, most of the old infrastructure has been demolished and replaced with brightly coloured town-houses and a new Canadian Forces headquarters. One of the last remaining buildings is the old Royal Canadian Legion Branch 56. It stands as sentry over its former commander.

Dr. Luke Gillespie ran past the Legion's memorial, deep in thought. *There is more going on here than meets the eye*, he thought as he ran the dirt trail around Quidi Vidi Lake. This 3.8-kilometre leg of the St. John's grand concourse always cleared his mind.

He had his best ideas when he was running, but this morning his head was foggy. He knew Sister Pius wasn't telling him the whole story. *Praying for his soul*, she had said. *What does that mean?* It wasn't his soul that was bleeding. Or was it? What did she know?

He ran past the boathouse. The early-morning rowers were pushing their shells into the water and gliding toward the start line. Several were already at the stakes, each practising beating the record-breaking time of 8:58:20 rowed by Outer Cove two years before. The fog was sitting lightly on top of the pond, and the water was as still as glass.

Luke picked up his speed and began to sprint toward the top of the lake. He could hear the coxswain yell his orders out to the boat crew. He turned his head to see them cutting through the lake like a bullet through water. He drew from his full strength and tried to race the historic shell, but he was no match for a six-man crew who could row 3,200 metres in less than nine minutes.

By the time he got to the top of the lake, his lungs were heaving and felt like they had collapsed. He bent over, placing his hands on his knees, trying to draw in deep breaths. Sweat ran down his forehead, burning his eyes. His morning coffee was back in his throat, then in his mouth and on the pavement. He staggered to his car, opened the trunk, took a towel out of his gym bag, and wiped the sweat and puke from his face.

"What just happened?" he asked himself out loud. He had pushed himself too hard. He wasn't as young as he used to be. The long hours in the hospital and lack of sleep were catching up with him. Making him feel older than he really was. He drove back to his condo thinking about Sister Pius. From all appearances, she looked humble and wholesome, but she had a layer underneath that she hid. *A layer of hate*, he thought. He could feel it when she spoke. This was a woman scorned, but by whom? He didn't know.

* * * * *

Gillespie started his shift in the ICU, and Nurse Agatha Catania was already waiting for him at the front desk with the archbishop's file in her hand. "The tests are all back." She handed him the file. He flipped it open as she continued talking.

"So, if a patient was losing weight for an unknown reason, had night sweats, fever, fatigue, enlarged and swollen lymph nodes, chronic diarrhea, unusual white spots in his mouth and dark spots that appeared all over his body for unknown reasons, what would you say he had?" She was out of breath.

"I know where you're going with this, but these symptoms are similar to those of many illnesses. It's not HIV." He had already thought of that. The archbishop was a celibate man, and he didn't fit the description of a drug user. Gillespie had still ordered the HIV antibody test, p24 antigen test, and PCR test.

"But they came back 'indeterminate.'" She pointed to the red writing on the chart.

"Indeterminate could mean anything," said Gillespie. "It may be from the blood transfusions he had over the past few days. He could have lupus or diabetes. Or it could be a problem with the test itself." He continued to speed-read through the file.

"Or he could have syphilis," she said with a wry grin. "They ran the tests three times. Each time it came back 'indeterminate.' I have more news," she teased.

He looked up from the file and straight into her eyes. "Well?"

"There's another one in the emergency on the way up. A sixty-one-year-old male with the same symptoms. A real bleeder with an unquenchable thirst."

"Is he a priest?" Gillespie inquired.

"Nope. Child psychiatrist." She smirked.

Gillespie let out a great sigh and closed the archbishop's file. It was then he noticed that the X-ray technician was standing outside the archbishop's room again, looking in through the window. "He has a visitor?" Gillespie nodded toward the man.

"Yes." Agatha turned around quickly. "But not him. There's a guy inside the room."

"Why? Is he family? Only family should be allowed in now." Luke kept his eye on the X-ray technician so he didn't sneak out.

"The archbishop seemed to know him."

Gillespie put the file under his arm and decided to deal with the X-ray tech first. "Cousin, isn't it?"

The man turned around. "Yes. Jermaine, please." He shook the doctor's hand.

"Not much has changed since your last visit. We still don't know what's going on with Archbishop Keating, but we're working on it." Gillespie looked closely at him. His eyes were red and his face was white, drained of blood like he saw a ghost. "Are you okay?"

"Yes. I'm fine." Cousin's voice was shaking. He turned to walk away.

"Sister Pius was here." Gillespie wasn't sure what kind of reaction he expected, but Cousin turned around and a smile came across his lips.

"She's a good woman," he said. "Stern, but a good person. Don't let her crusty exterior fool you."

"So, you know her?" asked Gillespie.

"She was the principal at my school. She was a tough bird, but fair," Cousin replied.

"A tough but fair penguin?" Gillespie added.

Cousin laughed. "You went to Catholic school, too?"

"Oh, yes. I know what nuns are like. I've felt their strap more than once."

"Sister Pius wasn't like that. She didn't hurt the kids. She protected them. She'd face the devil himself, and often did." He looked through the window at Archbishop Patrick Keating, who was sitting up in the bed and talking to his visitor.

What an odd thing to say, Gillespie thought. *Not a lot of people like this archbishop*. "Is he the devil himself?" The doctor looked at the priest through the glass.

He was startled when Cousin answered him. "He's one of them." Cousin's pager went off, and he took it out of his pocket. "Duty calls." He turned and walked away.

Gillespie wanted to talk more but didn't know what to say. *There is more than meets the eye to this archbishop*, he thought. He pushed the door open and walked into the patient's room.

Keating was sitting up with his head turned toward the window that faced the parkway separating the Health Sciences Complex from Memorial University. He looked perturbed.

His visitor sat in a chair at the foot of his bed. It looked like the chair was two sizes too small. Luke guessed he had to be over six feet tall. His hands were as big as a boxer's. When Gillespie came into the room, he looked up at him.

"You have a visitor?" Dr. Gillespie acknowledged the archbishop's guest.

Archbishop Patrick Keating put a sour look on his face and folded his arms in defiance.

"I am Nicholas Myra." The guest rose and shook the doctor's hand.

"You're a police officer?" Gillespie asked.

"Is it that obvious?"

It was that obvious. From his thick moustache to the deep lines around his eyes, it was easy to tell that Nicholas Myra was a cop. "Are you family? The archbishop is a very sick man. I just lifted the quarantine," Gillespie informed him.

"We're having a chat." Sgt. Myra put a small black leather notebook in his coat pocket.

"I hope the archbishop hasn't been a victim of a crime?" Gillespie was curious now.

"He's trying to crucify me!" exclaimed the archbishop. Spittle sprayed from his mouth as he shouted.

"Now, now. Don't play the martyr, Patrick. It won't work on me." Myra had obviously talked to this man before.

The archbishop turned his head toward the police officer. His face was red with anger. "Who do you think you are? Talking to *me* like that! I am the head of the Church in this province, and I answer to no one," he screamed.

Myra shot back, "He may have created you in His image, but that does not mean you are His equal."

"One call. One call . . ." The archbishop pointed his index

finger at Sgt. Myra. ". . . and you'll be walking the beat downtown."

"Those days are gone," Myra informed him. "There's no sweeping this under the rug anymore."

"Sweeping what under the rug?" the archbishop yelled, looking toward Gillespie, who was standing with his mouth open, caught in the crossfire. "I was helping those boys. You don't know how promiscuous they were with each other, with strangers. It was the only way to calm them down."

"Is that how you justified it?" Myra asked.

"It was how we calmed them down. Kept them under control." The archbishop was exasperated.

"Kept them intimidated and scared," Myra added to the archbishop's sentence.

"Hang on a second here," Gillespie jumped in, turning on Myra. "This is my patient. You can't do this."

"He agreed to speak to me," said Myra, standing up to his full height.

"Outside," Dr. Gillespie ordered. Both men left the room, shaking in anger.

"What are you doing?" Gillespie asked as soon as the door to the archbishop's room closed.

"Conducting an investigation. He consented to it."

"In an ICU room?" The doctor was pissed now.

"We started in his office a few weeks ago, then the police station. I am just finishing my file now."

"Are you charging him with something?" Gillespie asked.

"Yes," Myra said. "The formal charges will be laid shortly."

Gillespie was stunned. "He's the archbishop, for God's sake. How could he be anything but innocent?"

"All men are innocent till proven guilty in a court of law." Myra was sick of the privileges that were bestowed upon the archbishop. "But Doctor, I don't charge innocent men."

Nurse Catania had just finished getting her new patient settled when she heard the commotion in the hallway. She peeked out to see Dr. Gillespie and the police officer, both looking frustrated.

"The new patient is here," she interrupted.

Dr. Gillespie turned toward her. He ran his fingers through his hair.

"I am a little stressed." Sgt. Myra changed his voice to a softer tone. "There are fifteen victims. All who were young boys. All with the same story."

Gillespie believed he knew what that story was by now. More so than he wanted to. "He's still my patient."

Myra's cellphone rang, and he turned to answer it. Gillespie took the file from Agatha and began to read.

"He's sleeping now," she told him. "Fifty-three-year-old male, unbearable pain, uncontrollable bleeding, and unquenchable thirst. The exact same symptoms."

Doctor Gillespie stood in front of the new patient's open door. "Well, the first thing we do is try to find a common ground between our two patients. Did they work together? Did they visit the same place? Are they related? Do they even know one another?" Gillespie was at the beginning of his shift but already felt exhausted.

"They know me."

Gillespie and Catania jumped at the voice coming from behind them. Myra was putting his cell back in his pocket.

"They do?" Gillespie asked.

“They both know me quite well.” Myra stood about seven inches taller than Gillespie, and the doctor hated that he had to look up at him.

“So, the only thing these two men have in common is you.” He was shocked by the sound of his own voice.

“No. The only thing these two men have in common is that they are both part of a police investigation.” He straightened his coat and walked toward the exit. He pulled a business card from his jacket pocket and handed it to the doctor.

Gillespie watched him leave, then read the card. SGT. NICHOLAS MYRA, CHILD EXPLOITATION UNIT, ROYAL NEWFOUNDLAND CONSTABULARY. He felt sick in the pit of his stomach.

4

The whistle of the kettle boiling startled him. Dr. Gillespie realized he had nodded off while standing up making his tea. He poured hot water over the Tetley Tea bag in the porcelain cup, squeezing the tea bag to turn the liquid a dark red. He threw the bag in the garbage and poured in some tinned milk and sugar. This would calm his nerves. What a night it had been. Before he had a chance to think about what Sgt. Myra had told him, the new patient had gone into convulsions. Blood had flowed from his nose like a river, and he screamed out in pain and begged for water but spat it out, complaining it was vinegar. It was the archbishop's symptoms all over again, but what was the cause?

Gillespie stirred his tea. He was tired. He was an hour away from ending his twelve-hour shift, and he wanted to go home to sleep. He was drained, and it showed in his face. He was beginning to doze off again while sitting and holding his tea when his pager went off. He jolted awake and pulled it from his pocket. EMERGENCY ROOM, it read. He staggered to his feet and put his hot tea in the sink. As he hurried past the ICU desk, Agatha was running toward him.

"Another one!" Nurse Catania shouted, running to meet him as he hurried past the ICU desk. "In emergency. They want you down there now."

Dr. Gillespie picked up speed as he left the ICU. By the time he reached the elevator, he was in a full jog.

The commotion in the emergency department was familiar to him. He could hear a man's screams as he approached the room. The staff were already dealing with blood spraying over them. The white sheets covering the patient were red. He was sitting up and screaming, "Give me something for pain!" His face was distorted with agony, but his eyes were familiar. Even through the blood and the torment, Dr. Gillespie recognized this patient's face. John Duffy, the stepfather of his best friend from childhood.

A cold feeling came over his whole body. He walked toward the bed, but Mr. Duffy didn't recognize him. "The doctor, finally!" gasped Mr. Duffy. "Thank God you're here. These idiots don't know what they're doing," he complained, blood still dripping from his nose. "I asked for water and they gave me vinegar. I'm in incredible pain." He was holding a Styrofoam cup full of ice chips. Without notice, he threw it in the face of the nearest nurse. She jumped back and shrieked with a fright.

"Calm down!" Gillespie hadn't mean to shout so loud. The nurse grabbed a towel and dried her face as she walked out of the room. Luke could tell this was the last straw for her.

Duffy reached up and, with an extraordinary amount of strength, grabbed Luke by the front of his green scrubs. Grinding his teeth together in rage, Duffy informed him, “I am a very rich man. I have very important friends. You tell them bitches to show me some respect.” With each word, his blood sprayed over Dr. Gillespie’s face.

Luke grabbed Duffy’s wrist and pushed him away. He hated this man. He hated his arrogance and sense of entitlement. He hated what he knew about him. Most of all, he hated what this monster had done to his friend and how he had gotten away with it.

“You’ll get the care you’re entitled to,” Gillespie informed him. With that, Duffy gave a long, loud, piercing cry. He slumped down in the bed, his body went limp, his bottom lip drooped to one side, and a stream of blood flowed from his nostril.

“Bastard!” The nurse came back into the room, her hair still wet from the water. “What a bastard he is. Who the hell is he, anyway?”

“He’s a businessman. Very old money.” Luke looked at Duffy lying in the bed. “Did he come in with anyone?”

“No. He came by ambulance. There’s a family member in the lobby now waiting to talk to someone,” she informed him. “Do you want me to hook him up on a morphine drip?”

“No. Don’t do that.”

The nurse gave him a questioning stare.

“Morphine may make him throw up. Let’s wait. It may cause him to choke if he has another nosebleed at the same time.” Luke pulled the top of his scrubs out to survey the blood spray. They had escaped the bloodbath. His outfit was clean.

The nurse obeyed the doctor’s orders. “Don’t forget the family member in the lobby,” she reminded him.

“I’ll take it.” He picked up a face cloth from a shelf over the sink and ran warm water over it. The doctor looked in the mirror and was sickened by the spray of blood on his face. He scrubbed it off and threw the cloth in the garbage. Luke made himself as presentable as a doctor could while working twelve-hour shifts and walked into the lobby.

"Luke!" A familiar voice came from the crowd. Within seconds a big, rough-looking, burly lumberjack of a man came barrelling toward him. "Luke!" he called again.

A smile came across the doctor's face as he recognized his old friend. "Jack!" He reached out his hand to greet him, but he was already in a bear hug and lifted a foot off the ground.

"Put me down, you maniac," Luke laughed. Jack planted a big, wet kiss on his face and dropped him to the floor. Luke almost lost his balance, and they both laughed like schoolboys.

Then the awkward silence hit. Jack began. "The old lady made me come here. It wasn't my choice."

Luke could still see the hurt in his friend's eyes. Jack had had so much potential as a child until that monster got to him. He knew Jack could tell what he was thinking, and he cleared his throat uncomfortably.

"He's not well. I just got here, so I don't know what's wrong with him yet. But I can tell you he is the third one in two days with the same symptoms. I am starting to think it's an epidemic. Has he had the bleeding and pain for long?"

"For months," Jack told him. "Mom said the pain is excruciating, and he suffers with it almost every day." Jack grabbed his arm. "Let's go outside for a smoke."

Luke noticed that the waiting room was full, and all eyes were on them. "Sure."

The night air was cold, and they could see their breath. Luke and Jack were the only two standing in the designated smoking area. Jack put a cigarette in his mouth and pointed the open pack toward Luke. "Smoke?" he offered.

"Not in years," Luke replied.

"I suppose you can't have a doctor smelling like smoke anymore," Jack chuckled. "You've done some good, Luke. I'm some proud of you."

Luke knew in his heart Jack truly meant that. "I wouldn't have made it out of school without you, Jack. You always had my back."

Under the street light shining above, Luke could see Jack's face clearer now. He could remember him perfectly as a young boy attending Catholic school. Jack had struggled in school, but he had been as big as a bear. Luke had been smart, but small, and always the subject of the class bully. Until one day when Jack had put the bully up against a locker and told him to leave Luke alone. No one had bullied Luke again after that. Not with Jack around. Luke had followed him around like a puppy after that. They became the odd couple: Luke with his slight build and nerdy glasses, and Jack like a bull in a china shop scrapping through school.

Jack had lived with his mother downtown, far away from Luke's beautiful white house with its manicured lawn. Jack and his mom didn't have much, but they had each other. Luke remembered going to their small, old house with the worn furniture. Mrs. McGraw didn't use plastic covers to protect her couches like Luke's mother did, and she made the best Rice Krispies squares in the world. Luke would often go home with Jack after school to help him with homework. Mrs. McGraw always had a fresh batch of Rice Krispies squares on the table, waiting.

He envied their relationship back then. Mrs. McGraw wasn't anything like Luke's mother. Her nails were never painted, and she didn't wear makeup. She kept her hair in a bun on top of her head. Not like Luke's mom, who lived at the beauty parlour, constantly running late for manicure and hair appointments. She hadn't even known what a Rice Krispies square was. If she did, she would have asked the housekeeper to make them. It wasn't the same.

"Your mind's wandering," said Jack, startling Luke from his thoughts.

"I'm tired. This is the last hour of my twelve-hour shift. It's been a long, long night," Luke confessed.

"You're wondering why I am here?" Jack huffed through a cloud of cigarette smoke.

"That's your business," Luke answered.

"She made me come. You know I can't say no to her." Jack took a long inhale from his cigarette and blew it out with a sigh. "Every time she calls, I still hope she is going to tell me she's leaving him, but she never does." Jack couldn't hide his hurt, even now. "I can't stop loving her." Tears filled his eyes. "She's my mother, or she's the shell my mother lives in. I miss her." His voice trembled, and he caught himself before a tear fell.

Luke knew Jack was forever frozen as the young boy who lost his mother and his innocence. "I know." He wasn't sure if he should put his arms around Jack to comfort him or not. Luke remembered that he never knew how Jack was going to take being touched. Sometimes he would break down crying, and sometimes he would beat you to a pulp.

He remembered the first time he saw Jack cry. They were on their way home from school, but the route was different than normal. Jack was getting on the same bus with Luke now. His mother had met a wonderful man, Mr. John Duffy, a well-known local businessman. His mother used to clean his building downtown. He had taken an interest in her, constantly asking about her life and her son. At first she was too shy to talk to him, but he was friendly and eventually got the story out of her. She told him all about Jack, how he was big for his age but a little slow. How his father had left after the boy was born. How her family had turned against her for getting pregnant out of wedlock. She couldn't believe it when he asked her out. She told him she didn't own a dress or shoes good enough to go to a fancy restaurant, so he bought them for her. A beautiful red dress and black patent leather high heels.

Jack was beaming the next day when he came to school and told Luke how beautiful his mother looked. He was captivated by the gentleman's big white Cadillac, and he laughed describing how the neighbours peeked out of their windows and watched his mother getting into the brand new shiny car. On their second date, Mr. Duffy gave Jack a leather baseball glove and ball. It was the first time an adult male had been kind to Jack. Duffy spoke to him like an adult. Telling him how he admired the way Jack took care of his mother and was the man of the house.

Within weeks his mother was showing off her big diamond engagement ring. Shortly after, they became a family and moved two streets away from Luke's house. At first everything was great. Jack loved the attention of his new dad. His room was full of toys and games he hadn't even known existed. His new dad insisted on treating him like a man, even giving him alcohol when his mother wasn't around. His mother was going for weekly visits at the beauty salon now, too. Getting her nails and hair done by professionals. Her clothes were all new. She didn't make Rice Krispies squares anymore. No more cleaning offices for her. Jack and his mother were living the Cinderella dream life.

Luke's mother wasn't happy about it at all. At first, Luke thought she was jealous. She didn't want her son going over to Jack's house anymore. She told him to stay away from Mr. Duffy, but she wouldn't say why. Luke didn't tell her about the alcohol, because he knew she would throw a fit and stop their friendship altogether. He couldn't understand why she didn't want him to be friends with Jack just because he moved to their neighbourhood.

Then one day Luke noticed Jack crying on the school bus. He wasn't sure at first. Jack was sitting next to the window on their shared seat. Luke was going on about the new hockey cards he had bought over the weekend. Jack was quiet, gazing out the window. Luke saw his reflection in the glass and noticed tears running down his cheeks.

"Jack?" Luke pulled at the arm of his coat. "Are you okay?"

Jack hugged his arms around himself even tighter, burying his face in his jacket. His body began to heave slightly as he tried to suppress his tears.

"What happened? Are you okay?" Luke didn't understand.

Twelve-year-old boys didn't cry on school buses for no reason. And Jack didn't cry at all. Luke had noticed Jack was changing. Jack wasn't as happy-go-lucky as he used to be. He wasn't smiling that big goofy smile that made Luke laugh. He was falling behind in school, but he wouldn't let Luke come over to help him with his homework anymore. Maybe Jack didn't want to be friends with the school nerd, Luke thought at the time. Luke reached into his jacket pocket and pulled out a tissue. He passed it to Jack, who took it and quickly wiped away his tears. The two boys sat in silence for the rest of the way home.

When they got off the bus, Jack grabbed him by the collar. "Don't tell anyone I cried!" He gave him a forceful push back. Luke tripped, landing on his rear end. He was looking up at his best friend in stunned amazement, his mouth hanging open. Jack had never laid a hand on him before. He didn't know what to say. Jack turned and ran toward his house. Luke could tell he was still crying.

The next day, Jack didn't sit with him on the bus. A few days later, the rumour at school was that Jack had been suspended for showing up at school drunk. Luke didn't believe it. He walked over to Jack's house after school and knocked on his front door. At first he thought no one was home, but then he caught someone peeking out the front window when the curtain moved. A few minutes later, the front door slowly opened. Jack stood in the doorway.

"Heard you were sick," Luke lied. "Can I come in? I got some new baseball cards."

Jack opened the door a little wider, just enough to let Luke walk through. The house was grand. Even grander than Luke's. It was quiet. No one was home except for Jack.

Luke could tell he wanted to say something, but he couldn't get it out.

"Jack, you're my best friend. I don't know what's going on with you, but you'll always be my best friend."

Jack wrapped his arms around Luke and began to sob hysterically. Luke could feel the shoulder of his shirt getting wet from the tears, but he stood there, put his arms around his friend, and said nothing. It seemed like a long time before Jack stopped crying. He finally stood back, wiping his face with the sleeve of his sweater.

"Let's go to my room." He gestured toward the stairs.

They climbed the grand staircase, walking the long hallway to the room at the end. Far away from his parents' master bedroom.

"What's wrong, Jack?" Luke asked as they sat on the bedroom floor looking at baseball cards.

"I hate him." Tears began to well up in Jack's eyes again.

"Who? You hate who?" Luke didn't understand.

"John," he responded.

Luke had to think for a moment. Who was John? Then it hit him. Jack's new father. He never heard him call Mr. Duffy John before. He always called him Dad.

"Your father?" Luke asked, surprised.

"He's not my father!" Jack yelled back.

"Did he hurt you? Did he hit you?"

Luke couldn't believe Mr. Duffy, who was so kind to Jack and his mother, would hurt him.

Jack began to cry again. He was sitting with his arms wrapped around his knees. He started to rock back and forth. Luke didn't know what to do.

"Talk to your mom, Jack. She won't let him hurt you."

The tears began to flow even more. He blurted out, "She doesn't love me, she loves him. She loves this house. She loves her hair, but she doesn't love me anymore!"

Luke sat next to him on the floor and tried to put his arms around him. He didn't know how to comfort his friend. Jack pushed him away.

"Don't touch me." He coiled into a ball on the floor, like a dog that had been beaten.

Luke was afraid. He didn't know what to do. They both heard the car pull into the driveway.

"You better go home." Jack jumped to his feet, wiping his face with his sleeve again. "Now!" he yelled.

Both boys hurried down the stairs just as Jack's mother and Mr. Duffy came in through the front door. They were laughing. She was carrying shopping bags from a ladies' clothing store in each hand. When Jack and Mr. Duffy locked eyes, they both froze. The smile left Duffy's face, and Jack stood still in fear. Luke could feel the tension.

"Hello, Mrs. McGraw," was all Luke could think to say.

She put her bags on the floor. "I'm Mrs. Duffy now, Luke," she corrected him.

"I'm sorry. I forgot."

Luke noticed that Mr. Duffy and Jack had not broken their stare during the exchange.

"Jack?" Duffy hissed. "Are you allowed to have a friend over without asking me first?"

Luke looked back at Jack. His face was white, and he was shaking.

"It's only Luke," his mother interrupted. "They're like brothers."

"Did I ask for your opinion?" Duffy shot her a look, and she knew what it meant. "You have your prizes, now go play with them. Jack and I will go have a conversation about rules in this house."

She picked up her bags and walked toward the kitchen. Jack turned and ran up the stairs. Luke could hear his bedroom door slam. Mr. Duffy looked mad. Luke knew he had to leave in a hurry.

The next day, Jack didn't get on the school bus. Mr. Duffy drove him to school and picked him up at three o'clock. He didn't talk to Luke anymore. He always blamed himself for showing up uninvited and getting Jack in trouble. Jack failed grade seven that year and had to repeat it while Luke moved on to grade eight. Jack developed a reputation for being a wild child and a fighter. Luke heard he had quit school shortly after grade eight began.

Luke never had a best friend like Jack again. Over the years, he would hear rumours of Jack getting arrested, being thrown out of the house, or landing in some kind of trouble. Whenever Luke ran into him, Jack would turn and go in the other direction.

Then one day he picked up the newspaper. "PROMINENT BUSINESSMAN CHARGED WITH SEXUAL ASSAULT." Mr. Duffy's picture was on the front page.

Luke was sick as he read through the article. Mr. Duffy's adopted son had alleged that Duffy had started molesting him at twelve years old and continued to do so until he was sixteen. The article went on to say that Mrs. Duffy was standing by her husband, stating that her troubled son had been in and out of jail for years. He was sick, she told the reporter, and needed help. Mr. Duffy was a good man who tried to help him.

Luke was at university then. He thought about calling Jack. It all made sense to him then. But he didn't know how to start the conversation. He followed the trial in the media, anxiously waiting for the paper each day and watching the evening news every night. He saw Jack going in and out of the courthouse.

Years of alcohol abuse and hard living had turned him into a sore sight.

Then it came. "PROMINENT BUSINESSMAN ACQUITTED."

Tears fell from Luke's eyes as he read the judge's decision. Jack was not credible, the papers wrote. His story changed. He couldn't get his facts straight. Mr. Duffy's lawyer presented a solid case when he accused Jack of trying to blackmail his stepfather. He had proof of Jack saying he would go to the police with the allegations if he didn't give him money. The picture on the front page showed a triumphant Mr. and Mrs. Duffy leaving the courthouse, arm in arm, smiling. Jack's picture appeared on page three with the second half of the story. It was the size of a postage stamp, simply stating Jack McGraw had used blackmail, then false allegations, to extort money from his stepfather.

Life went on. Luke finished medical school and started long hours as an intern, moving up the ladder until he became a doctor. He'd never heard from Jack again until now.

There he stood, smoking a cigarette, like no time had passed.

Jack knew what he was thinking. "I didn't know how to tell you, Luke. I didn't understand myself." Jack hung his head. "I didn't know what the words were. What you called it. No one talked about men like that back then."

Luke didn't know what to say. "I followed the trial. I wanted to call you, but I didn't know what to say."

"You didn't need your good name caught up in that garbage," Jack assured him. "It made me happy to know you were doing well."

"Did your mother know, Jack?" Luke couldn't help but ask.

Jack threw his cigarette on the ground and stepped on it. "Yes. She knew." Jack looked sadder than before. "She traded my childhood for new clothes and fancy hair. She won't admit it, but I know she heard me crying when he came into my room." He looked like a boy again. "She'd take a sleeping pill to knock herself out. Then she'd smile at me in the morning like nothing happened. Every time she came home with a new dress or new shoes, I knew I was going to pay for it. No one knew the horrors that went on in that house."

"My mother knew." The words came out of Luke's mouth before he could stop them.

Jack gave him a blank look.

"My mother never wanted me to go to your house after your mother married Duffy. She never said why. I thought she was jealous. She warned me to never be alone with him. When the trial was happening, she made a comment one night that everyone knew he was a pedophile."

"She was right, Luke. Everyone did know he was a pedophile, but no one would help. His good name was more important than my childhood."

"I wish we had stayed friends, Jack. I wish I had known. I would never have stopped being friends with you."

"I had to stop being friends with you, Luke." Jack's words surprised him. "He was getting tired of me. He wanted me to start bringing you around again, but I wouldn't do it."

Luke was frozen. He felt an icy chill go up his spine. Jack had not pushed him away. He had protected him. Like he always had.

"Is he in pain, Luke?" Jack asked with wide-eyed innocence.

Dr. Gillespie nodded.

"Good. I'm glad. I hope he dies. I hope God makes him suffer for what he did."

Luke looked his friend in the eye. For a moment they were back to being twelve-year-old boys again, but this time Luke would protect him.

* * * * *

Luke was incredibly angry when he returned to emerg. He walked into Duffy's hospital room and stood by his bed for a long time. No nurses were around. Duffy was sleeping. His breath was laboured. He sounded like he was drowning. The only other sounds came from the hospital machinery. Luke imagined himself taking the pillow off the bed and putting it over Duffy's face, pressing hard. He wouldn't make any sound, and Luke would walk out of the room and go for a coffee. By the time he got back, Duffy would have been found dead by a nurse. Luke would pretend to try and revive him, then call the time of death. It seemed so easy. Then he remembered the oath he took the day he graduated from medical school: *Doctor, do no harm.*

He jumped like a scared cat when Nurse Catania walked up behind him and said, "How are you doing?"

Agatha began to laugh when she realized she had scared the doctor. "My God. You're some jumpy!" she laughed.

"You're not supposed to sneak up on people like that." He was shaking, not because Agatha scared him, but because his own thoughts scared him more.

She was still laughing when she asked, "So, is he another diddler?"

"Diddler?" Gillespie asked.

"Yes. Diddler. That's what we used to call pedophiles back in the day."

Luke looked toward the bed. “We don’t know for sure if any of these patients are involved with that.”

“Luke, there’s something to this. This is not a coincidence. There’s something going on here.” She spooked herself with her own words.

“I think it’s time I started calling around to other hospitals. Someone may be doing something to diddlers.” He sighed.

“Could there be a disease that kills people who touch kids?” She was thinking out loud. “Remember when AIDS first came out in the 1980s?”

“This is nothing like AIDS,” Gillespie reminded her.

“I know, but when AIDS first hit the news, everybody thought it came from men having sex with monkeys in Africa. Then the Catholics jumped on board and said it was God’s way of punishing homosexual men. There are still people who believe that today.” Agatha was on a roll now.

“Not from having sex with monkeys,” Gillespie stated. “From eating tainted monkey meat. There was so much misinformation about this disease in the beginning, I can’t believe people believed that crap.”

“We know that now, but that’s not what the rumours were back in the age of disco dancing and leg warmers,” Agatha said. “We didn’t have Google.

“I was in high school when people started talking about AIDS,” Agatha went on. “If a person said they had AIDS, the rest of the community wanted to put them on an isolated island away from everyone. Sure, Mom warned me not to drink out of water fountains at school. We had this one guy in our class who was obviously gay—we called them ‘mama’s boys’ back then. No one would even hold his hand after the AIDS epidemic hit.

Everyone was too afraid they would catch it by touching a gay person."

Luke remembered those days, too. It was a hateful time, and not one he would ever want to live through again. Suddenly, the heart monitor began to beep a warning that their patient was in trouble.

The room filled with health care professionals hooking up equipment to Mr. Duffy's body. Dr. Gillespie forgot his earlier thoughts of smothering this man and began do what came naturally to him: saving a life. He worked on him until Mr. Duffy came to. He was still groggy and incoherent. Then, suddenly, Mr. Duffy was howling so loudly they could hear him in the waiting room. Convulsions of pain shot through his body until his eyeballs bulged from their sockets. The nurses couldn't keep the heart monitor clasps attached to their pads because blood was gushing down from his nose so fast it was covering his chest and making it slippery. He drew deep breaths, and with each gulp of air he began to drown in his own blood and then throw it back up again. His body finally reached its exhaustion point and went limp in the bed. His heart stopped, and he couldn't be resuscitated. It happened so fast the health care team stood around with bewildered looks on their faces.

After fifteen minutes of feverishly working on him, they gave up. Gillespie called the time of death. Mr. Duffy's body lay limp on the hospital bed, his face distorted like a gargoyle from the pain.

Luke went back out to the waiting room, where Jack was sitting down watching TV.

"Jack?" Luke called out to him, then gestured toward the

front door. Jack followed him outside the hospital to the smoking area.

"He's dead," Luke told him.

"Dead? Really?" Jack was filled with disbelief. Could the monster in his room really be dead?

"Has he been in hospital before with these symptoms?" Luke asked.

"No. Mom said he wouldn't leave the house when he was like that. She called an ambulance today because she couldn't take it anymore." Jack lit a cigarette. He felt a strange calm come over him. "Luke, you said he was the third one like this. Can you tell me who the others are?" He was curious now.

"I'm not supposed to give out that information about patients, but now I have to start linking these cases together. You don't happen to know Archbishop Patrick Keating, do you?"

Jack's face went white. "That bastard!" he exclaimed. "That's another one. He used to come to our house all the time."

"Really? I don't remember you being overly religious."

"Nothing religious about him!" Jack spat out. "He used to come over with his boy."

"His boy?" Luke was getting that sick feeling in his stomach again.

"His name was Charlie Horan. He was an orphan. Keating used to take him out of the orphanage all the time. People thought he treated him like a son."

Charlie Horan, Luke thought to himself. *Father Charles Horan, the archbishop's assistant.* "Did he treat him like a son?" Luke knew the answer before he asked the question.

"Like a whipping boy, more likely." The veins in Jack's neck were bulging, and his cheeks began to turn red as the anger swept through him. “He was doing the same thing to Charlie that Duffy was doing to me.”

“How do you know for sure?” Luke asked.

“Because they would take us on camping trips to a cabin in the woods, and they would take turns with us.” Jack hung his head.

“No one was suspicious?” Luke couldn’t believe what he was hearing.

“More like no one cared,” Jack told him. “Keating had a good supply of orphans whenever he wanted them, but Charlie was his favourite.” Jack lit another cigarette off the flame from the first. “No short supply of perverts, either.”

“What?” Luke was in shock. A tremble ran through his limbs.

“Duffy, Keating, other priests, teachers, even the doctor who used to check us over at the cabin could pick his favourite boy. All respected men. Some even married. They all came to the cabin.” Jack looked exhausted.

“I am so sorry, Jack.” Luke shook his head in disbelief.

“Did he suffer, Luke?”

“Yes.”

“I mean, did he really suffer? I always dreamed of that bastard dying a hard death.”

“Yes, he suffered,” Luke answered back.

“How do you know for sure, Luke?” Jack looked like a little boy asking if the monster under his bed had really been slain.

“Because I didn’t order any morphine for him, Jack. I wanted him to feel your pain.” Luke turned and walked back into the hospital.

Jack smiled, watching his friend go through the door. He

would go to his mother's house now for the first time without feeling sick or scared. He imagined her wrapping her arms around him when he told her they were both free. Maybe she would ask him to live with her, and tomorrow she would make him Rice Krispies cookies again.

* * * * *

The next morning, Luke sat down with his morning coffee and paper. There it was on the front page: HALL OF FAME BUSINESSMAN DIES UNEXPECTEDLY. Under Duffy's smiling picture, the article listed his many achievements in business. Leaving to mourn his wife of many years, Mary. They had no children.

Luke felt the rage rise to his cheeks when he read the last line of the story. "Mr. Duffy, a devout Catholic, left his entire estate to the Church."

Jack and his mother were back where they started. With nothing but each other.

5

Father Charles Horan sat in the private family room outside the ICU where Archbishop Keating rested. Dr. Gillespie stood in the hallway watching him through the viewing window. He took a deep breath and exhaled it with a heavy sigh. Horan had asked to meet with him. Gillespie dreaded it after what Jack told him.

Horan looked more like a nervous son waiting to hear about his beloved father than an assistant to the archbishop. He was wearing jeans, a white shirt, and boat shoes. He looked much younger than the first time he saw him. The priest was sitting on the couch, bent over with his forearms resting on the inside of his thighs. His gaze was on the floor. He sat erect when Dr. Gillespie walked into the room and sat across from him.

"Thank you for taking the time to meet with me. I know you're busy." Horan spoke with sincerity, and it showed in his face.

"I realize you're frustrated," Gillespie began. "So am I. You want to know what's going on with Archbishop Keating, but I don't know. I've run every test I can. Everything is inconclusive."

"I've heard you have other cases like the archbishop's?" Horan inquired.

"Yes. We have three cases," Gillespie informed him.

"I've heard one died?" Horan's voice shook when he asked this question.

"Yes," Gillespie answered. Without thinking, he asked, "Did you know John Duffy?"

Horan's eyes widened with shock. "He was a parishioner in our church and a friend of the archbishop," he stammered.

The priest sank back in his chair. Luke studied his body language, noting that he looked more like a twelve-year-old boy than a man. Duffy's name caused this man a lot of pain.

"I guess you'll be meeting with Mr. Duffy's family, then? I heard you were friends with his son," Gillespie inquired.

He was surprised at Horan's quick response. "No. I don't know them," he lied, then paused. "I knew his stepson years ago, but I haven't seen him in years. He is a lot of trouble. He didn't like me." Horan realized he had said too much. Archbishop Keating would be angry with him for talking. He suddenly bolted straight up in his chair. His eyes were locked on the open door of the waiting room. A look of fear came over his face.

"Hello, Charles."

Gillespie looked over his shoulder to see Sgt. Nicholas Myra. He was an imposing-looking man. He was older than Luke, probably mid- to late fifties. The sergeant was tall. Luke had originally thought he was around six feet, but he was easily six foot four, very fit, and well-dressed in a sharp suit and tie with polished shoes. He obviously took a lot of pride in his appearance, but the years of police work showed around his eyes.

Father Horan sank back in his seat and folded his arms. He looked at the floor without answering.

"Sgt. Myra, to what do we owe the pleasure of your visit?" Gillespie was not happy with Myra's surprise visits.

"Well, I heard one of my clients died last night, but I still have two more in your ICU. Thought I would drop by to see if they are ready to talk to me."

"Not today," Gillespie informed him. "They are both sedated." Gillespie was startled to hear that John Duffy was one of Myra's "clients."

"Maybe Charles would like to talk to me." Myra was intimidating Father Horan, and Gillespie knew it.

Horan looked at the police officer with the spite of a boy. "No," was all he said. Myra locked eyes with Horan, like he knew a secret that Charles desperately wanted him to keep.

Myra and Dr. Gillespie left the room and found a private office not far away.

Gillespie felt like Myra was reading his mind when he asked, "Don't you find it funny that all three of your patients have the same symptoms and are under investigation for crimes against children?"

"Why is that?" Gillespie needed something to tie these cases together.

"What do you think?" Myra asked.

"I don't know. That's why I am asking you," the doctor responded with a snarky tone.

"What have you heard? Any rumours yet?" Myra wanted to find out what the doctor knew before he gave him any information.

"Heard? I haven't heard anything." Luke's life consisted of

working or running. He didn't pay attention to rumours. "Why? What are the rumours?"

Myra decided to throw it out there to see what Gillespie's reaction would be. "There's a rumour that only pedophiles get this disease."

"That's crazy!" Gillespie laughed. "Who would believe that?"

Myra shrugged his big shoulders. "I'm just telling you what I heard. I never said I believed it."

"How come Father Horan doesn't have any symptoms, or is he my next patient?"

"I don't think so. Charles is a victim. And it doesn't seem like he has followed in the archbishop's footsteps. Keating took him out of the Christian Brothers' orphanage and raised him. I did a little digging, and it looks like Charles's mother adopted him when he was born, but she died when he was twelve. She was a single mother with no family. That's how Keating kept him without anyone asking questions. No one looked for him."

"That's so incredibly sad." The whole conversation was depressing to Gillespie.

"I wish I could get Charles to talk," said Myra. "He is the smoking gun I need to bring the archbishop and others like him down, but he won't give it up."

"Why not?"

"He has been with the archbishop since he was about twelve. Maybe it's loyalty. Family. Maybe it's fear. Maybe it's love. Or the only definition of love he knows." Myra put his hands in the pockets of his neatly creased dress pants. "I don't understand it, myself."

"I know a victim of John Duffy. I know his stepson, Jack. I

wanted to ask him if he had any symptoms, but I couldn't," Gillespie confessed.

"He doesn't," Sgt. Myra responded. "I've been busting Jack since he was a teenager. He was a lost kid, and he is a victim. He didn't continue the abuse. Jack was an unlikely criminal."

"How so?" Luke was still heartbroken over Jack.

"He just didn't have the heart of a criminal. He wasn't mean. He was acting out. I always thought he committed crimes so his mother would come bail him out. It seemed to be the only way he could spend time with her." Myra thought for a second, then added, "People think criminals come from the poor part of town. They think people who live in big houses raise law-abiding kids. In my experience, those are the worst kids. They are the most neglected and act out for attention. The poorer kids are too busy working minimum-wage jobs to act out. Too many people measure their success by the size of their house and the price of their sports cars. People should measure their success by how their kids turn out."

"Interesting theory." Despite himself, Gillespie was beginning to like Sgt. Myra. He recognized that this cop had a lot of experience dealing with the underbelly of society.

"Every time I bring an out-of-control teen home to his house, it only takes thirty seconds with his parent before I say to myself, 'Oh, that's where he gets it from.'"

"So, are you saying you believe this disease only affects child molesters?" Gillespie blurted out. "It's not possible."

"I am saying that's the rumour." Myra was challenging him now. "These are not the only three cases of this, you know."

"What?" Gillespie was stunned.

"I attended two suicides in the past three months. Both were registered sex offenders. Both had the heavy nosebleeds, according to their families. There are others, too. You just don't know about them."

Luke was curious. "What do you mean by others? Where?"

"Whatever this disease is, it has been going around for about a year or more. This is a tight-knit group. They have been sharing their symptoms with each other, trying to find out what is going on as securely as they share their child pornography. They won't go for medical help because they are scared. They think that only the molesters get it, not the victims." Myra was obviously well versed in this world.

"Sgt. Myra, I can't believe what you're telling me." Gillespie was numb. *What have we stumbled on?* he wondered.

"Call me Nick. I got a feeling we're going to be good friends. We need to talk."

"Can you do it now?" Gillespie asked.

"I need to get my files, but I can meet you back here in a few hours, and I'll brief you on some of my reports. I suggest you get on the phone to your medical colleagues and start asking other hospitals and doctors if they have patients with these symptoms."

"I guess it's about time to start doing that now. When you come back, page me and I'll drop whatever I'm doing to meet you." Gillespie had a heavy heart. "What have we stumbled on?" he asked, this time aloud.

"Pandora's box, I think," answered Nick.

* * * * *

Luke felt like he had told the hospital administrator that the world was flat. Her eyes were wide, her mouth hung open, and she stood still, like she was frozen. He understood her reaction.

"I understand that you are shocked, but I think we have to act on this, and quickly," he warned her.

Mrs. Furey had been with the hospital for thirty years. She couldn't believe what Luke was saying.

"So," she reiterated, "you're saying you think you've uncovered a new disease, and we have had three cases in the past week. Two still in our ICU, and one dead?"

"I'm running every test I can think of, but one explanation on the table is from a police officer," said the doctor, knowing this was going to sound crazy. "He knows all three of the patients and says there is a possible connection." Luke was aware he sounded like Chicken Little saying the sky was falling.

Mrs. Furey sat back and stared at Luke as if she was waiting for him to say, "April Fools!" But she knew he was serious. Dr. Gillespie was a good and respectable doctor.

"Tell me again," she said, and closed her eyes as if to let it all sink in without interruption.

"All three patients have the exact same symptoms. I've run every test known to the medical profession, and everything comes back inconclusive. The only connection these men have is they are all under investigation by the RNC's Child Exploitation Unit. I don't know if they are all known to each other. I have also heard from the same police officer that there are more cases that are not being reported." He had gone over this in his head a hundred times, and by now it was starting to sound sane to him.

"There has to be another reason." Mrs. Furey opened her eyes and looked at Luke again.

"The police officer, who is very knowledgeable in this area of crime, is meeting with me this afternoon. He claims to have files on pedophiles that prove this disease has been around for over a year, but the victims have been hiding it.

"All I'm asking for is a video conference with other hospitals and permission to contact the Association of Physicians to ask if they have encountered the same symptoms. We'll need our own serious disease doctors to attend the video conference, too." Luke knew she wasn't buying it.

"I won't mention that the patients are being investigated by the police unless they bring it up first." He suspected that this was going to be an uphill battle. "If nothing else, we may have an epidemic on our hands, and we have to deal with it. We wouldn't want anyone to say we knew first and did nothing about it."

Mrs. Furey tapped her fingers on her desktop. "All right, I'll set up the teleconference, but don't say anything about a disease that only targets child molesters." She sat back in her chair. "I can only imagine the media coverage this would get. It would be the first time the public raised money to stop us from curing a disease."

Luke was questioning himself on beginning this process. It could generate many complicated problems as the result of his interference into something he knew nothing about.

"That's all I am asking for. I just want to discuss it with other doctors to see if there is anything I am missing." Luke was satisfied. His hospital pager went off, and he knew it was Sgt. Myra back with his files.

6

Sgt. Myra's desk was covered in files. Months of notes and investigative work were neatly stacked inside each folder. He didn't have to read through them. The sergeant knew from memory, and too many nightmares, what each of them contained. He opened his desk drawer for some elastic bands to put around the bigger files so they would stay intact.

It was still there. The picture frame he had put in the drawer, face down, a year ago.

Myra was a third-generation cop in the Royal Newfoundland Constabulary. His father had retired from a proud, forty-year career, and his grandfather before that had served for thirty-five years. There was no doubt from the day he was born what his career would be.

The Royal Newfoundland Constabulary is the oldest civil police force in North America. It was modelled after the Royal Irish Constabulary with the secondment in 1844 of Timothy Mitchell of the Royal Irish Constabulary to be inspector general. Myra's dress uniforms, right down to his pith helmet, still resembled those of his Irish brothers and sisters.

Myra knew from a young age that the only reason his father had a son was to carry on the family business. His mother was a devout Irish Catholic who knew she would have little say in what her son would grow up to be, but that didn't stop her from becoming the greatest influence on his life choices. His mother was a schoolteacher who loved children, often spending a good portion of her meagre salary on crayons, chalk, and other items for the students in her class. She had desperately wanted children ever since she was a child herself. Although she and her husband tried like good Catholics to conceive, they could only get pregnant once. When she gave birth to her only child, she knew what his name would be. Nicholas. Nicholas Myra. She would name him after the patron saint of children.

When he was growing up, his mother would tell him the story of Archbishop Nicholas, who was known to have returned lost children to their parents, resurrected children from the dead, and rescued them from kidnappers and other dangerous situations. His official feast day was December 6, Sgt. Nicholas Myra's birthday.

Sgt. Myra was now in his thirtieth year of policing. He had joined the RNC at twenty-one after attaining his psychology degree from Memorial University. Throughout his childhood, he would watch his father get ready for work. Putting on his freshly starched uniform with pride. Shining his parade boots and silver badge. Nick grew up playing cops and robbers with the neighbourhood children, always being the cop.

During his last year in high school, a seed of doubt nagged at him. He wasn't as sure about policing as he once was. He would discuss it with his mother sometimes, but never with his father. His mother knew he wasn't as hard on the inside as the other Myra men. Despite his intimidating size, Nicholas had a soft interior that he desperately tried to hide.

His mother spent many nights watching her husband sit in his easy chair staring at the TV screen, not even knowing what was on the screen. Deep in thought about the files he worked every day. Sometimes she would hear him late at night, downstairs in the kitchen, crying. Crying over the things he had seen throughout the day. The things that never left his mind. The things that no one should see. As the years went by, it became harder and harder for him to put on his uniform. But he did. In the tradition that his father had passed on to him. He put on his uniform, choked back his tears, swallowed his fears, and went to work. Always smiling. Always dedicated. Always a police officer of the highest regard. His son would carry on where he left off.

Nicholas had always been a devoted son. Respectful of his father. Tender toward his mother. Never ashamed to hold her hand, even as a teenager. He was the perfect combination of his mother's caring spirit and his father's rugged good looks. All through high school and university, girls would fawn over him, but he was shy. Finding his height and dangling, long limbs awkward, their attention would make him nervous. A quality that seemed to add to his attractiveness. A more confident boy with his looks could become quite the ladies' man, but not Nicholas. His mother had raised him to be a gentleman. His father had raised him to be a policeman.

His mother talked his father into letting Nicholas get a university degree before going into policing. She convinced his father that a university education would help their son rise through the ranks quicker. She was buying time, allowing her son to reconsider the family business. His father agreed, secretly hoping his son would not follow in his footsteps. The day his father stood before the graduation parade and handed his son his badge was the both the happiest and saddest day of his life. Inspector Myra welcoming Constable Myra into the force, while Superintendent Myra sat in his wheelchair, looking on with great pride. The family was back in business.

His first year on the job, he met his wife, Maria. She was a legal secretary he was introduced to during a Christmas party. She instantly fell in love with the tall, handsome police officer who blushed when he caught her eye. Within a year, they were married. He loved her more than anything, except the job. He forgot to come home. Rarely making it to special occasions that were important her. Ten years later, she'd had enough. She filed for divorce. He was devastated. Not knowing what he had done wrong.

He provided for his family the best he could. He told her from the beginning that no one marries a police officer for the money or quality family time. She didn't care in the beginning. She did in the end. Even when he was home, he was working. Always alone in his thoughts. Always running through the door when his phone rang. Never able to discuss his cases. Never wanting to. He thought he was protecting her. She thought he was shutting her out.

Ten years later, two people who loved each other divorced each other. She found comfort in the arms of a lawyer she worked with. He found comfort in the files that surrounded his desk. He put their wedding photo in his desk drawer, face down.

Over the years there would be other women, but he was married to his job. They would all leave after a while. They would cry, he would go to his office, work, and occasionally turn the photo over when he missed her.

7

Dr. Gillespie and Sgt. Myra met in a private boardroom on the fifth floor that overlooked the hills surrounding the Health Sciences Complex. The long cherry wood table was bare except for a conference calling speaker. A dozen black leather chairs surrounded the table and were perfectly arranged for the next meeting of the medical minds who would sit in them. Myra reached down into his large black briefcase and lifted out about two dozen file folders, stacking them on the table.

He sat down and took the first file off the top of the stack. A legal-size, white file folder with a blue form printed on the outside cover that allowed police officers to document the status, jurisdiction, personal data, and diary dates of each investigation.

"Are you going to meet with your counterparts about the nose-bleeding disease?" Myra asked him.

"I just came from a meeting with the hospital administrator. She thinks I'm crazy now—thank you for that, by the way. She's going to set up a teleconference with other hospitals and doctors. But I'm not allowed to say they are being investigated by the police for anything."

"I'm not surprised. I don't really believe the connection myself," Myra confessed. "I mean, come on. I think someone who was sexually abused as a child is getting to these people somehow and poisoning them with something."

"So, you don't really believe there's a new disease killing pedophiles? Then why are you pushing that theory?" asked Gillespie.

"It scares the crap out of child molesters. Ever since the rumours of this disease started circulating, their online chat groups have all but dried up. They are scared to death. No pun intended."

"So, you used me?" The colour drained from Luke's cheeks.

"No, not at all. I never said I believed the theory. I just told you the rumour so that other people could hear it. By the way, I'm not even sure about them being poisoned. All I know is, something or someone has declared open season on pedophiles, and they are dying before I can charge them. Now I have to find out how, and I think you can help." Sgt. Myra laid his file down on top of the stack in front of him. "We can help each other here. We both need to find out why these people are dying, even if it is for different reasons."

Gillespie relaxed a little. "I suppose you're right."

"This is a file I started about twelve months ago." Myra opened the thick folder and read from memory. "This was when I first noticed the symptoms." Luke was struck by the incredible penmanship on the top page. Observing the inquisitive look on his face, Myra confessed, "My mother was a teacher. We practised handwriting and spelling every night. I have been accused of typing my handwritten notes on occasion, but it is ink." Then he added, "Yes. I do think I have OCD, and no, I have not been tested."

"I'll leave you with your self-diagnosis," said Gillespie. "Meanwhile, what do you have there?"

"I won't go into too much detail, but basically, a ten-year-old girl tells her teacher her stepfather is hurting her at bedtime. The teacher alerts Child Protective Services, who in turn alert us." Myra leaned back in his chair. In addition to keeping impeccable notes, he also had a photographic memory and could recall, with detail, any scene or interview after just a few seconds of looking at the file.

"I interviewed the child, and over time she told me her mother worked a night shift, so her stepfather would put her to bed. And then play games with her. He started out touching her inappropriately and made her touch him. Within a month, it had escalated into intercourse. A medical exam proved her story. The stepfather had severely bruised and ripped her vagina. I charged him with sexual assault on a child, but I wished I could have charged him with the sexual torture of a child, because that's what it was."

"Why didn't you charge him with the sexual torture of a child?" the doctor innocently asked.

"Ask our federal politicians. The sexual torture of a child is not a charge a police officer can lay. There are only degrees of sexual assault. If police officers made laws instead of politicians, pedophiles would never see the light of day again, and drunk drivers who kill would automatically be charged with murder. Politicians must please the bleeding hearts who vote them in. Police officers don't care about who they piss off. They are just trying to do their jobs." Myra was getting worked up just talking about it. Thoughts like this kept him up all night. He was trying to learn to let go.

"My God. How do you do this day after day?" Luke looked away from the file in disgust. Just looking at the words on the page made him queasy. Gillespie had been involved with several child abuse cases over the years. One stuck with him. He had to examine a baby who had been sexually abused and fill out a report on the assault for the police. She was an eighteen-month-old baby girl. He had followed the trial in the media. It was the boyfriend of the child's seventeen-year-old mother who raped her.

The most shocking thing that remained with Luke was the little girl's crossed eyes. Yet there was no record of her being born like that. He combed through her medical file from birth to the day she was admitted to emergency, and nothing. He called the child's family physician, who had seen her four times, and was told the child did not have crossed eyes. After re-examining her, Dr. Gillespie concluded that the force of the rape had been so severe and traumatic that the impact had detached the child's retina, and her eyes crossed. Once he put it together, he began to shake uncontrollably. He felt a hot stream of liquid run down his leg and realized that he had urinated on himself. He ran to his locker and showered in hot water while tears ran down his face. To this day, the memory of that child haunted his dreams.

"I focus on saving the child," said Myra. "If people like us sat down and cried every time we had to investigate a crime like this, nothing would get done. At the end of the day, my job, or your job, is not for the faint of heart. It takes a hard-hearted, determined person to do what we do." Sgt. Myra knew the best thing was to leave the files on his desk when he left work. The problem was he never left work.

For the first time, Myra showed his Achilles heel. "I interviewed the stepfather at the station. As soon as I started asking him questions, his nose began to bleed. It started as a trickle first, but within five minutes it was flowing like someone had turned on a tap. I just figured he was a hemophiliac or something." He closed the file.

"After interviewing the mother and the stepfather, I found out she had met him on a local dating site. She advertised she was a single mother with one daughter. He answered the ad. The mother said all of them got along in the beginning. He showered both of them with gifts. Things they could never afford before she met him. After he moved in, the daughter started to become withdrawn. The mother says that's when the nosebleeds started with the stepfather.

"She thought the daughter was being defiant and jealous because she never had to share her time before. Eventually the daughter became more and more defiant and the stepfather became sicker. She said the blood would drain out of his nose, and he would scream for water but constantly complained it tasted like vinegar." Myra moved the folder to the bottom of the pile. "That's the first time I heard of it. I didn't pay much attention to it then. I was more interested in finding out if he molested his stepdaughter than I was in finding out what his nosebleeds were about."

Luke couldn't help but ask, "Did he? Did he molest her?"

"Yes. It started as soon as he moved in. When we analyzed his computer, we could prove that he was trolling for single mothers on dating sites. He was targeting ones that worked shifts so he could get the kids alone in the nighttime." Myra took the next file off the stack and opened it on the table. Once again, meticulously taken notes were pinned to the inside of the file, and the outside form was filled in with dates and times all written with the finest of penmanship.

"Just as I was wrapping up that case, this one came in." He pointed to the writing on the page inside the file folder. "Ten-year-old boy, involved in hockey since he was five, loved the game, suddenly refused to play anymore." He read it out like a grocery list.

"That's not a crime, is it?" Luke tried to lighten the mood.

"He complained his coach made him angry. His father said the coach always showed him special attention. Coach claimed he was the next big thing. Kept him for extra practices and really built him up. The father thought he was a great guy and trusted him completely. Neither of the parents were educated, and both worked minimum-wage jobs. All extra money, or what little there was, went to pay for their son's hockey lessons. It was an investment in his, and I guess their, future.

"He and his wife even invited the coach into their home for meals on several occasions. They noticed their son stayed in his room when the coach came over. They thought he didn't like him because he was a tough coach. Then the son refused to play hockey, and after some arguing, he finally told them why. The coach had been molesting him for about a year." Myra closed the file and slid it under the stack.

"When I interviewed the coach, his nose started to bleed. He asked for water. I could tell his mouth was dry, because he could barely say a word. I gave him bottled water. After he drank, he spat it out on the floor. It was followed by a gush of blood.

My counterparts in the unit joked that I was roughing up my suspects, but I didn't lay a hand on him, as much as I would have loved to. But a good investigator knows you have to pretend to be the friend of these guys to make them confess." He looked straight at Luke. "Molestation is never about sexual gratification. It's about power. Having power over someone. That's what drives them. As an investigator, I have to get the power back."

"Really?" Luke was surprised.

"It's always about having power over the weak, the defenceless, and the innocent." Nicholas Myra stood up and put his hands in his pants pocket. He was an intimidating-looking man, even when he was trying to be friendly. He rarely smiled, and even when he tried, his thick, brown moustache covered his top lip completely. Smiling didn't come naturally to him. He had decided long ago he achieved more in life by frowning.

"Case after case, I couldn't help but notice that the nosebleeds were constant. Other investigators in the unit also made note of it in their files. Each molester said water tasted like vinegar. Then one time I asked a suspect about it. This suspect was picked up in a pedophile ring. He told me the symptoms were becoming more common among his type, but they were afraid to go to the doctors. He referred to it as Wormwood."

"Wormwood?" asked Luke. "What the hell is Wormwood? I never noticed any worms on these patients."

"It's some kind of Biblical reference," Myra informed him. "You'll have to talk to someone who knows more about the Bible than me."

"Well, the one who knows the most about the Bible is lying in ICU, bleeding to death," declared Luke, "and I don't think he is going to talk to me about Wormwood."

Sgt. Myra gathered up his files and put them back in his large square briefcase. Dr. Gillespie sat back in his chair with his hands locked behind his head, deep in thought.

"It's a lot to think about, isn't it?" Myra asked him.

"Yes. I am a doctor, not a detective. My job is to save lives, not research the Bible."

"Well, I am a detective, not a doctor, and my job is to protect lives, not research the Bible. But right now, I would take advice or help from anyone who could help me do my job."

Luke stood up. "I have to go do my rounds. I need to think about this. The hospital is organizing the teleconference for tomorrow afternoon. Maybe I'll know more then."

"Can you let me know what you find out?"

"As long as it's not about individual patients." Then Luke had another thought. "Maybe it would be good for us to share information and keep it between ourselves for now."

"I think there is a benefit for both of us in that. Not telling you how to do your job, but could you test their blood for poison? The results may change the course of both of our investigations."

8

Dr. Gillespie picked up his files in ICU. Archbishop Keating's was on top. He opened it up and started to read through the notes written by the nurses and other doctors. Nothing was new. No one knew why the archbishop continued to bleed.

"Hello, Dr. Gillespie." Sister Pius startled Luke, and he almost dropped the file. She was a small woman with a big presence. Sister Pius, a proud member of the Sisters of Mercy, preferred to maintain the old ways. She wore the older tunic that touched the floor and the veil that covered her hair. Her face and hands were the only flesh that showed. Although the younger Sisters teased her about wearing such a restrictive dress, she took pride in her uniform of God. She looked friendlier now as she waited for Luke's response.

"Sister Pius, it's good to see you again," Luke lied. He was hoping he'd never have to see her again. She made him feel like he was a ten-year-old boy standing in the principal's office. "Is the archbishop awake?"

"No, he is sleeping. The nurse gave him something to quieten him down about an hour ago," she informed him.

A thought entered Luke's mind. "Sister, can I talk with you in private?" She looked surprised to hear his request.

"Sure. You have something on your mind?"

"Yes. I need an expert, and you may be the one." Luke pointed her in the direction of a private room next to the ICU.

He closed the door behind them and pulled out a chair for Sister Pius to sit on. He sat across from her.

"What is Wormwood?"

Sister Pius blinked several times, and a sound escaped her lips like Luke had said a vulgar word. Her lips moved as if she was trying to say something, but nothing was coming out. Finally, she asked, "What do you know about Wormwood?"

"Nothing," Luke answered. "That's why I am asking you. I truly know nothing about it."

She closed her eyes and began to speak like she was chanting an ancient proverb. "And the third angel sounded, and there fell a great star from heaven, burning as it were a lamp, and it fell upon a third of the rivers and upon the springs of water. And the name of the star is called Wormwood, and a third of the waters became bitter and many people died of the waters because they were made bitter." She opened her eyes and looked at Luke. "Revelation 8:10, 11."

He was stunned. A star from heaven? Bitter water? What did this have to do with child molesters or patients bleeding to death? He looked confused, and Sister Pius decided to fill him in.

"Where did you hear that name?" she asked him.

"I hear that's what pedophiles call this disease," he boldly answered her. Dr. Gillespie didn't know how this Catholic nun would react to him referring to the archbishop as a pedophile.

The implications of what he said, how it could impact his career, maybe even end it, never came into his mind.

She sat sternly in her chair. He could tell she had heard the word before.

"What is this disease? What is Wormwood? If you know something, just tell me, for God's sake!" Luke was tired of riddles from this woman.

Sister Pius had prided herself on staying humble and wholesome throughout her calling. She told her own mother when she was five years old that she wanted to enter the convent. All through her teenage years, when her school friends delighted in wearing lipsticks and being asked to dances, she stayed home and faithfully prayed her rosary. When she was sixteen, she met a boy who changed her mind. An awkward situation occurred. The relationship ended. She went back to wanting to join the convent. When her friends teased her, she would answer, *It's my calling*. She never regretted her decision.

Often, as her own brothers and sisters married and had children, they would ask if she ever missed what she didn't have. She would go to her school, into her classroom, and tell herself, *I have everyone's children. I don't need any myself.* She meant it, but in her heart, she kept a secret that could never be revealed. She had truly answered her calling to God. She was serving Him the best way she knew how. Except when Archbishop Keating came to visit.

Sister Pius knew she was not supposed to hate, but she didn't know how to stop hating him. She understood some priests had relationships with each other. She was aware that some nuns had relationships with other nuns. And she was even aware that some priests and nuns lived together like man and wife. She turned her head. In the end, she would have to answer only for her sins. Others could worry about themselves. But the children, that's where she would draw the line. No one would hurt them while she was in charge.

Every night she got down on her knees and prayed that God would answer her prayers. Send her a miracle. Make it stop. Finally, He did. The answer came with a tiny drop of blood that fell from Archbishop Keating's nose. She didn't understand in the beginning, but eventually she put two and two together. She knew it would only be a matter of time before God unleashed a plague upon the earth. The plague was here. The plague was Wormwood.

Sister Pius looked into Dr. Gillespie's blue eyes and began to explain. "Some people think the term 'great star' represents an important political figure, while others think it means Jesus or God Himself. I think, in this case, it's the Holy Spirit." She continued, "Every generation of theologians refers to Wormwood as an event from their time, like a war. Some think it refers to an asteroid's collision with earth. Others believe that the Chernobyl disaster fulfills the prophecy because 'Chernobyl' translates to 'Wormwood' in Russian."

Luke's head was starting to hurt. "But why do they use the term 'Wormwood' to describe this disease?"

"Religious people consider Wormwood to be a symbolic representation of the bitterness that will fill the earth during troubled times. Only God knows the troubled times children have seen at the hands of these sick people. In the Bible, there is a plant called Wormwood. It is a Biblical metaphor for things that are unpalatably bitter. These people taste bitterness in their mouths first. Then it turns into a thirst that can't be quenched.

Water tastes like vinegar to them. That's when their noses start to bleed uncontrollably and the pain starts." She seemed to be more of an expert on this than Sgt. Myra.

"These people?" Luke questioned.

"Pedophiles," she answered. "Yes, pedophiles, if that's what you're getting at. They seem to be the only people who contract it."

"Are you sure?" Luke still wasn't sure if he was connecting the dots.

"It's my job to work with the lepers without judgment. I pray a lot," she added.

"Do any of the scholars say how to stop the blood and the pain?" Dr. Gillespie asked.

"No," Sister Pius answered, "but the Bible does."

"Really? This is in the Bible?" Luke was surprised.

"Sort of," Sister Pius informed him, and then she began to site a verse from memory. "Then I heard a loud voice in heaven, saying, 'Now the salvation, and the power, and the kingdom of our God and the authority of His Christ have come, for the accuser of our brethren has been thrown down, he who accuses them before our God day and night. Our brothers conquered him by the blood of the lamb and by the word of their testimony, for they did not cling to their lives even in the face of death. For this reason, rejoice, O heavens and you who dwell in them. Woe to the earth and the sea, because the devil has come down to you, having great wrath, knowing that he has only a short time.'"

"What the hell does that mean?" Luke was frustrated.

"Well," Sister Pius began, "it means different things to different people."

"How does it apply to this situation? I don't care how it applies to anything else." Luke was tired all of a sudden.

"I'll try to explain it the best way I can," the nun said, her brow furrowing as she tried to sort it out in her own head. "What I think it means is this: God has decided to come for the pedophiles. Not for those accused, only those who are guilty. He can look into their hearts and see their sins. He doesn't need a detective or court to decide the innocent and the guilty. Being washed in the blood of the lamb means to have your sins forgiven so you can enter Heaven. I think the blood is meant to be both literal and figurative in this case. He is showing the world who the guilty are by marking them with the blood of the lamb. At the same time, if they confess their sins, the blood stops. But for those who do not confess, they die in a pool of blood. A person with this disease doesn't last more than a year."

She stood up and walked toward the door, then added, "I truly believe this disease marks the child molesters and, at the same time, gives them the opportunity to confess to get into heaven. If they refuse, they die a slow, painful death and they go to hell."

"That sounds reasonable," Luke joked. "You know the archbishop molested children, including Father Horan, so why do you come to pray for him every day? Or are you just coming to enjoy his suffering?"

Sister Pius looked vexed, as nuns do when they are mad. "I don't enjoy anyone's suffering, Dr. Gillespie. I come to pray that he confesses his sins to free his soul, to free Father Horan's soul."

"Do you honestly think he would confess to molesting children? He is the head of the Catholic Church."

"Imagine if he did," she replied. "Imagine the souls that

would be set free if he confessed and showed true remorse. Even victims who are not his would find release from that confession." She raised both her hands toward heaven, as if she were delivering a new commandment to the followers.

Luke stood up, too. "One last question. If they confess, does the bleeding stop? Does the disease go away? What happens?"

"From what I've seen, the blood and the pain stop, but the person still dies. I've only seen four cases where this has happened. They each died of a heart attack." Now Sister Pius looked tired.

"So, whether they confess or not, they still die! So, why would they confess and have their names ruined?" Luke asked.

"Ruined in this world," she informed him. "On their deathbed they get one final chance to save their soul and the souls of their victims or die with the sin. Remember, the Bible says, 'The devil has come down to you, having great wrath, knowing that he has only a short time.' They get one final chance to be washed in the blood of the lamb or be sent to the fires of Hell. The symptoms of this disease are only a taste of what Hell is really like."

Luke couldn't believe that she was making sense to him. He opened the door and let Sister Pius go before him. He watched her walk through the corridor of the ICU toward Archbishop Keating's room. She was singing softly to herself, "Have you been to Jesus for the cleansing power? Are you washed in the blood of the lamb? Are you fully trusting in His grace this hour? Are you washed in the blood of the lamb?"

9

When Dr. Gillespie started his next shift in the ICU, the first person he encountered was Jermaine Cousin, the X-ray technician. He was keeping his usual vigil outside Archbishop Keating's door. The nurses were doing their rounds, and no one was on the front desk. Except for the hum and beeps of various medical equipment keeping people alive, and the soft snoring of patients, the ward was quiet.

Dr. Gillespie decided to take advantage of the quiet to talk with Mr. Cousin. Maybe today he might get some real answers.

"Hello, Jermaine." He startled the visitor, who had been deep in thought. Jermaine turned with a jolt toward the doctor, like he had been awakened from a deep sleep. His eyes were wide with surprise, and Luke, in turn, stopped in his tracks.

"Dr. Gillespie! You scared me," he exclaimed, putting his hand over his heart as if to stop sudden palpitations.

"You've come back to visit the archbishop again?" Gillespie noted as he also took a place in front of the viewing window.

"Yes, just curious about his condition," Jermaine admitted.

“We didn’t get to finish our conversation the other morning,” Luke informed him. “You were telling me about Sister Pius and what a good school principal she was. How she protected the children.” This time, Jermaine Cousin looked like he was about to have a real heart attack.

The air in the ICU ward felt stale and constantly smelled of bodily fluids. The odour of everything from blood to urine lingered in the air. At times it was so thick it could stick in a person’s throat for days. The temperature was always up on bust to accommodate the patients going through shock and those who shivered when their blood pressure fell. After a short time in the ICU, a person either felt the urge to puke from the stench or fell asleep from the heat. Standing in one spot for a long period could leave one feeling overwhelmed and faint.

Jermaine Cousin felt beads of sweat running down his face and was beginning to feel himself sway as his legs lost their strength. “I don’t recall what I was saying. I should get back to work.” He turned to leave.

“Don’t go. I know why you come here. I know about Wormwood.” Luke waited for his reaction.

Cousin slowly turned on his heels and faced the doctor. It was the first time Luke realized that Jermaine Cousin was twice his weight, and broad as a truck. He looked to be about thirty years old, and he had deep, dark circles around his eyes. Cousin had pulled his shoulders back and stood as strong and tall as a maple tree. His big hand came up, and he pointed his finger directly at Luke’s nose.

“I don’t have Wormwood! There’s no blood on me.” He ground his teeth as his head turned toward the archbishop’s window. “He has Wormwood. That’s why he is dying.”

Gillespie wasn't sure if Jermaine was going to punch him or take the window out. "I am not saying you have it. I am asking if you know about it," Luke stuttered.

"I know about it. It's how we tell the monsters from the rest of us," Cousin answered.

"He molested you," Luke stated. "In school. You were one of his victims. You come here to watch him die." Now Gillespie was looking directly into Cousin's eyes.

"Yes," the X-ray technician said with a nod. "I was one of his victims. So was my older brother." His eyes began to moisten. "My brother could never deal with it. Or talk about it. He filled his body with alcohol and drugs, but nothing could stop the torment of Keating coming into his room at night." Tears began to roll down his face.

"We were put in the orphanage when we were young. I was five, and he was nine. Our mother had fallen on hard times, and she needed a break just until she could get her life back in order. She warned him to watch out for me."

Luke was frozen on the spot. He wanted to suggest they move to the private room nearby before the nurses returned, but his mouth wouldn't move. Cousin continued.

"At first Keating was like the father we never had. He gave us candy and toys. He always gave us extra attention. I thought the other boys were jealous, because they teased us so much. They called us 'Kissing Cousins.' Afterwards, I realized they were warning us not to get so close." He hung his head. In telling his secret, this massive man had reverted to a five-year-old boy. His body changed. His shoulders slouched, his head hung, and his big hands were shaking.

"It started with my brother first. I noticed he was changing a week after we got there. He started to get violent. Lashing out at everyone. Even when Mom came to visit. He would beg her to take us home, and when she refused, he would attack her physically. Screaming things at her that I never heard him say before. She would leave, crying, and Keating would reassure her she was doing the right thing.

"He changed overnight." Cousin sighed. "I didn't know why. One night Keating came into my room. In the orphanage, the rooms were divided up according to age. My room was the five-to-seven-year-olds. My brother was in the eight-to-twelve. Keating often came into the room late at night and tucked the boys in. Sometimes he would sit by their bed, and sometimes he would take them out for a walk. I didn't know why."

The tears had dried on Cousin's face, and his speech had slowed down, like he was describing a picture he could see out the window. "One night he sat by my bed. He asked me about my day. How school was. All the while he was rubbing the blanket on top of me. I remember feeling uncomfortable. Then his hand slid under the blanket. That's when my brother came running toward me. He grabbed Keating by the arm, and he was crying. Keating threw him to the floor, but he got up and grabbed his arm again. Other boys started to wake up. Keating jumped up and grabbed my brother by the arm and dragged him out of the room. The next day his eye was black, and he was limping. He said he fell over the stairs, but the rumours were rampant. He had stood up to Keating, and he took a good beating for it. It was the first of many."

Jermaine Cousin turned toward Luke. "Years later, I went to counselling and told the psychologist that story. It was the one memory I had that was as real as the day it happened. I didn't realize until she pointed it out. My brother was trying to save me. He knew what Keating was up to. At nine years old he stood up to a monster and tried to protect me. Just like Mom told him to do." The tears came back to his eyes.

Luke thought back to his conversation with Jack. Hearing him say that Mr. Duffy had grown tired of him and asked Jack to bring Luke around still sent shivers down his spine. Jack's refusal to follow his orders may have saved Luke from the same life Jermaine was describing. These two young boys had shown more courage than all the adults around them, Gillespie thought.

"The abuse started the next night. Keating was vicious and cruel. Other Christian Brothers who were so nice in the daytime, when the staff were around, would change into animals in the nighttime. The boys would beg them to stop. There were some decent ones who would try to stop it, but they wouldn't last long at the orphanage. Sister Pius suspected something bad was happening. I don't think she knew the extent of the sexual torture that we were subjected to, but she knew something wasn't right. She would comfort me when I cried at school. She asked me over and over again what was happening. I didn't know how to tell her. At one point she asked Archbishop Keating if my brother and I could stay at the nuns' house to help with the chores, but he said no. Our mother finally took us out after two years, but the damage had been done."

Gillespie hadn't expected to hear this kind of story from Jermaine Cousin. Despite the morbidly warm temperatures on the ward, Luke's whole body was shivering. A bead of sweat was running down his back. A lump formed in his dry throat, and he fought back against the tears welling in his eyes. "What happened to your brother?"

Cousin wiped the last remaining tear off his cheek. "He killed himself." He looked through the glass pane at the sleeping archbishop. "The molestation lasted two years, but the torture lasted a lifetime. He couldn't get over his hate for Keating and those like him. The hate he felt for himself and the guilt of not protecting me. Even though we left the orphanage, Keating still came into his room every night for the rest of his life. The abuse never stopped in his mind."

"And you?" asked Luke.

"I don't know how I got through it. I tried to put it out of my mind. I went through counselling when I got older, but I never got past it. I never married like my friends. I was afraid to have children. I am afraid the monster lives in me, too."

Cousin's eye pierced the window that separated him from Keating's sleeping body. "Every time I stand here, I am five years old again. I can still smell his breath on me. I want to go in and put my hands around his throat and watch his eyes bulge as I squeeze the life out of his body. But I have no strength in my arms. I'll never be free until he is dead."

Cousin looked at his watch. "I'm late. I have to go."

He started to walk toward the door. They were both surprised to see Sgt. Nicholas Myra standing behind them. Neither had heard him come in. The policeman said nothing. As Jermaine walked past, Myra reached into his pocket, took out a business card, and handed it to him. "I would like to talk to you at your convenience," Myra whispered.

Cousin took the card, put it in his pocket as he opened the door, and left the room.

10

Mrs. Furey had arranged Dr. Gillespie's video conference for the next morning at 11:00 a.m. She had given her assistant strict orders that the only people allowed in the room were Dr. Gillespie, herself, and the hospital's disease specialist. An email invitation followed up by a phone call confirming their attendance was sent to all specialists in Nova Scotia, New Brunswick, Prince Edward Island, and Ottawa with the same strict regulations. Only doctors were allowed in the room—no interns, and no technical people to operate the phones. In total, thirteen specialists accepted the invitation.

Mrs. Furey started by making introductions. Nova Scotia and Ottawa had four doctors attending, New Brunswick had two, and Prince Edward Island had one. She thanked everyone for attending, then referred to Dr. Gillespie, again explaining that he had come across a situation and was looking for advice and guidance from his counterparts throughout the country.

"Dr. Gillespie will take the floor now."

Gillespie had been up since 5:00 a.m. trying to come up

with his first line, but he couldn't find one that didn't make him sound crazy. He cleared his throat and decided to present the cases as he had outlined them in his notebook.

"I have three patients," he began. "My first patient came in through the emergency department. He is sixty years old and was unconscious at times. He complained of an unquenchable thirst, but each time he was given water, he would spit it out, complaining it tasted like vinegar. He is in constant pain and has extreme nosebleeds. He is presently in our ICU under observation."

Gillespie could see the other doctors on the video screens were talking among themselves and taking notes.

"My second patient is also male, approximately sixty years old, with the same symptoms. He died within hours of entering the emergency. The third patient is a fifty-three-year-old male, same symptoms."

Gillespie put the notebook down and looked directly into the camera. "Information gathered from their medical files shows that all three men report an unexplained weight loss over the past year, cold or flu symptoms, fever, enlarged and swollen lymph nodes, unusual white spots in their mouths, heavy nosebleeds, and chronic pain. They also complained of an unquenchable thirst and that water tastes like vinegar."

Luke could see the other doctors were chatting at a furious pace with the colleagues sitting next to them.

"I have tested all three for a variety of diseases, and they all tested negative. I am at a complete loss to find any similarities in these men." He paused, knowing there was one similarity that he couldn't speak of. He could feel Mrs. Furey's eyes on him. He did not look toward her.

"The one who passed away was a businessman. The second man in the ICU was a child psychiatrist, and the third man is the archbishop for the province. The archbishop and the businessman knew each other, but I have no indication that the psychiatrist knew either one of them." He took a deep breath.

"Morphine seems to give them relief from the pain, but not for long. Nothing seems to stop the nosebleeds. They come on quick and heavy, and they complain there is no relief from the thirst."

Luke let out a deep sigh. "I am asking my colleagues from across Atlantic Canada and our national's capital to help me put a name on this condition and to inform me of any similar cases you may have. I will open the floor for comment now."

Doctors from all four provinces had their mics open and ready to jump at the chance to be the first to talk. Mrs. Furey pressed the master control mic, which muted everyone else. "Let's start with Ottawa, then work our way east."

"Good morning, everyone. I am the head of Infectious Diseases Unit at the Ottawa Regional Hospital. My colleagues and I thank you for organizing this video conference. We were discussing doing the same thing." She opened a file on the table in front of her. "We have seen similar cases. We have had sixty-three cases in the past twelve months. We have twelve in care now. All with the exact same symptoms. They don't get better, no matter what the treatment. They all die." She paused, then added, "Very slow, painful deaths."

"Have you taken any action?" Dr. Gillespie asked.

"We have tried to track this disease back to an original source so we can isolate it and keep it from spreading, but we can't find one. We have notified the Department of Health that we have some sort of an outbreak, but they want us to pinpoint a source before going to the media and public."

"Do any of the patients know each other? Did you find they participated in a common activity that could have led to them being infected?" Gillespie knew he was on a fishing expedition with this line of questioning.

"There are a couple of similarities. They are all male. All professionals: teachers, priests, a lawyer, and one was a gymnastics coach." She took care when saying the next sentence, as if she, too, had been warned about what she could and could not say. "Out of the sixty-three cases, fifty-five were either under investigation or charged with sexual assault on a child. The other eight did not have any criminal background, to our knowledge. A lot of the victims either did or do know each other, but they were not sexually active with each other. So, this is not a sexually transmitted disease situation. We are at a loss as to how it is spread. I will pass the mic to our colleagues in Nova Scotia for their input."

She muted her mic, and Luke noticed her hand was shaking when she reached to touch the button. She nervously exchanged nods with the other three doctors sitting around the boardroom table.

"Okay. Nova Scotia, can you add to that?" Gillespie moved on.

"Hello from Queen Elizabeth II Health Sciences Centre in Halifax. We have forty-seven cases with the same symptoms. Ten are still in care. We are wondering if anyone thinks this disease is contagious. We are worried about our health care workers interacting with these patients. We've taken precautions and ordered everyone who cares for them to wear protective masks, gloves, gowns, etc. Just because the nosebleeds are so severe."

Dr. Gillespie unmuted his mic to say, "We don't think it is contagious, but we are taking the same precautions with our health care workers as well."

"Thank you," the doctor from Nova Scotia continued. "It's funny you mentioned the criminal background of these men, and yes, all our victims are male, also. Out of the forty-seven cases, forty had known criminal records for child molestation. We know because the Halifax police department disclosed this information to us about nine months ago. They were noticing these symptoms in a pedophile ring they targeted. They thought that an epidemic was hitting the city, but we found the same results that you did. The patients didn't test positive for any of the known diseases.

"Many of the victims do know each other, but all have said they are not sexually active with those they know. Our victims are also mostly professional men. Most are married to women and heterosexual. We have asked the police if we can test some of the children who were victimized by these men. Some are now adults, and five allowed us to take their blood to test, but all results came back negative."

The Nova Scotian doctor nervously looked around the table at his colleagues. "From what we can tell, those accused of being pedophiles have these symptoms, but it is not transferred to their victims. Having said that, we do not have any proof that the seven without criminal records are pedophiles."

The doctor muted his mic and sat back in his chair. Luke could see he was relieved to have that over with. "Let's go to New Brunswick," he said, anxious to keep the conversation going.

"Bonjour from Dr. Everett Chalmers Regional Hospital in Fredericton." The new speaker pushed the file folder in front of her away and began. "We have fifty-one cases like yours.

All male, all with the same symptoms. Many do have criminal backgrounds that include child molestation; a few don't. We met with the RCMP, who notified us they also thought we were facing an epidemic, and instructed all their officers to use protective gloves, masks, etc. when dealing with or interviewing pedophiles or suspected pedophiles. We have instructed our health care workers to do the same. I am just wondering, have any of you spoken to colleagues in other parts of the country about this? Surely it's not only happening on the east coast. Has the World Health Organization been notified?" She leaned back in her chair and muted the mic to let others speak.

They all spoke among themselves, shaking their heads. The doctor from Nova Scotia pressed his mic. "I did speak to a colleague in Vancouver. They have cases, too. She told me they notified the federal Department of Health."

"Thank you. That's all we have to add right now," the doctor from New Brunswick said before muting her mic.

Luke looked over at Mrs. Furey. She was white as a sheet. Her mouth was open, but she said nothing.

Luke's hand trembled as he unmuted the mic. "My esteemed colleagues. Do we all agree we have a health crisis on our hands? If anyone disagrees, please voice your opinion now." All the doctors nodded. "Why haven't we received anything from the federal Department of Health yet? Why hasn't it leaked to the media? It seems impossible to me that so many cases exist but no one knows about it or made a connection."

The doctors stared solemnly into their screens.

"Can we agree that we all believe this disease, whatever it is called, seems to only affect a certain group of people?" Gillespie asked.

"Wormwood," the doctor from Ottawa replied, unmuting her mic. "The disease, according to police officers, is called Wormwood. They tell me it is what the pedophiles call it."

Luke almost fell off his chair. He couldn't believe he'd heard someone say it out loud. It seemed like they were all waiting for someone to say it, because within seconds they all unmuted their mics to confirm that Wormwood was the name they had heard from police and the victims of the disease.

"We can't say it only affects pedophiles, because there are victims with no known criminal histories. We have to be careful," Luke warned. "Now, what do we do?"

He stared blankly at the video conference screen. All the doctors seemed to chime in at once, and their words were swirling around in his head. Lack of resourcing. Who takes the lead? What if the media finds out and reports on a disease that kills child molesters? There were more questions than answers.

Mrs. Furey muted everyone's mic at once. "As the hospital administrator and the one who organized this group, I will immediately write to the provincial Health Department and ask them to notify the federal department, in turn setting up a national investigative committee ASAP. We need to get this under control. We need to trace this back to see when it first appeared, who had the first symptoms, and where they lived. We also need to find out if anyone has been successful in containing it or curing it."

The doctors were busily taking notes. "The federal Department of Health may already be aware of this. It will be their job, obviously, to track the disease on a national level. No one hospital would have the resources, human or financial, to do this. They may already have a computer database of cases across the country, and maybe the world. I suspect there are lots of cases that have gone undiagnosed. We can't be the only ones wondering what's going on here." If there was an epidemic, Mrs. Furey wanted to be at the forefront of it.

Furey closed off by saying, "We need to keep track of all new cases, and the nosebleeds seem to be the one thing that sets it apart from other diseases. We will form our own east coast committee and stay in touch with one another. We may be looking at a pandemic here. Who knows? What I ask you all is to go back to your existing patients and question them, as well as any new patients. In addition to when their symptoms started, ask what their profession is. Take notice if there are any pedophile investigations or charges against the person. I realize we are all just grasping at straws here, but let's document our own cases as well as we can. If this is an epidemic or a pandemic, I would like us to be the world experts on it. Thank you all for coming, and keep in touch." She muted the mic, then ended the call.

Luke knew what she was thinking. A new disease discovered by this hospital would bring financial resources through grants and donations. But would people give money to cure a disease that killed pedophiles? Luke highly doubted that. He also knew Furey was resourceful and would come up with an angle to frame this like a good-news story. That's what hospital administrators did.

The call had gone longer than expected. He still had rounds to do, so he decided he would call Nick Myra in the morning.

11

The Basilica of St. John the Baptist, in the heart of the city, was the most beautiful church that Dr. Luke Gillespie had ever seen. This was the church his mother had brought him to as a child. Every family event had been held here, from baptisms to funerals. He had been in other churches over the years for events, but none of them matched the gilded splendour of the Basilica of St. John the Baptist.

He sat in the front pew, sprawled off with his head tilted as far back as it could go. He always marvelled at the workmanship in the ceiling. The basilica was in the shape of a crucifix. Every inch of the ceiling was covered in ornate gold designs and paintings. *Who did this work?* Luke thought to himself. *They must have spent months on top of scaffolding, painstakingly planning and etching each golden swirl and stroke.*

His gaze fell to the statues framing the altar. Each of the Apostles was carved from the finest marble and stood guard over the church: Matthew, Mark, Luke, and John. They each had a corner and stood high up on marble shelves, carrying a message of their own. What was it? Luke couldn't remember. Only that he was named after St. Luke the Evangelist. The patron saint of artists, physicians, and surgeons. Was it a coincidence that his mother named him after the patron saint of physicians and surgeons, or had she planned it from the beginning? She had always told him he was going to be a doctor.

Why was he even in this church? he wondered. He started the morning with his regular run to clear his head but decided to take a different route today. He ran up Military Road to take advantage of the steep inclines and hills in that area. When he reached the top of one incline, he stopped, put his hands on his hips, and filled his lungs with deep breaths of salt air from the Atlantic Ocean. As the sweat ran off his forehead and down his face, he wiped it back with his hands.

He couldn't sleep last night. He kept going over and over the information he had gathered from the video conference with the other doctors. Everyone seemed to know what this was, but no one wanted to say. Everyone was waiting for the other person to admit some of their patients had been charged with sexual assaults on children. Then, how was it spread? Was it through blood, semen, or other bodily fluids? Was someone infecting pedophiles on purpose? That couldn't be. They couldn't travel all over the country to do this. Was it a curse from God? Luke refused to think that way. *God doesn't create diseases. They are created by our environment, infection, unhealthy lifestyles, or a person's genes.*

The sweat was blurring Luke's vision. He tried to wipe it away with his T-shirt. When his vision became clear again, he looked up and saw the ten-foot-high, pure white marble statue of St. John the Baptist standing on top of a triple arch constructed of enormous blocks of granite. Luke remembered Sister

Francis, his fourth-grade teacher, explaining that the statue represented St. John preaching penance as he held a baptismal shell in his left hand. Sister Pius's words came back to him. *Are you washed in the blood of the lamb?* He walked through the biggest arch onto the piazza, past the twenty-foot marble statue of the Immaculate Conception on its granite pedestal.

He slowly mounted the steps, wondering if the basilica would be open. He pulled at the large wooden door and was surprised to find it unlocked. He entered the vestibule and looked around. To the left in a niche stood a life-size marble statue of *Christ with Doctors*. It stood on a base displaying five identical sculptured faces. Luke remember his mother telling him the name of the marble statue when he was young.

He pushed the main door open and entered the basilica itself. The beauty and elegance of the church, bathed in the sunlight streaming in from the stained glass windows, was overwhelming and immediately filled Luke with a feeling of peace.

Luke walked down the main aisle toward the altar that enshrined one of the most revered and valuable pieces of statuary in the basilica, *The Dead Christ*. He sat in the first white oak pew. His mind was full of questions and no answers. He lost track of time as he admired the architecture and tried to sort out the thoughts in his head. He was so caught up in the beauty of the basilica that he didn't notice the man standing ten feet away from him.

"You're a little early for Mass."

Luke snapped to attention in his seat and looked around frantically to see who had spoken. An older man was walking toward him. He was dressed in jeans and a plaid shirt. Luke assumed he was the caretaker.

"I was passing by and decided to come in. The door was open. I hope you don't mind." Luke wasn't sure if he was allowed to be there.

"The doors are always open, son." The man gestured toward the back. "It's a church. You're welcome any time." He reached his hand out to Luke. "I'm Father Peter Cooke."

Luke stood and shook his hand. "I'm Luke Gillespie." He suddenly felt embarrassed by his appearance and looked down at his sweat-stained T-shirt and running shorts. "I'm sorry," he apologized. "I'm not dressed for church."

"That's okay. I'm not dressed for church either." Both men stood in an awkward silence.

Luke turned to leave the pew. "I better get back to my run."

"What are you running from?" Father Cooke inquired.

"I'm not running from anything. Just exercising to clear my head." Luke wasn't convinced by his own answer.

"Well, if you ran here, there must be something on your mind. People run to the church when they need hope, courage, or strength to face a challenge."

Is that what he was doing here?

"Father . . ." Luke hesitated, then decided to go with it. "Do you have nosebleeds?"

Father Cooke gestured to Luke to move farther into the pew. "Sit down and let's talk nosebleeds." Luke sat down again, and Father Cooke sat next to him.

"No. I don't have nosebleeds. Do you?" The priest looked into Luke's eyes like he could see his whole soul.

"No. I don't," Luke stammered. "I am a doctor."

"Oh. Then the medical field is catching up with this crisis, finally." Father Cooke nodded and sat back in the pew.

"You know about the nosebleeds?" Luke asked.

"Yes. I know about Wormwood, if that's what you're asking. What do you want to know?"

Luke looked at the priest and for the first time noticed how kind this man's eyes were. "Everything," he replied.

"Wormwood is the name of a star in the Revelation to John 8:10, 11. 'The third angel sounded his trumpet, and a great star, blazing like a torch, fell from the sky on a third of the rivers and on the springs of water—Wormwood is the name of the star.'" The priest recited the information just as Sister Pius had.

"Who wrote Revelations?" Luke was curious now.

"People originally thought it was John the Baptist, the builder of this church, but the writer was identified as St. John the Divine," replied Father Cooke.

Luke looked around again. It was all coming together, but what did it mean? Why was he at *this* church? Was it all a coincidence? Walking by the *Christ with Doctors* statue, meeting this priest, learning that St. John the Divine wrote about Wormwood in Revelations, and now he stood in John the Baptist's church under the very statue he was named after. Was this all planned? He felt light-headed and unsteady. A wave of sweat came over him, and it dripped from his forehead onto the pew. He frantically wiped it away with his hand.

"Are you okay?" Father Cooke asked. "Do you need some water?" He started to stand.

"No. I am okay. Do you believe in coincidence?"

"No, I don't," answered the priest as he sat down again. "I believe we are where we are supposed to be at all times." He knew Luke was troubled. "You are here in this church, in this pew, talking to me for a reason. This is not an accident, Luke. It is not a coincidence. Maybe it is serendipity." He looked toward the great altar. "Maybe there is a benefit to you being here."

"What is it, then?"

"We both want to find out more about Wormwood, don't we?" Father Cooke raised an eyebrow.

"Yes, I guess we do. How do we stop it or cure it?"

"We don't. We let it run its course."

Luke was surprised to hear him say that. "What? Let these people suffer and then die? What kind of priest are you?"

"One who is sick of constantly facing accusations of being a child molester." Father Cooke rose from his seat and walked to the other side of the pew. "I was called to follow God. I never doubted that. I wanted to teach children about science and math in addition to religion. I was good at my job. Then, suddenly, parents are telling their children not to come near me because I am a priest. I can't get altar boys to stand at Sunday Mass anymore. I am painted with the sins of evil men." Now the priest was sweating. "They ruined my calling. They ruined my church. They crucified my God all over again, and we can never come back from that." He lowered his head to catch his breath. "Our Lord suffered on the Cross." He pointed to the back of the church, where a huge wooden crucifix hung. "Why shouldn't these child molesters suffer and die like he did?"

Gillespie was shocked. He hadn't expect a priest to say such things. "What about forgiveness? What about 'love your enemy as yourself'?" To Luke, these people were his patients, and all this talk of Wormwood was nonsense not proven by science.

"What about it?" The priest waved his arms around. "Look around this church. Every Sunday it used to be packed with parishioners who came to be part of a community. To love God.

Where are they now? I am lucky if twenty pews are filled on Sundays. Families don't come to church anymore. They can't forgive us for not protecting them. Even little old ladies don't come to church anymore because they can't forgive us for not giving them a prominent role in the church. They set up the altar and sing in the choir. My God, the Virgin Mary is the most powerful of all Catholic figures, and we can't let a woman say Mass?"

Father Cooke was pacing back and forth in front of Luke's pew with his hands on his hips. He had some pent-up frustration that he wasn't keeping in anymore.

"Don't talk to me about forgiveness. Let God forgive them. Those bastards destroyed the lives of little children. What's wrong with letting them die?"

Luke was speechless. He sat back to let the priest's words sink in as Father Cooke continued his tirade. "Jesus said, 'Let the children alone, and do not hinder them from coming to Me; for the kingdom of heaven belongs to such as these.' He wanted to protect the children. He wanted us, as his followers, to protect the children, but we didn't." He paused. "We protected the child molesters, and now we are damned for all time. Just like Judas. We betrayed Him again and again. Is there any wonder He unleashed this plague upon the earth?"

"Are you saying you believe God is punishing pedophiles by infecting them with this disease? How? How does He infect them? Where did it start?" Luke couldn't believe he was having this conversation.

"Yes, it is God. They are infected when they molest a child. It's not transferred by any bodily fluid. It doesn't matter if it is a boy or a girl. The molester feels the pain a thousand times stronger than the agony of their victims. Every time the victim or molester thinks about the abuse or cries out from the memory, the molester is tortured for their sins." The priest was pale and almost foaming at the mouth as he spoke.

"What about those who are not pedophiles who have the symptoms? Not everyone affected is being investigated or accused of abusing children," Luke informed him.

"Yes, they are! They just haven't been caught," Father Cooke shot back.

"What about the blood? Why the blood?" Gillespie was also standing now and pacing next to the pew.

"The blood is how God tells you if they are guilty or not. It is how He marks them, so others will know. It doesn't matter how rich or powerful the molester is. He can never hide from the blood of the lamb. He is marked for all time. It will only stop when he confesses. Then he dies with absolution. If he doesn't, he goes to Hell, where he belongs."

Luke was standing still, staring at him. "Father, if a child molester came to you and asked for forgiveness, would you give it?" He really wanted to know the answer to this question.

Father Cooke stood straight and gave his answer like he had rehearsed it many times. "Only if they asked their victims for forgiveness first and were granted it."

"Really? As a priest, isn't it your job to give forgiveness?"

The priest had a vacant expression. "No. It's God's job to give forgiveness. I am just the middleman."

"Life is funny, isn't it, Father?"

"No. Life is horrible. Life is damn horrible and hard. I can't help the victims any more than you can help your patients with bloody noses. I prayed and prayed for an answer. Why? I kept asking God. Why are You letting them destroy Your Church?" The priest sat down, and Luke sat next to him.

"He finally answered me, didn't He? He'd finally had enough. He sent this disease to rid the world of pedophiles. Now you are here praying for a cure. Why would you want to cure them?" The priest grabbed Luke by the arm as if to shake him awake.

"It's my job," said Gillespie. "I have a calling, too. I cure people. I took an oath. I am a doctor." Luke had no problem defending his duties as a physician.

"Well, I guess you've come up against a mighty opponent. Let's see who wins." Father Cooke stood tall to end the conversation. "I'd say may God be with you, but I know God is with the children on this one."

Luke fell back on his medical training. "Let's see about that. Science still has a say."

As he was walking back toward the front doors, Luke heard Father Cooke call out to him, and he turned around.

"Luke, are you going to explain this to the media?"

"What? No. We are in the beginning stages of discovery right now. We're not ready for the media. It would cause mass panic."

Father Cooke raised an eyebrow. "Really? Too bad, because I already have my media strategy ready to execute. This time the church will not be the last one at the podium."

"What are you saying? You're going to the media without scientific explanation? You're going to tell the public that God created a disease that kills pedophiles? You can't be serious!" Luke was shocked by the man's arrogance.

"Are you kidding me? This is the opportunity every church has been waiting for. It's a miracle! Should we wait until the

Muslims claim it? Or the Jews? Not this time. I prayed for this miracle, and I got it. As word spreads, people will come back to the church in droves."

"You're going to use this disease to bring people back to church?" Luke couldn't believe it. "What are you going to do? Stand in front of the cameras with the new Commandments on stone tablets?"

"Luke," the priest laughed. "God doesn't use stone tablets anymore. I am posting it to my blog tomorrow. Then, Facebook. The media will call me. By the end of the week, I'll be an international saviour."

Luke knew he was right, and he kind of supported him, in a way. What was wrong with killing off pedophiles? He contemplated the United States government executing prisoners and the public supporting it. The people who opposed it always said there was a chance they were wrongly accused, but there were no wrongly accused here.

Luke left the basilica and ran down Harvey Road toward Quidi Vidi Lake, where he had parked his car. He considered Father Cooke's stand on this. *God looks into your soul. God judges your soul. God washes you in the blood of the lamb. Case closed.*

He still had to meet with Sgt. Myra. He wondered if Nick knew Father Peter Cooke.

12

Luke got off the elevator on the fifth floor at the same time Nurse Agatha Catania was running down the hall. The two bumped into one another.

"Oh, my God, I am sorry." Nurse Agatha Catania was in her own world, deep in thought, and on a mission to get to the ICU as quickly as she could. It took a second before she realized it was Luke she had run into.

"What's your hurry?" Gillespie asked. "You almost took me off my feet."

"Walk with me to the ICU. I have something for you to do this morning," she teased. "We have a new patient on the way up from emerg."

"Another bleeder?" Gillespie asked.

"Yes, but not like the others. This one will throw you for a loop."

"Why? What's so different about this one?" Gillespie's curiosity was getting the better of him. "Not another archbishop?"

"Nope. A female! This time the bleeder is a female." Agatha

used her building access pass to get into the ICU. The buzzer sounded, and she opened the door to let herself and Luke in.

"When did this one come in?" Luke asked, flipping through the patient's files on the ICU's desk.

Agatha updated him. "Late last night. Emergency couldn't get the bleeding to stop, and they were aware we had two patients with the same symptoms. They are sending her up. She should be here any second now."

"I have to call Sgt. Myra this morning, too," Luke said. He looked at his watch and hoped to get it done soon, because he wanted to discuss the pedophile theory more.

"Sgt. Myra is in the room with the child psychiatrist," the nurse behind the counter informed him.

"Let me check on that patient." Agatha was becoming smitten with the police sergeant. "I loves me some Sgt. Myra first thing in the morning."

"Really?" Luke was surprised. "You're into older cops?"

"Have you seen the size of his hands? I love a man with big hands. The moustache is kind of hot, too. Find out if he's married," she said with a flirty smile.

"I will not," Luke replied.

"He does have those rugged movie-star looks," the nurse behind the counter joined in.

"Is that how he gets into ICU all the time? Because you all think he is a hot cop?" Luke asked.

"Why, yes! We don't let the ugly cops in at all."

Agatha picked up the patient's file and went to the room to meet with Sgt. Myra. At the same time, the two doors to the ICU flung open, and two attendants quickly pushed a gurney through with a woman lying on it.

"Your new patient is here," the gurney operator said. "Which room is she going in?"

"This one over here," said a nurse. She hurried from behind the counter and pointed to an empty room next to the archbishop's. The attendants followed, and Luke could hear them in the room transferring the new patient to the hospital bed that awaited her. Luke took the file from one of the attendants and started to read through it.

Sixty-one-year-old female, school principal, lived in coastal Labrador for thirty-five years, recently retired, started having severe nosebleeds about a year ago. Luke read through all the same symptoms that the other patients had shown.

Nick Myra and Agatha exited the other patient's room, smiling at each other. "Luke," Myra asked with a grin, "do you have time to chat now?"

"I did until this new patient came in." Gillespie pointed at the room. "This one doesn't fit your profile. The new patient is female."

"Why? Do you think women can't be pedophiles?" Myra was surprised.

"I suppose. I've never thought about it, really. Either way, I must go take her vitals. Give me an hour, and I will meet you in the cafeteria for a coffee. By the way, why were you in the psychiatrist's room?"

"He was coherent this morning, and I had some questions to ask him." Sgt. Myra put the black notebook he was carrying in the inside pocket of his blazer. "He was actually quite forthcoming today."

"He asked to put his lawyer on the visitors list," Agatha informed them both.

"That's his choice. Now I must go see my new patient and prove your theory wrong." Gillespie picked up the file and went to see his new patient.

She was groggy but awake. Luke thought she looked like a typical schoolmarm. Her grey hair was tightly pulled back in a bun on the top of her head, and the crease was neatly combed down the middle. A small, pink, childlike bow pinned the bun to her head. Even a night in the emerg hadn't caused a hair to go astray. She wore tiny circular glasses with gold rims, and her scrawny, birdlike hands had the blanket pulled up to her chin. Her chart said she was five foot six and 130 pounds. Gillespie decided she looked more like a nun than Sister Pius. There was no next of kin noted on her chart.

"How are you feeling, Mrs. Power?" Dr. Gillespie asked.

"Oh, I'm all right, Doctor," she said, giving him a coy look. "I have an awful nosebleed and a lot of pain sometimes."

"I know, and I am trying to get to the bottom of that for you. Can I ask you a few questions before I order some tests to see what's going on?"

She nodded yes, and Gillespie opened her file again. "It says here you're a retired school principal. Where did you teach?"

"I taught up through coastal Labrador for thirty-five years." She pointed a bony finger toward the ceiling. "All Aboriginal communities. Hard children they were to teach, too. You know what they're like." The new patient pursed her lips and shook her head, like she was disgusted with something. She put one hand over the other and cracked her knuckles, making a godawful sound.

Gillespie was taken aback by her racist undertones. He had seen stories in the media about children in Labrador's indigenous communities who sniffed gas and had to be removed from their homes and school, but he had also worked with a native doctor when he was an intern who turned out to be one of the best mentors he'd ever had.

"Is it all right if I listen to your chest?" Gillespie took the stethoscope that hung around his neck and put it in his ears. Mrs. Power let go of one corner of the blanket, and he tugged it out of her other hand, then pulled the coverlet down to her chest. She was still wearing a hospital gown, and she had it tied tightly in the back. "I am going to have to untie the gown to examine you."

She turned her head to the left and rolled onto her side. Gillespie could tell she was terribly uncomfortable with this. He untied the string at the neck and slid the stethoscope down to her chest. Her breathing was laboured but clear. There was no sign of fluid on her lungs. He moved the stethoscope and she jumped a little, like she had been startled. Gillespie decided this must be the closest she had ever been to a man.

"Your chest sounds fine right now, Mrs. Power. Can you tell me how long you've had those dark spots on your back and chest?"

"Ms. Power," she corrected him. "I have never been married. Those spots showed up about a year ago. I believe they are age spots, but they are awful big for age spots, don't you think? I also have diarrhea almost every day. I have lost so much weight over the past year."

"Okay, I will let the nurses know, and they will take care of you, Ms. Power." Gillespie was careful to use *Ms.* instead of *Mrs.* "I will check the spots for you. You don't have any next of kin noted on your chart. Can you give me the name of someone I can put there in case of emergency?"

"No. I don't have any family." She leered at him. "I was married to my job. Devoted to the children I taught."

"Yes, of course, but is there a friend, a neighbour, maybe an old student, anyone we can call to let them know you're in hospital?"

"No. I kept to myself, really. I live alone. I like it that way. I don't want anyone in my business. I am tired now. Go away." She pulled the blankets back up to her chin, then closed her eyes.

Who's taking care of your fifty cats? Dr. Gillespie wanted to ask, but he bit his tongue. He walked out of her room and headed toward the cafeteria to meet up with Sgt. Myra.

13

Dr. Luke Gillespie bought an extra-large coffee and looked around the cafeteria for Nick Myra. He spotted him at a corner table talking to Agatha, and even from that distance he could tell the sergeant was flirting with his nurse.

"Excuse me. Am I interrupting anything?" Luke asked as he sat at the table.

Agatha began to blush, and Luke realized that she really was quite caught up with this police officer. "So, are you making daily trips to my ICU to take statements, or are you just looking for an excuse to see my favourite nurse?"

"I cannot confirm or deny your suspicions at this point in my investigation, Dr. Gillespie," Nick answered in an official tone. "Now tell me about your newest pedophile."

"Not this time," Luke answered. "She's a retired school principal who spent her entire career teaching in coastal Labrador. Never married and has no family. She is an old spinster and can probably eat the pillars out of the church."

"You're still convinced that she's not a pedophile because

she's female, aren't you? What do you think the number one profession of a pedophile is?"

"I don't know . . . priest?"

"No. School principal. Teacher is second. Priest is actually not on the list," Myra informed both Luke and Agatha. "Children who are abused are almost always abused by their caregivers, meaning their own parents, step-parents, relatives, babysitters, even camp counsellors. Priests don't have access to children anymore. They don't teach in public schools like they used to, and there are not as many altar boys or choirboys at church."

Luke and Agatha were shocked by the information, but neither one had children, so they'd never thought about it before.

"As a matter of fact," Nick continued, "out of all my files that I've investigated over the past five years, not one victim mentioned a priest, until last year, when the archbishop's name came up and victims started to come forward."

"I would never have thought of a teacher as a child molester," Agatha said. "I loved all my teachers. I guess you tend to trust a female more than a male around kids."

"Most times child abusers are teachers, a neighbour, a friend of a parent, or someone a parent has been dating. I have four cases where the children were molested by a handyman a parent had hired to do repairs around the house, and it wasn't the same handyman, either. I'm talking four different cases. Each time the guy took just a little too long to finish the job. Gained the trust of the parent. Befriended the child and took note of what park they went to, where they hung out, and then conveniently ran into them. You'd be surprised at how quickly parents will trust strangers even though they tell their kids never to do it."

"I would never suspect a handyman or a good friend of

mine." Agatha was shocked by her own lack of knowledge on the subject.

"Children are more likely to be molested at home or school than church. Nine out of ten times the child and parent know the molester well. What always kills me is every time I take a statement, the parent will say, 'I had a funny feeling something was wrong, but I didn't want to insult my friend, neighbour, brother, etc.' They would rather put their head in the sand and pretend everything is okay."

"My God, you learn something new every day, don't you?" Agatha felt a chill run down her spine.

"I still don't think my new patient meets the profile of a pedophile." Luke just couldn't picture this little old lady abusing kids.

"Okay," Nick stated. "She lived alone all her life in isolated communities. Rather than cling to family or friends to maintain contact with the outside world, she isolated herself. As a principal, she would have had unlimited access to kids and would have been the only authoritative voice over them. It would always be her word over theirs. Now does she fit the profile?" Sgt. Myra could see Luke was thinking about it. "If she were a man, you would agree with me, but because she is a little old lady, you can't get your head around it!"

Luke's pager went off and startled all three of them. He hurried for the nearest phone and had a quick conversation before rushing back to the table.

"The archbishop is crashing! We need to go to ICU."

Luke and Agatha bolted for the nearest elevator. When they arrived, Father Horan was standing outside the archbishop's room with his hands over his mouth and tears streaming down his face. Sister Pius was standing next to him, looking intently through the viewing window. Jermaine Cousin was standing farther down from them, watching, and doing a poor job of pretending to be there on other business.

Nurses were busy hooking up monitors and other equipment to the archbishop's frail body. He was awake and coughing, gasping for air. Blood trickled from his nose and mouth. Every few minutes he would cry out in pain.

"He is hooked up to a morphine drip," the lead nurse informed Dr. Gillespie. "Will I increase it?"

"Yes, give him more and see if we can get the pain under control, then the blood may stop," he ordered.

Archbishop Keating abruptly sat up in bed and let out a terrifying shriek as the pain hit him again. Blood began to gush from his nose. He choked as every breath he took through his mouth was full of his own blood. The morphine wasn't helping and seemed to make the pain worse. He gave another loud, piercing cry like a man who was being brutally tortured.

Sister Pius ran into the room. "For God's sake, make it stop!" She stood shaking with fear.

Gillespie never saw her coming until she was standing next to him. "We're doing everything we can," he shouted back.

Sister Pius grabbed Luke by the arm. "There's nothing *you* can do." She looked him in the eyes "He has to stop this himself!" She grabbed the archbishop by the arm and shook him. "Confess! Ask for forgiveness. Free your victims. For God's sake, free your own soul. You're going to Hell!" She was shaking with anger as she locked eyes with the archbishop.

"Bring Charles in," the archbishop said weakly to Sister Pius. Archbishop Patrick Keating looked frightened for the first time since Gillespie had met him. Sister Pius turned and gestured for Father Charles Horan to come into the room. He walked slowly to his archbishop's side.

A tear rolled down the archbishop's cheek when Father Horan looked at him. "I am sorry, Charles. I am sorry for what I did to you."

Father Horan began to weep uncontrollably. His whole body shook with each heavy sob. He couldn't speak.

"I don't know how it happened. I couldn't control myself. I have ruined so many lives." The archbishop looked his victim in the eye. "Will you please forgive me, Charles?"

"Yes, Father," Horan sobbed. "I forgive you."

Luke, Agatha, and the other nurses stood around the bed in shocked silence. No one had noticed that Sister Pius had left the room until she came back with Jermaine Cousin by the hand.

"You need to ask forgiveness from all your victims," she said sharply as she pushed a shaking Jermaine Cousin toward the bed.

Archbishop Keating looked at Sister Pius with pure hate in his eyes. "What, did you go looking for them?" he spat at her.

"There's so many, they are not hard to find," she snapped.

Jermaine Cousin didn't cry. He stood firm at the side of the bed. He had dreamed about this moment for most of his life. He could feel the spirit of his brother standing next to him. Protecting him. He waited for the archbishop to ask him the question.

The archbishop looked away from Sister Pius and changed his facial expression from one of defiance to one of a sweet old man on his deathbed. He gently looked at Jermaine and in a sickly sweet voice asked, "Will you forgive me?"

"Who am I?" Jermaine asked.

"I am old. My memory fails me at times," the archbishop said, vaguely recognizing something in the X-ray technician's eyes.

"You don't remember me, do you?"

"I can't think of your name right now. Refresh my memory for me, son?"

"My God, you have molested so many boys you can't even remember who they are!" Cousin felt a sour gall rise in his throat.

"I know you, and I see your saucy brother standing next to you, too," Archbishop Keating said, pointing a bloodstained finger at Jermaine. "He was nothing but trouble. He asked for what he got. I am the true victim here!"

"You are a victim of your own ego!" Sister Pius grabbed the archbishop by the hospital dressing gown. "Release these boys, you rotten bastard. Give them peace!" Dr. Gillespie grabbed her from behind and pulled her off the archbishop.

A wave of pain like no other came over the archbishop, and his whole body curved at a horrible angle. His eyeballs bulged from their sockets, and from his nose came a gout of blood so thick that the nurses were sure his whole body had to be empty by now. As he fell back in the bed, he finally realized he knew what had to be done. He looked directly into Jermaine's eyes and in a sincere voice asked, "Please forgive me. I am sorry for what I did to you and your brother. I beg you for forgiveness."

Jermaine walked to the side of the bed and stood next to Father Horan. He glared at the old archbishop and said, "No. Go to Hell!" Then he spat in the old man's face and turned and walked out of the room. There was a collective gasp of astonishment in the room.

The archbishop reached up to wipe the spittle off his face. "Charles, help me. Get a tissue," he ordered his assistant.

"No. No. I won't help you. This is not remorse. This is you trying to get out of pain. You lied to me!" Horan shouted. "You lied to me my whole life! You ruined my life. You saddled me with your crimes and sin." He moved back from the bed. "I don't forgive you. I will never forget what you did to me and all the others. I will never forgive you!"

For the first time in Father Charles Horan's life, he made a decision on his own. He turned and walked out of the room. Sister Pius ran behind him. Another wave of pain came over the archbishop, and as he sat up to brace for it, he collapsed back on the bed. He drew a deep, laboured breath, filled with his own blood, that caught in his throat. It would be his final breath.

The machine signalled a flat line, and Dr. Gillespie called the time of death.

As Luke walked out of the hospital room, Agatha pulled the blanket up over the archbishop's face. Looking at him one last time, she saw that his face had frozen in pain and he looked every bit like Lucifer himself. She threw the blanket over his head and ran out of the room.

Sgt. Myra was standing outside the ICU with Father Horan and Jermaine Cousin. They couldn't help but notice the look on her face. "He's dead?" asked Sgt. Myra.

"Yes." Agatha was trembling. "His face will haunt me till the day I die. You should have seen it. I've seen lots of people die, and they always look peaceful, like they're sleeping. Not him. His face was pure evil."

"Well, most people go to Heaven. This is the first time you've seen someone go straight to Hell," Sister Pius enlightened them.

Charles and Jermaine stood in silence, both unsure what to do next. Nick Myra stood in front of the two men.

"You're free now. You're free to live your lives and put this behind you. You were both victims. Neither of you asked for this monster to come into your lives. He preyed on the helpless. He sought you out. This is not your fault."

Neither could utter a word of reply. Father Charles Horan reached out his hand and shook Sgt. Myra's. He faked a smile as he choked back tears, then walked toward the elevator. Myra wondered if he would stay in the priesthood.

Jermaine Cousin also shook his hand. "Thank you," was all he could say. As he walked away, Myra could swear he felt the presence of another person walking with him.

Luke joined Agatha and Nick in the hallway. "What is it? Myra, what do you see?" Luke asked.

"I just got this gut feeling that Jermaine Cousin has a guardian angel." He was surprised by his own words.

"He does. He has a brother who protects him. Maybe more than he knows. I think they both found peace today." Gillespie watched Jermaine get on the elevator.

"But neither gave him forgiveness," Agatha stated. "I don't get it. I thought to find peace you had to give forgiveness."

"Not always," answered Nick. "Sometimes you find peace through retribution and justice."

14

Father Peter Cooke was pacing up and down the vestibule inside the great doors of the Basilica of St. John the Baptist. His eyes were closed as he ran through the script in his mind. Had he covered everything? Had he anticipated all possible questions? The priest reviewed his speaking notes every few steps, hoping he wouldn't forget anything. He would have one chance to get this right, and he didn't want to fail his Lord and Saviour. This time, *he* would save the Church.

His morning had started with the news of Archbishop Keating's death. It was perfect timing. Father Cooke knew God Himself had aligned the stars in his favour. With Keating out of the way, he was now free to protect the children and let the world know that God was unleashing His plague upon the world.

When he posted the news release to the basilica's website and social media pages that morning, he hadn't expected the phones to light up so quickly. Within seconds of posting the announcement, his elderly receptionist was inundated with calls from the media.

In between questions from reporters, the new, temporary archbishop called and demanded he answer the phone. Father Cooke whispered, "I am not here," to the poor lady who was doing her best to keep up. The Church was still reeling from the death of Archbishop Patrick Keating. Media outlets had been announcing his death all morning. Several asked for permission to shoot footage inside the basilica, and Father Cooke saw this as his sign from God.

Not this time, he thought. *You will not stop me this time.* Beads of sweat dripped from his forehead, and he mopped them away with a cotton handkerchief he kept in his pocket. He decided to wear his Eucharist vestment today instead of his normal choir dress. *After all*, he thought, *this will be the most important central act of divine worship that I will take part in.*

He stood still for the first time, statue-like, in front of the great wooden doors at the front of the Basilica of St. John the Baptist. The sun beamed in from the top windows. He prayed for guidance. He prayed for strength. He prayed for hope. He prayed that this rebellious act was rooted and grounded in his love for the Church and not vengeance against those who had hurt it.

Father Cooke closed his eyes and took several deep breaths to calm his nerves. His eyes opened slowly, and his focus was intense. His jaw was clenched like a fighter walking into a ring. His breathing was slower, deeper than usual. It was as if someone else had taken possession of his whole body. He raised his arms, his steady hands grabbed the two large handles, and he pulled the massive doors open, causing a downdraft to rush into the vestibule and swirl his robes around him. The priest calmly walked toward the media storm, basking in the glow of the camera's lights, knowing he was now in control of the whole Catholic

Church. The entire foundation of the Roman Catholic religion, and Christianity itself, would implode and be rebuilt today.

He recalled Matthew 16:18. *And I tell you, you are Peter, and on this rock, I will build My church, and the gates of Hell shall not prevail against it.* He was indeed Peter—Father Peter Cooke—and this rock was the island of Newfoundland and Labrador. The most easterly point in North America. Father Cooke envisioned himself as the gatekeeper.

The steps in front of the Basilica of St. John the Baptist were full of reporters, camera people, and TV camera tripods. They were scurrying to set up before Father Cooke came out to speak. His news release inviting them to attend his news conference was short and to the point:

> **Blood of the lamb: God has arrived to kill pedophiles**
> Father Peter Cooke, Diocese Priest at the Basilica of St. John the Baptist, is holding a news conference on Tuesday, May 1, 2018, at 10:00 a.m. on the steps of the basilica to discuss Wormwood, God's revenge on pedophiles.

The news conference notice shot through newsrooms throughout the province and the country like a bullet. Wide-eyed reporters sat staring at the screens on their phones, wondering if this was a prank. Calls to the basilica office verified that it was indeed real. Every other story happening in the country went on the back burner. News directors were barking out orders to dig out footage of past interviews with church officials, victims, or anyone who could add to what they rightfully predicted was going to be the biggest story of the year.

Reporters staked their spots on the steps of the basilica, each trying to get a front-row seat to Father Cooke's show. When the doors to the grand basilica opened, they were not disappointed. This Catholic priest walked toward them like he was the Pope himself. He looked calm and fierce, more like a warrior than an ordained man of God.

The great doors stayed open behind him, and the photographers were pleased to see how this priest was framed by the long aisle that led to the statue of *The Dead Christ* lying across the altar. It was as if he had planned it that way.

Father Cooke stood in front of the media. A hush came over the pack. All microphones and lenses were on him.

His eyes were dark and hypnotic. He took a deep breath, and his lips parted. Everyone who stood in front of him held their breath, waiting on his first word. Nobody moved. He tilted his head toward the sky, as if asking for permission to speak. Lowering it, he looked directly at the crowd gathered in front of him. His voice at first was calm and low.

"My name is Father Peter Cooke. I am a Catholic priest. A servant of God. I have come to talk to you about Wormwood."

As he spoke, his preprogrammed social media updates appeared every five minutes on the basilica's Facebook and Twitter streams. Each one was shared and retweeted by the dozens, then hundreds, then thousands, then tens of thousands, until Father Cooke began to trend worldwide. By the power of God, and social media, he would own this story.

His voice took on a strong, authoritative tone. "Wormwood is the name of a star in Revelation 8:10, 11. The third angel sounded his trumpet, and a great star, blazing like a torch, fell from the sky on a third of the rivers and on the springs of water—the name of the star is Wormwood. A third of the waters turned bitter, and many people died from the waters that had become bitter."

He looked around at the baffled faces in the media, each one standing still with mouth open and microphone pointed at him, not knowing what was coming next.

"For many years, scholars had interpreted this passage as a comet, meteorite, or a natural disaster striking the earth." His voice took the tone of a backwoods preacher. "I am here to tell you, today, that those scholars are all wrong! They are wrong." He lifted both arms toward the heavens. "Wormwood is not a natural disaster. It is a disease. A disease that affects only pedophiles!" The reporters looked cynical, as if unable to decide if this was real or not. Then a huge, cold gust of wind swept over the crowd. It was as if Father Cooke's news conference came with special effects. It took a second to process what the priest had just said. Then the reporters went into overdrive.

Father Cooke felt a power inside him that he had never felt before. The true meaning of his life was unfolding before his eyes. He felt like his body was being lifted toward heaven. Words were coming out of his mouth, and he had no idea who was speaking. He continued with his sermon.

"The very saint that this basilica was named for, John the Apostle, wrote about Wormwood in Revelations. About a year ago, I became aware of symptoms that some parishioners were having. Every now and again someone would ask me to pray for their father, brother, uncle, or aunt who was suffering. After a while I found it odd that these people all had the same symptoms, but no disease was ever attributed to their suffering. Until one day a man came to confession and told me his sins. He confessed that he had molested his nephew. As he spoke to me, his nose began to bleed profusely. He told me every time he thought of the molestation he would experience nosebleeds, severe pain, and an unquenchable thirst."

The media people stood silent with their mouths agape. They could hardly believe what they were hearing. They never uttered a word, but they were tweeting out quotes as fast as Father Cooke explained.

God creates disease to kill pedophiles #Godisback, tweeted a TV reporter.

John the Baptist wrote about a disease that kills pedophiles called Wormwood #Godisback, tweeted a newspaper reporter.

Father Cooke knew he had the media where he wanted them. He took strategic breaths and paced himself to allow them time to update their social media feeds. He knew by the time he walked back in through the basilica doors he would be famous worldwide.

"Then, I was giving the last rites to a dying man. He was in great pain, suffering nosebleeds, and called all water poisonous. On his deathbed, he confessed that he, too, had been a child molester and felt insurmountable remorse toward his victims. Once he confessed his sins, the bleeding and pain stopped. He sipped water without issue and died peacefully."

Disease is cured when pedophiles confess #Godisback, tweeted a reporter.

Cooke waited for the reporters to look at him again, then continued. "I began to notice a trend. When each sinner confessed, the pain and suffering stopped. When they didn't confess, the pain and suffering worsened. They were being tortured for their sins by God Himself."

God is torturing pedophiles, claims priest #Godisbadass, tweeted a young reporter in the back of the crowd.

The priest settled back on his heels, enjoying the heat of the limelight. "I started investigating and found the community of pedophiles referred to this disease as Wormwood. In Revelations, wormwood is a well-known bitter taste. They call the disease Wormwood because it makes all water taste bitter, and without water a human can only live for three days."

He watched as they took notes with a vengeance. "This disease only affects pedophiles, not victims. They suffer great pain that cannot be calmed with drugs or alcohol. Which is God's way of punishing them for their sins. Then He afflicts them with unstoppable nosebleeds. Jesus said He would wash us from our sins in His own blood. The blood of the lamb."

Pedophiles being killed by the blood of the lamb #Godisback #Godisbadass. Twitter was on fire worldwide with news of the disease created by God to kill pedophiles. Google was breaking from millions of people searching *Basilica of St. John the Baptist* and *St. John's, NL.*

Kevin Macy sat in his hospital bed watching the news conference on his small rented TV. He nervously put his hand to his face and could feel the thick blood dripping from his nostrils. It was followed by a sharp, stabbing pressure in his chest. His monitor began to beep, indicating distress. The nurses ran into his room and tried to stabilize him.

Father Cooke was in his glory. "The information you want is in the old hymn "'Blood of the Lamb.'" He began to sing softly, "Have you been to Jesus for the cleansing power? Are you washed in the blood of the lamb? Are you fully trusting in His grace this hour? Are you washed in the blood of the lamb?"

His dark eyes scanned over the crowd of skeptical and elated reporters. Many would make their careers based on this news conference. "Do you have any questions?"

Every mouth moved at once as a wind swept over Father Cooke. A reporter in the front of the pack asked, "What do you mean by 'washed in the blood of the lamb'?"

He responded, "The phrase 'washed in the blood of the lamb' refers to being washed by virtue of the blood of Jesus. His blood was spilled upon His death to cleanse the sins of humanity. So, when you are washed in the blood of the lamb, you are forgiven your sins."

Reporters began to fire questions at him. Who does this affect? Priests who molest? Or others?

The priest replied, "Wormwood affects *anyone* who molests a child. Take note that 'molest' does not just refer to the physical inappropriate touching of a child, but the lustful thought of molesting a child by watching or creating child pornography. Their profession does not matter. Only the act of molestation matters. Remember, there are pedophiles who have not acted upon their urges. So, this disease does not affect them unless they act on it through their body or mind. Once a pedophile acts upon their urges, they will suffer by God's Hand."

A reporter jumped in. "This is the first I am hearing of this disease. How long has it been around? When did this start happening?"

Father Cooke pondered the question. "I believe it has been around for the past two years. This year I started hearing about it more and more. I did some investigation after giving numerous last rites. It struck me as odd that so many people who were dying started confessing to these crimes against children. There was no rhyme or reason to it. For some, the offences had happened within the last year, but for others it happened decades ago. Some were repeat offenders, and some committed one offence."

"So, you're saying Wormwood not only affects recent offenders but historical offenders, too?" questioned another reporter.

"Yes. From what I understand, any time the victim or the abuser thinks about the abuse, the abuser is hit by a torturous bout of Wormwood."

Reporters were looking at each other, trying to get their facts straight and process the information. "A disease is a disorder that produces specific symptoms. How can one person remember a traumatic event in their life and have it affect another person who caused the event? It doesn't make sense," advised a senior reporter in the pack.

"None of this makes sense, my son," teased Father Cooke. "God works in mysterious ways. That's all I can tell you."

"What if I don't believe in God?" the reporter yelled back at him.

"Then I suggest you start." Father Cooke was a natural in front of the cameras.

"Are health professionals aware of this disease?" interrupted another reporter.

"Yes, health professionals are perfectly aware of this disease. A young doctor stopped in here this week to ask me about it. They want to cure it," fretted the priest.

The idea of a credible source excited the crowd. What doctor? What is the name of the doctor? Can you tell us the name of the doctor?

"I can't give you his name. As a priest, I can't give you the names of those I speak to. It is part of my oath. I will leave that up to the health care professionals. They can deal with that part of it." The gauntlet had been dropped.

Another question came from the back. "What about the police? Are they aware of it?"

"I believe so," continued Father Cooke. "I have had conversations with a police investigator about this."

Once again, the questions came at him rapid-fire. Can you name the police officer? Which police force does he work for? Was it part of an investigation?

"You will have to contact the police about that," Father Cooke countered. He was feeling elated. "I will take one last question." His gaze swept across the sea of reporters.

"Father, does your nose bleed?"

Father Peter Cooke's eye twinkled. "No."

With that, he turned and walked back into the Basilica of St. John the Baptist, closing the big wooden doors behind him.

"No," he happily repeated to himself. "No."

15

It was as if someone had let the air out of the room. Dr. Luke Gillespie, Sgt. Nicholas Myra, and Mrs. Furey stood transfixed by what they were watching on the television.

Dr. Gillespie could not believe that Father Cooke had gone through with his plan. Sgt. Myra was trying to mentally prepare himself for the onslaught of victims who would be coming forward. Mrs. Furey was envisioning the media that would soon be swarming the hospital.

The doors of the great basilica had closed. Reporters and camera people stood in different areas around the church doing closing shots so they could file their stories. The female news anchor looked pale when the studio camera came back to her. She stumbled through her words as she ad libbed through the wrap-up on the biggest story of her career.

"If you're just tuning in, Father Peter Cooke, a Roman Catholic priest from the Basilica of St. John the Baptist in St. John's, Newfoundland and Labrador, has just made a stunning announcement on the steps of that church." She cleared her throat. “Father Cooke has just proclaimed that *God* has created a disease called Wormwood that seeks revenge on pedophiles and possibly kills them.” The news anchor could not believe what was coming out of her mouth. She struggled to keep up with the information appearing on the teleprompter in front of her. “Father Cooke claims he became aware of the disease when some of his parishioners started showing signs. The main sign of this disease is a bloody nose.”

In the news control room, a producer was screaming, “Find me some pedophile victims who will talk! Find me someone with a bloody nose! Goddamn it, get me the Pope on the phone!” Producers and reporters were scrambling in all directions. The producer put his microphone, a direct line to the anchor person’s earpiece, close to his mouth and slowly said, “So God has created a disease that marks pedophiles, then kills them . . . about time.”

The news anchor stared solemnly into the camera pointed directly at her and repeated the sentence word for word, even though the producer hadn’t meant for her to repeat the last two words. Now it was out there. The media had taken sides. The lynch mob was starting to form. People throughout the world watched in shock. Taking to social media, one by one, they lit their torches, picked up their pitchforks, and joined in. Until every tweet, every Instagram update, every Facebook status became a sworn allegiance to the support of Wormwood.

For the first time in social media history, God began to trend.

The media did not have to wait long for a person to interview on the street. Before they had a chance to pack up their trucks parked around the Basilica of St. John the Baptist, people began to flock to the church where it was all happening. Cars began to block Military Road on both sides as the faithful came to the church in hordes and droves. They stood with their phones stretched out to the end of their arms taking selfies with the *Blessed Virgin* in the background. Then with the saint himself, John the Baptist. Within a short time, the road was blocked, and the police showed up to direct traffic through the narrow streets.

The doors of the basilica were soon flung open, and people began to fill the church. For the first time in years, staff opened the two balconies on either side of the altar. Father Peter Cooke, like the Apostle John himself, was perched on the ornate gold chair behind the marble altar. He sat quietly and prayed. He prayed for forgiveness. He prayed for guidance. But mostly he prayed a prayer of thanks.

Once it was standing room only, he stood up. Still dressed in his Eucharist vestment, he walked to the grand pulpit on the left of the altar. The church suddenly went quiet, and all eyes watched this priest climb the steps to the pulpit and stand in front of the microphone. He surveyed his church. Not a seat available. He had dreamed of this moment. He thanked God, cleared his throat, and began.

"Then Jesus came from Galilee to John at the Jordan to be baptized by him. John would have prevented Him, saying, 'I need to be baptized by You, and You come to me?' But Jesus answered him, 'Let it be so now, for it is proper for us in this way to fulfill all righteousness.' Then he consented. And when Jesus had been baptized, just as He came up from the water, suddenly the heavens were open to Him and He saw the Spirit of God, descending like a dove and alighting on Him. And a voice from Heaven said, 'This is My Son, the Beloved, with whom I am well pleased.' Matthew 3:13-17." Father Cooke never took his intense stare off the crowd the whole time he spoke. He didn't need any notes or the Bible in front of him. He had practised for this moment his whole priesthood.

"Welcome back to the Church, my brothers and sisters. Welcome back home."

All of a sudden, the quiet was broken by sobs that started out muffled but turned into great cries as people began to feel they were a witness to something great. Something bigger than themselves. A feeling of anticipation hung over the basilica, the hairs stood on the back of people's necks, and shivers went down their spines. They could feel the presence of something unworldly.

"Let us renew our own baptismal covenant." Father Cooke lowered his head. "Do you believe in God the Father?"

The crowd voiced loudly and in unison, "I believe in God, the Father Almighty, Creator of Heaven and Earth."

"Do you believe in Jesus Christ, the Son of God?"

The thunder of voices reverberated through the arches of the church as the faithful recited, "I believe in Jesus Christ, His only Son, our Lord. He was conceived by the power of the Holy Spirit and born of the Virgin Mary. He suffered under Pontius Pilate, was crucified, died, and was buried. He descended to the dead. On the third day, He arose again. He ascended into heaven and is seated at the right hand of the Father. He will come again to judge the living and the dead."

Father Cooke looked toward the heavens. "Do you believe in God the Holy Spirit?"

The media had set up cameras throughout the church to capture people in prayer. They recited by memory, "I believe in God the Holy Spirit, the Holy Catholic Church, the communion of saints, the forgiveness of sins, the resurrection of the body, and life everlasting."

"Will you continue in the Apostles' teaching and fellowship, in the breaking of bread, and in the prayers?"

Nobody noticed the media cameras, because every second person had a phone stretched high in the air, recording the service, either streaming it live to a social media account or recording it to post as soon as it finished. Others were taking pictures and posting them as fast as they could. They answered, "I will, with God's help."

Father Cooke was basking in the glory of it all. "Will you persevere in resisting evil and, whenever you fall into sin, repent and return to the Lord?"

Church etiquette had flown out of the stained glass windows. "I will, with God's help," they responded.

"Will you proclaim by word and example the good news of God in Christ?"

The chants were getting louder. "I will, with God's help."

"Will you seek and serve Christ in all persons, loving your neighbour as yourself?"

Throughout the world, people were watching the service on their TVs and speaking in tandem with the mass of people at the basilica. "I will, with God's help."

"Will you strive for justice and peace among all people, and respect the dignity of every human being?"

People of all religions tuned in through social media, and the response began to trend worldwide. "I will, with God's help."

"Will you strive to safeguard the integrity of God's creation, and respect, sustain, and renew the life of the Earth?"

The warrior cry could be heard throughout the world. "I will, with God's help."

"Brothers and sisters. Jesus told us He would come again to judge the living and the dead. You may have believed that He was coming back in the form of a man, as He did before." Father Cooke surveyed his audience, who hung on to his every word. "This time, He has returned in the form of a disease called Wormwood. This disease will judge the living and the dead." The audible gasps could be heard outside the church.

"Jesus said, 'Let the little children come to Me, and do not hinder them! For the kingdom of Heaven belongs to such as these.' Well, the children came to Him, didn't they?"

Heads nodded throughout the church.

"What did we do?" He took on the tone of a TV evangelist. "What did we do?" he asked louder.

Shouts could be heard from the pews.

"We turned our backs. We protected the perpetrators and hated the victims. We were wrong."

The people jumped to their feet and cheered.

"We were wrong! And we are sorry!" His voice became gentle as he choked back tears. "I come to you today to ask for your forgiveness for my Church. I beg you for your mercy." Throughout the basilica, people wept openly as they finally heard the words they had waited their entire lives to hear.

"God will have his revenge on those who sinned in His name." Father Cooke's voice rose again. "He will show no mercy." He took a deep breath and said the words that would damn sinners for all time. "You will know the sinners by the mark of the blood of the lamb. They will have severe nosebleeds to show their sins, severe pain to pay for their sins, and an unquenchable thirst until they confess their sins."

The cheering from inside the Basilica of St. John the Baptist could be heard as far away as the St. John's waterfront.

*****

"Jesus, Mary, and Joseph!" cried Mrs. Furey. For the first time in her career as hospital administrator, she doubted her abilities to do her job. Her thoughts were in overdrive as she almost fainted into the nearest chair. "What the hell are we going to do?" She looked toward Sgt. Myra and Dr. Gillespie.

At the same time, her assistant flung open the door to her office and came barging in. "The hospital lobby is full of reporters! They are running through the emergency department looking for patients with signs of this new disease!" She was visibly shaking as she continued. "The emergency doctors are asking for security. Other floors are calling for security, too. Patients are fighting patients! Anyone who is showing signs of Wormwood is under attack! What are you going to do?"

Mrs. Furey felt her stomach turn, and bile rose to her throat. She choked down the taste of her own vomit. "Call security. Tell them to bring in everyone they can get. Call Code Black. The hospital is on lockdown." Her assistant ran to her office and began making calls.

Sgt. Myra's cellphone began to vibrate. He grabbed it from its holster and put it to his ear as he hurried to a corner of the office, as if he could talk privately. It was a habit. He answered with quick yes and no responses, then put the phone back in its holster. "That was the chief's office. I have to get back to headquarters. Apparently, our lobby is full of reporters, too." He looked from Luke to Mrs. Furey. "Get ready for a crisis of epic proportions."

As Myra left the office, Mrs. Furey closed the door behind him, locking herself and Luke in the office. "I need a spokesperson. It has to be you."

Luke's mouth fell open. "I am not media trained," he protested.

"I don't care. You're a doctor. You are now the official expert on this. We are staying in here until we get our story straight, then we are going in front of the cameras." Mrs. Furey sat behind her desk and pulled out the tray to her keyboard.

"Why are we speaking? Wouldn't it be best to wait and see how this plays out?" Luke knew this was a bad idea.

"Wait for what? This is a crisis. You heard Sgt. Myra. We have about two hours to respond, or the reporters will go elsewhere and create a story we can't control." She picked up her phone and pressed the direct line to her assistant. "Get me the PR and communications people. *Now!*" She banged the receiver down so hard Luke jumped. "Look at the TV screen."

She stared transfixed by what she was watching. Father Cooke had finished his sermon and was walking through the crowd gathered in the basilica. People flocked around him taking pictures, shaking his hand, reaching out to touch his vestment.

"Look at him," Mrs. Furey said. "He looks like Jesus riding into Jerusalem on a donkey. I'm surprised they're not singing hosanna, waving palm branches, and spreading their coats on the ground in front of him to walk on." A knock came on her office door, and her assistant showed the PR and communications team in.

Luke sat quietly, thinking. He knew the story of Palm Sunday, when Jesus rode the donkey into Jerusalem. He feared Mrs. Furey didn't know the whole story. Luke knew from his Catholic upbringing that Jesus did this to mock the Romans. When the Romans marched home after violently conquering a territory, they would ride their stallions through the streets as people waved palm branches as a sign of victory. Jesus knew this would enrage the Romans.

What Luke knew, which Mrs. Furey didn't, was they were now the Romans.

16

Sgt. Myra sat in the private waiting area outside the office of the chief of police. The chief's assistant sat behind her desk staring at him, not knowing what to say. An adrenalin rush of excitement, a level that only a police officer could understand, was coursing through the veins of everyone who wore a uniform due to the news of a disease that targeted pedophiles.

Sgt. Myra leaned back in his chair, running through his statement in his mind. Fact checking, repeatedly. The phone rang, and the assistant picked up the receiver, answered with a simple, "Yes sir," then nodded toward the chief's closed door.

"You can go in, now, sir."

Sgt. Myra stood to his full six-foot-four height. But he knew Chief Robert DeSilva had his own brand of intimidation. He was well respected by the front line as a cop's cop. He had climbed his way up the policing ladder and strategically spent time in general patrol, major crime, drug section, commercial crime, then went to the policy side of policing in strategic planning and criminal operations. There was no area of policing that he hadn't spent time in. He was also a master of navigating the political landscape of his masters.

DeSilva was not as tall as Myra, coming in at only six feet, but he was broad across the shoulders and had hands the size of baseball gloves. He had strikingly bright blue eyes that could look through you when he wanted answers, and he was known for not being able to smile. He had one look: very serious and very intense.

Sgt. Myra marched into Chief DeSilva's office, saluted as a sign of respect, then reached across the chief's desk and shook his hand.

"Nick, have a seat," DeSilva said. He pointed toward two chairs in front of a large window that overlooked downtown St. John's. They could see the basilica and the circus now surrounding it from this view. The two men sat across from each other, both not knowing what was going to happen next.

Chief DeSilva looked Sgt. Myra in the eye and started with, "What the hell, Nick?" He was flabbergasted. "We have been together a long time. We started out in training together. You're one of my best cops. Are you losing it? Do you need time off?"

Myra was a little taken aback by the line of questions. "I don't need time off. I need more resources for my unit. Other than that, I'm fine. I also didn't speak to the media."

"Okay, let's start from the beginning. Father Cooke says he spoke to the police, so I am assuming that's you. Am I right?"

"Yes, I spoke to him. As a witness. Several of the targets in my investigation mentioned they spoke to him. I knew he couldn't tell me what they said because of his oath, and I respected that, but I had to try." DeSilva would never question Myra's ability as an investigator. He knew he left no stone unturned.

"Okay, my recommendation is to set up a task force." The

chief picked up his notebook and began to make a list. "You will be the lead. I will authorize a profiler to put together a rundown on each victim and perpetrator, two criminal analysts to start putting together the puzzle pieces and create a timeline, and two major crime investigators to help with the interviews."

"Thank you!" Myra had wanted a team like this for years. "We need to get ready for the onslaught of victims coming forward."

The chief cut in, "The purpose of this task force is to investigate and substantiate the accusations of the victims. Myra, I am not prepared to put God on trial. More than likely we have some sick, vengeful bastard on the loose who is poisoning these animals somehow."

"Of course. I have considered that." Myra already had a plan in his head. "But how do you explain victims in other parts of the country? If we have a serial killer who is targeting pedophiles, how is he criss-crossing the country finding his victims?"

"Well, that will be one of the objectives of the task force, won't it?" The chief realized this was going to be a monumental undertaking that would more than likely define the reputation of his police force and his own personal legacy. "I want your team to start tracking the circles and squares in this investigation that will put together a strong case. We are going up against the Catholic Church and the medical field here. Your conclusion has to be bulletproof."

Myra was making his own notes. "I know some of the circles and squares are not going to pan out, but I'm hoping some of them will start to link together. Where there's smoke, there's fire."

The chief put down his pen. "Nick, my gut tells me this is vigilante justice. We need to look for someone who was molested as a kid and is now hunting down suspected pedophiles and somehow getting to them. There could be a group of them. We need to get a warrant for the medical files of the ones who have died and the ones in hospital to see if any of their bloodwork shows poison or a foreign substance." DeSilva stood up and looked out the window at his city. Then to the crowds surrounding the basilica. "What's your take on this priest, Peter Cooke?"

Myra leaned back in his chair. "My thoughts are someone is setting him up. I think someone went to him and confessed the whole Wormwood theory, then went about making it come true. So now he thinks it is real."

The chief's job was to always be one step ahead. "I would suggest to you that no matter how airtight you make this case, your conclusion is not going to be accepted by the majority of the public, who want to believe this is a miracle."

"I realize I can't prove that God created a disease that kills pedophiles, because first I would have to prove there is a God." Myra looked directly at the chief. "To be honest, over my career and what I have seen people do to each other, I could make a strong case that there is no God more so than I can prove there is one."

"Well, if the medical community proves there is a disease that only affects pedophiles, then that proves Father Cooke right and he gets his miracle. But where does that leave us?" The chief was pondering his own question. "Does Jesus Christ become a serial killer?"

"The task force's main objective is to find a serial killer who hasn't died on the Cross," chuckled Myra. "I really don't want to have to issue a warrant for the arrest of Jesus Christ. That didn't work out so well for the last cop who did that."

"The task force will have all the resources it needs to succeed. You will deal with the facts, you will put them all together, and if you find out over the course of the investigation that there is no sick bastard killing pedophiles and this is a disease, then we will leave it to the medical community. They can confirm the symptoms and the outcome."

Myra had a thousand thoughts flying around in his brain. "So, if it is a disease that only kills pedophiles, do I arrest God, or do we tell the task force to stand down?"

"We will deal with that on a day-by-day basis," replied the chief. "Right now, you need to get started and get your people in place. I will put together the necessary paperwork and inform the Department of Justice. Let's just hope the goddamned politicians don't start jumping for Jesus to get votes."

"Yes, sir. I will get started as soon as I get back to my office. Thank you, sir, for the resources. I know this will be a financial drain on the force, so I will do my best to keep our reputation intact." Myra stood up and opened the door to the chief's office and began to leave.

The chief walked behind his big wooden desk and sat heavily in his chair. He called out to Sgt. Myra as he was leaving the office.

"Sgt. Myra . . . Godspeed!"

17

Luke could feel his legs shaking. His mouth was dry. Sweat was trickling from his hair into his eyes. He had never walked into a room full of reporters before. *I have walked into a room full of car accident victims covered in blood with limbs missing*, he thought. *This can't be worse.* He was wrong.

The minute the door opened, a hush fell over the room. Instantly, all cameras and microphones were on him. He walked to the front, laid his notes on the podium, and looked out at the room full of media people. There were about fifty crammed into the hospital's media centre. The PR team had grossly underestimated their attendance.

"Good afternoon. Thank you for coming," he began. He looked up at the room again. There were no smiles, no friendly faces. Just a room full of people sitting quietly, holding their microphones and monitoring their cameras. "My name is Dr. Luke Gillespie. I am an emergency medical specialist, and I have treated several patients with symptoms of this disease."

Reporters were busily writing down everything he said.

"We currently have treated four patients with these symptoms. Two have passed away. I can't give you any personal information on the patients due to doctor-patient privileges and hospital privacy policy."

He stopped to take a drink of water. "The symptoms include an unexplained weight loss, enlarged and swollen lymph nodes, chronic diarrhea, white spots in the mouth, and some had dark spots that appeared on their body, heavy nosebleeds, and chronic pain. They also complain of an unquenchable thirst. Not all patients have *all* of these symptoms. The two symptoms they all do have are heavy nosebleeds and an unquenchable thirst."

He finished with, "We are asking anyone who has those symptoms to go to the closest emergency department or to your doctor." As soon as he finished, the rapid-fire questioning began. He was like a deer in the headlights.

"What are you calling this disease? Is it Wormwood?"

"There's no name on it yet. It seems to be an accumulation of several diseases," Luke answered.

"Are all your patients male?"

"No. One is female," he said. His answer sent a shock wave through the room.

"So, you're saying one of the pedophiles is a woman?"

"I am not saying anyone is a pedophile," he sternly responded. "I said they are patients."

"Are the police questioning your patients?" A murmur of laughter could be heard when the reporter said "patients."

"You'll have to ask them," Luke quipped. He knew if he spent another moment at the podium he would explode.

"Thank you for coming." He bolted from the room as fast as he could.

* * * * *

Gillespie and Mrs. Furey sat in her office, both looking shell-shocked. "I am never doing that again," he informed her. "I have to go do my rounds now and feel like I have been sucker-punched. I am afraid to look at my news feeds. I am turning my phone off."

"I know how you feel," Mrs. Furey mumbled. "Why us? Why now? Why couldn't this happen to a hospital in a bigger city with more resources? I am three months away from retirement. I just wanted to go quietly and end my career on a good note."

"I am twenty years from retirement, and I am afraid that I've ended my career at that podium." Gillespie sighed.

Luke was running through the last few days in his mind. "Maybe it's because we are so isolated. This disease may have gone unnoticed in a larger city. The population of St. John's is just a little over 200,000 people. There is not a huge transient population like there is in bigger cities. The only way to get off this island is by boat or plane. From a scientific point of view, it's easier to do a case study here."

"So, you're thinking God wants us to do a case study on the population of St. John's?" questioned Mrs. Furey.

"I think we need to stop bringing up God and deal with what we know—science," responded Dr. Gillespie.

"You're right. It's hard not to get caught up in the drama of God's vengeance on pedophiles, isn't it?"

"Not when you're a man of science. To answer the questions

'why us and why now' is not easy. Maybe because our population is so small it came to our attention quicker. It has nothing to do with God's wrath on people. We simply found it first."

Mrs. Furey sighed. "Yet Father Cooke is selling it as God's cure and punishment for pedophilia, and people are buying it by the pound."

"I hope Father Cooke realizes at some point that it is the height of cruelty to sell false hope." Luke was exhausted. "There are victims of sexual assault who are now thinking God is on their side and handing out punishment to their abusers. What if the accused does not develop this disease or show any symptoms? Does the victim now become victimized by themselves? Questioning their own details of their horror?"

Mrs. Furey sat back, pondering his questions. "I never thought about it from that angle. So, if victims don't see any symptoms in their perpetrators when they focus on their trauma, does it prove them liars? This is going to be one big mess."

"Will victims spend time constantly reliving the horror of their molestation and rapes, hoping their attackers will suffer?" Dr. Gillespie stood up and headed toward the door. "I have to do my rounds. I can honestly tell you this is the first time I walked onto a ward and had security checking my ID and credentials. This hospital is starting to feel like a penitentiary."

"Well, hopefully it is only a short-term thing. I know the cost of all these extra resources is driving my overhead through the roof." Furey was exhausted herself. "I'm going to get started on writing new policy for our own employees on how to deal with this and remind them to stay professional. I do not want to hear of any patient being denied care because they have a bloody nose."

"There's always one who makes everyone look bad. I don't think you should worry about that. Our health care professionals are too overburdened with work to have time to deny anyone of anything."

Mrs. Furey sat in front of the computer, wondering where to start. Dr. Gillespie walked back to the ICU, also wondering where to start.

18

Sgt. Myra's news conference was quick and to the point. "We cannot confirm that people with the alleged symptoms are pedophiles. I will refer your medical questions to the medical community. A high-level task force has been established to find answers. The Royal Newfoundland Constabulary will dedicate six police resources to it. To protect the integrity of the investigation, no further details can be released at this time."

The media had their talking head, a few good quotes, and a task force to keep tabs on. They dubbed it Operation Wrath of God. Sgt. Myra named it Operation Wormwood.

A room was cleaned out next to the major crime unit adjacent to Sgt. Myra's office. Four desks, computers, and other equipment were set up. The criminal analysts already had victim and perpetrator organizational charts on the wall. The door was closed in order to keep the looky-loos out.

Sgt. Myra knew from experience that the criminal intelligence analysis would be the heart of the operation. He needed the best in the business for both operational and strategic support. The investigation was no longer a city file—they would now be looking at this on a provincial and national level. This would mean consulting with police forces across the country. To do that, the task force would have to be a joint forces operation and include members of the Royal Canadian Mounted Police, who also shared the policing duties in the province.

He chose an operational analyst from the RCMP and a strategic analyst from the RNC. Their main objectives would be to help the task force deal effectively with the volume of information, warn them of threats, and support the operations activities and the investigation in general.

Sgt. Myra wanted the operational analyst to focus on the disruption of any pedophile groups and any person or persons targeting them. She would identify any links between suspects and their involvement in this type of criminal activity and prepare profiles of known or suspected pedophiles.

He instructed the strategic analyst to keep him informed, warn him of threats, and deal with any emerging sex crime issues. Her focus would be to identify the modus operandi of suspects and to keep track of crime trends, patterns, and emerging threats.

The Royal Newfoundland Constabulary had one criminal profiler who was already overburdened with files. His office was situated close by, so Myra let him stay where he was, but his directive was clear: Build a profile of someone looking for vigilante justice; identify the top likely suspects, and then analyze the patterns that may predict future victims. He would be given access to all evidence collected and victim reports to develop the offender description. Myra wanted to know what personality traits, psychopathologies, and behavioural patterns to look for, as well as demographic variables such as age, race, and geographic location.

Myra chose investigators from each force. He had already contacted the RNC and RCMP records departments to give them a heads-up. His task force investigators would be looking into historical sex crimes from the past five years that involved children as well as recent assaults. They would examine the outcome of the cases and health of the perpetrators. They had to re-interview witnesses and suspects, look at the evidence again, and write a report on each file. They would also consult with their major crime sections on current sex files. That information would be shared with the profiler and analysts, who would then start filling in the circles and squares.

Sgt. Myra sat at his desk, putting together the information that would convince a judge to give him a search warrant. The warrant would allow him to go to the Department of Health and seize the files of people who had died from or who were suffering from symptoms of Wormwood and other specified evidence that would be relevant and material to his investigation.

His focus this week, and the focus of his team, would be the two patients in intensive care at the Health Sciences Centre: the female principal, Mary Power, and the psychiatrist, Kevin Macy. He wanted everything on both of them. His team did not disappoint.

Mary Power was sixty-one years old and had taught in coastal Labrador indigenous communities for thirty-five years. She had no family and lived alone. Neither the RCMP nor RNC had anything on her. She was completely clean. "No one is completely clean," declared Sgt. Myra. He instructed the RCMP investigator to dig further. "Talk to other teachers she worked with. Find out who the RCMP detachment commanders were in the communities she taught in. Track them down and ask them about complaints, gossip, rumours."

The psychiatrist was a different story, the members of the task force warned him. He was a child psychiatrist who specialized in counselling abuse victims. "No victims have come forward concerning him, unless you count the one who can't make a complaint," one investigator warned him.

Myra's eyebrow went up. "One who can't make a complaint?"

The investigator explained that the child psychiatrist had been charged by the RNC with two criminal counts of possessing child pornography and mailing obscene matter, and two charges of smuggling and possession of prohibited goods contrary to sections 159 and 155 of the Customs Act by the Canada Border Services Agency. He explained the psychiatrist had ordered a child sex doll from China, and the possession of a sex doll depicting a child is illegal in Canada because it is a form of child pornography. The investigation began a year ago when CBSA officers at the International Mail Centre in Toronto intercepted his package. A police search of his home found the doll, which had not only been used but now had two broken legs from excessive and violent use. The psychiatrist was taken into custody and charged.

"So, did he sexually assault a child? Because Father Cooke is claiming that Wormwood only affects pedophiles," inquired one of the analysts.

"Not according to our investigation. Now, victims are coming forward all the time, so one may show up, but right now it's only the child sex doll," replied the investigator.

"That doesn't make sense," protested Sgt. Myra. "It doesn't fit the profile." He looked at the analyst. "Read back Father Cooke's statement to the public."

She flipped through the transcription of what they now referred to as "The Sermon on the Mount" and found the quote. "He says: 'Wormwood affects anyone who molests a child. Take note that '"molest"' does not just refer to the physical inappropriate touching of a child but the lustful thought of molesting a child by watching or creating child pornography. Their profession does not matter. Only the act of molestation matters. Remember, there are pedophiles who have not acted upon their urges. So, this disease does not affect them unless they act on it through their body or mind. Once a pedophile acts upon their urges, they will suffer by God's Hand.'"

Myra paced back and forth in the office. "So, the psychiatrist didn't molest a child; he molested the child sex doll. So, his lustful thoughts of molesting a child and using child pornography is how he became a victim of Wormwood, if you go by Father Cooke's theory. Even though he did not molest a child, he is still a pedophile, according to the law, and apparently according to God, if Cooke's theory is true." He thought for a moment. "We are not using Father's Cooke's information during this investigation. We need good, hard facts. If Macy is a victim of Wormwood, we need to find out how he got it and if it was a criminal act. We need to stop with the God crap.

"Let's get back to the law we know," Myra stated. "The Canadian Criminal Code's definition of child pornography includes any written material or visual representation that advocates or counsels sexual activity with a person under eighteen years of age."

"It is still child pornography even though no actual child was involved," insisted the investigator. "He is pleading not guilty and says the doll is his right to free expression. The doll is legal in other countries, but not in Canada. Our law states that the possession of a sex doll is just another form of depicting a child for a sexual purpose and therefore would meet the criteria for child pornography."

"If he had used the doll in the USA, would he have nosebleeds?" queried the analyst.

"The fact that he is using a child sex doll tells me he has an erotic attraction to prepubescent children no matter what country he is in," warned the profiler. "Clinically, he is a pedophile. He is using the doll to surrogate and fuel his fantasies. That makes it dangerous for him to be counselling abuse victims or be close to children at all."

Myra picked up the psychiatrist's file, knowing he would have to study it and the law surrounding it. "I will interview him myself," he informed the two investigators. "In the meantime, get me something on Mary Power. My gut tells me she is not as pure as she pretends."

The team went back to their desks and the arduous task of digging deeper and deeper. Sgt. Myra gave another order. "Take your time. Take your breaks. Do what you must do to protect your own mental health from this sickening subject matter. I know you are all committed, and I know by the end you will be mentally exhausted, but I don't want any one of you getting lost in what we are about to uncover. Stay removed from this file."

Sgt. Myra walked back to his office, knowing he would have a hard time following his own order.

19

Beyond the Sacred Heart Altar in the Basilica of St. John the Baptist stands the shrine of Our Lady of Fatima. The shrine was a gift from the Portuguese people to mark the centenary celebrations in 1955. Thousands of Portuguese fishermen formed a procession to the basilica from their ships docked at the St. John's waterfront. It is believed by the devout that if you pray at this shrine, Our Lady of Fatima will answer your prayers.

Father Charles Horan sat on the marble step in front of the shrine. He was curled up in a ball with his back toward Our Lady of Fatima. His arms were wrapped around his legs, and his head lay on his knees. His eyes were tightly closed as he prayed for guidance. He was so wrapped up in his own misery that he never noticed the dark form walking toward him until he felt someone sit next to him.

His head bolted upright, exposing his tear-stained face.

Sister Pius took some tissues from her pocket and handed them to him. Charles begin to wipe his tears, when suddenly a smile came across his lips and a chuckle came from his throat.

She looked at him questioningly. He pointed toward the floor. The long black skirt to Sister Pius's tunic had pulled up past her ankles when she sat next to him, unveiling a pair of white running shoes.

"You do have feet!"

"Of course I have feet!" she huffed. "How do you think I get around?"

"Hovering," he snorted back at her.

They looked each other in the eye with an air of unsureness, then broke out laughing.

"Shush." She put her finger to her lips. "I don't want to get thrown out!"

They both laughed harder, knowing there was nothing either could do that would get them thrown out of the church.

Sister Pius looked into his eyes again. She didn't see the grown man sitting next to her. All she could see was the suffering of an orphaned twelve-year-old little boy who had stopped growing the day he smiled at Archbishop Keating. Her heart went out to him. She had watched over him since he first came to the orphanage. He showed no signs of physical abuse but always seemed distant. She figured he was a loner and Archbishop Keating kept him by his side to protect him. She had never understood the relationship until this past year, when she started putting things together. That was when she started hating Keating with a passion.

"What do you want, Charlie?" she asked.

Tears began to fall from his eyes again as he tried to respond.

"I want to go home. I want to find a home." His body shook harder with each word.

She put her arms around his shoulders, hugging him tightly, and rocked him like a child. He was twice her size, but her capacity to love was bigger than the whole church.

"I got you, Charlie. I'll be your home."

Emotions that had been suppressed for years began to surface for both of them.

"You have a lot of healing to do, Charlie, a lot of lost time to make up for."

"I want to leave the priesthood," he confessed.

"I'm not surprised."

"I'm not a child molester." He looked at her without blinking.

"I know, Charlie."

"I am terrified that I am going to do to a child what was done to me. I would rather die than continue this cycle of abuse." Sister Pius knew he meant what he said. "I don't know how to be normal. I don't know how to be with a woman. I don't know how to be part of a family. I was raised by a monster." His eyes were blank as he stared into space.

"Charlie, we are a fine mess, you and I." The nun handed him another tissue. "You without a mother, and me without a child. I watched you grow up. I should have grabbed you and ran."

"I know you tried. I watched him stop you."

A pang of guilt came over her. "Families are not made from blood, Charlie. Families are made from love." In her heart she wished she had done more to save him. She wished she had spoken out more, gone to the media, done something.

"I put my papers in. I'm retiring," she said, surprising him.

"You can retire from the nun-hood?" Charles asked jokingly.

"I'm retiring as a teacher but also giving up my vows as a Sister of Mercy." She surprised herself when she said it out loud. "I have a house that was left to me by my mother, and I will be moving there soon." She took out a tissue to wipe her own face. "Charlie, there is a room there for you. There will always be a room there for you, Charlie."

Charles reached over, took her by the hand, and held it tightly in his. "I have to talk to Sgt. Myra. It's too late to stop the path of destruction left behind by Keating, but I have to give his victims closure."

"You have to do what feels right to you, Charlie. It's a chance to start over. You're an educated man. No one needs to know your story unless you choose to tell them."

He stood up and extended his hand to help Sister Pius. They began to walk in silence down the long main aisle in the centre of the Basilica of St. John the Baptist. They both stopped next to the baptismal font and dipped a finger into the holy water and blessed themselves. Then they walked toward the wooden doors in the back of the church.

A large statue of Jesus on the Cross hung next to the back door. As she passed, Sister Pius looked at the face of Jesus. For an instant she thought she could see a tear roll down his cheek. It sent a shiver throughout her body. She stepped into the sunshine, holding little Charlie Horan's hand. She began to sing sweetly to herself. *Have you laid down your burdens? Have you found peace and rest? Are you washed in the blood of the lamb?*

20

Dr. Luke Gillespie had been given his orders by the hospital administration and the provincial Minister of Health: *Trace the disease back to its origins and keep victims of Wormwood from giving it to anyone else.*

"Wormwood?" he said out loud. "Great, now even I am calling it that," he said to himself. He had submitted blood samples from all four victims to the lab so they could be tested for poison. He wanted to make sure these victims were not being targeted by some sick serial killer. He needed to find the similarities. Luke knew it was the only way to truly find out what this disease was and how it had been transmitted.

Nationally, the federal Department of Health finally started tracking the disease. They committed to creating a database that listed each case and its particulars, such as province, victim's sex, occupation, blood type, other diseases, known criminal activity, etc. First rule of order was to determine if each patient had Wormwood and not something else.

Luke would now be working with a national team of infectious disease experts. Once they were able to find the origins, then they would be able to stop or at least contain the disease. When all information was combined, they would hopefully get a better understanding on how it was spreading. Now that the federal government was backing them, there would be money to assign research studies, put out warnings to potential victims, and stop false information from spreading to the public and the media.

I don't understand why the federal Department of Health had this information for a year or more and did nothing with it, Luke pondered.

One thing all involved agreed on was this disease, whatever it is, didn't discriminate. It didn't matter who the victim was, what province they were from or ethnic background, whether they were rich or poor. Luke was happy the national group was in charge of finding out if it was a virus that was causing the disease to spread. Everyone feared a pandemic.

He put together a medical form for doctors and nurses to use when dealing with any patient who had the Wormwood symptoms. He had to find out who the patient had contact with, when they got sick, and where they were when the first symptoms appeared.

Once doctors across the country had their facts together and shared into a national database, they would start getting answers and create a plan. The number one mystery was, *How are people getting infected?* Once they had an answer to that, they would be able to control the spread of the disease. Everyone involved knew this was not going to be solved overnight.

Each province was required to send weekly reports to the federal Minister of Health, and his office would compile a monthly report for the medical community and update the media with any new information. The minister would be the keeper of all information concerning Wormwood, and his office alone would decide who would know what and when they would know it. Rumours were spreading faster than the disease, and the government needed to keep on top of it.

Mrs. Furey had issued gloves, masks, and protective gowns to all staff who were to have contact with patients who showed signs of Wormwood. She had directed her informatics department to install whatever was needed on their computers so Luke's team could stay in contact with teams across the country.

The team was already interviewing patients, looking through their hospital records, and talking to their families. Several team members were assigned to go back through historical files to look for the symptoms in past patients or deceased patients. Blood and other bodily fluids had been taken and sent to labs and were waiting to be analyzed. Eventually the puzzle would start to come together.

The national team did have one breakthrough: the disease was not contagious. There was no fear of catching it through accidentally touching blood or body fluids or by touching a person affected in any way.

Mrs. Furey would oversee the hospital's response to the crisis and coordinate the efforts of all other hospitals in the province. Luke would remain the spokesperson.

Questions and requests for interviews came in daily from the media to the hospital's public affairs office. There were no answers to give them, but Luke did his best to make at least one weekly appearance at a media outlet. Although it was eating up his valuable research time, he knew people wanted to know what was happening. Everywhere he went, it was all anyone spoke about. People were getting sick and dying. People didn't really understand how it was being spread, but that didn't stop them from spreading rumours. Every doctor involved knew they had to make quick progress with this mysterious illness.

He put the finishing touches on his weekly report to the federal Minister of Health and emailed it to Mrs. Furey for final review. Once she had given it her seal of approval, she emailed the encrypted report to the federal Minister of Health.

* * * * *

The report landed directly in the inbox of Minister Ronald McKenzie. He was anxious to read its contents and opened the message with great anticipation. *This Dr. Luke Gillespie seems to know what he's doing. Maybe a little too much.*

McKenzie knew he had to slow down the progress of this research. He would have to consult the network to find out how to derail a medical and police investigation all at once. This wasn't going to be easy. He put the report in a secret folder he hid on his computer from his assistant and secretary. He would have to put a stop to all of this. The network demanded it. They had threatened to release certain information and pictures concerning his digressions.

Minister Ronald McKenzie wondered how he would do this discreetly. He felt something hit his chest. Looking down, he saw a deep red bloodstain on the front of his white shirt. He quickly reached for his box of tissues and grabbed a bunch, putting them to his nose. Lately, the blood was thicker and darker than ever. *My God, I am so thirsty*, he thought to himself.

21

Sgt. Nicholas Myra answered the phone on his desk. He was focused on carefully reading through the stack of files in front of him. He did not want to miss one detail. The phone ringing made him jump, and he grabbed the receiver. "Myra," he snapped. "No, I am not expecting anyone." He then leaned back in his chair, and a rare smile came across his lips. "All right, then," he said. "I'm on my way. Please sign them in." He placed the receiver back down and thought, *I have waited ten years for that call.*

Sister Pius was dressed in jeans and a neatly pressed plaid shirt. Her short hair had a modern style, and Sgt. Myra didn't recognize her when he entered the front lobby of the Royal Newfoundland Constabulary headquarters. Father Charles Horan also wore jeans and an untucked plain white shirt, and he carried a small black briefcase. Anyone else in the lobby would think they were mother and son, there to report a property crime, but Myra knew better. He knew this day would come.

As he approached Charles, Myra reached out his hand. "Welcome to RNC headquarters, Father Horan." It was the first time Myra had used Charles's official title. He looked down into the face of the lady standing next to Horan and laughed. "Sister Pius, I would not be able to pick you out of a police lineup in your civilian clothes."

"Jeans," she corrected him. "Police wear civilian clothes, clergy wear jeans when we are off-duty," she laughed.

"Well, this is a surprise. I know you're not here because you miss me. So, what can I help you with?" Myra noticed Charles was nervous.

"We would like to talk to you in private," whispered Sister Pius.

"By all means." Myra gestured toward the door. "We can speak in my office." He used his building pass to open the secure door to the private hallway and led his guests through the maze of offices. He swiped his card on a box outside his special section. His team was busy working, but each member popped their head up to look when they realized who was with the sergeant.

"Come in and take a seat." Myra pointed to the two chairs in his private office and closed the door. "Before we start, I have to ask you if I can record our conversation."

"No," exclaimed Charles. "I am not ready for that yet." He placed the briefcase on his lap. Myra couldn't help but stare at it.

"Okay. Then, let's talk."

"I will start." Sister Pius sat straight in her chair. "Charlie and I have had a long conversation. I want you to know that he has been a victim of Archbishop Keating's for years. I had no idea how sick and twisted this whole thing really was." Her eyes filled with tears, and Myra passed her a tissue from a box on his desk. "Charlie would like to make a statement."

Sgt. Myra sat back in his chair. He glanced back between Sister Pius and Father Horan. He didn't know how to tell them. "Sister . . . Charlie . . . the archbishop is dead. I can't charge a dead man. It's too late." Myra was disappointed in his own words.

"No, but you can charge the rest." Charles slammed the black briefcase onto Myra's desk. "Here's everything you need."

Myra jolted upright and put his big hands on the briefcase. He unzipped it and looking inside. "What is this?"

"The archbishop was good at one thing: keeping files. He kept explicit details of everyone in his pedophile ring, their names, the dates, their perversions, pictures, names of the boys they molested. It's all there." Myra bit his bottom lip as Charles continued. "The night he died, I went back to the rectory and cleaned out the filing cabinet. I was going to burn everything, like he told me to. It was the look on Jermaine Cousin's face that stopped me. I slept in the bed next to his brother. The sound of him crying at night still haunts me." Charles was as white as a ghost. His voice was shaky, and his whole body trembled. "Everything you need is right here."

Even Sister Pius hadn't seen that coming. She had no idea what was in the briefcase.

"You're kidding me." Myra didn't know what else to say. He took the files out and thumbed through the tabs. Each one had a name on it; some he recognized, and some he didn't. Some names shocked the crap out of him.

"There's thirty-two files there. Twelve are dead now, counting John Duffy and Archbishop Keating," Charles informed him.

"Seven are in their late eighties or nineties and don't participate anymore. Thirteen are still active."

"This is quite a bit of information," said Myra. "Give me a minute. I have to think." He stood up and turned toward the big window in his office overlooking the city of St. John's. He nervously ran his hand over his face, pulling at the short hairs in his moustache, his form of a nervous tick. He turned around and looked at Horan. "Do you know Mary Power or Kevin Macy?"

"No, they don't ring a bell. Why?"

"Take a second to think about it. Mary Power was a school principal in Labrador, and Kevin Macy is a child psychiatrist." He thumbed through the names on the files as he asked Charles.

"No. Nothing. I have never heard of them."

"Okay." Myra stood next to his desk. "I don't know how to thank you, Father Horan. I can say you have saved a lot of children by coming forward with this information. I'm going to need some time to go through these files, and I will need to talk to you again." He looked at the files, and then at Charles. "Thank you. I know this wasn't easy."

Father Horan lowered his head. "I should have done it years ago. I do have one request, Sgt. Myra. Can I speak to you alone?" He nervously glanced at Sister Pius, who was still in shock.

"Sure. Sister Pius, would you mind?" Myra opened the door to his office and caught the attention of an investigator on his team. "Would you mind walking Sister Pius to the front lobby for me, please?"

"Yes, sir." The investigator opened the main door and led the nun away.

Myra went back in his office and closed the door. He lifted the chair that Sister Pius was sitting in and turned it toward Charles so they could be face to face.

"I didn't want to discuss this in front of Sister Pius," Charles confessed. "I want to ask you something." His hands were still trembling, and a bead of sweat trickled down from his forehead onto his cheek. He wiped it away and stared at the floor. "I am afraid. I am afraid I am going to fall."

"What do you mean?" Myra prodded.

"I am afraid one day I will look at a young boy and something evil will stir in me." He lifted his head and looked at the sergeant. "How often do victims continue the circle of abuse?"

Myra was beginning to realize how isolated Keating had kept Horan. "I don't have statistics on that, Charlie. I can tell you that every time I read a pedophile their rights, they start singing from the same old book with the 'I was molested as a child' song."

He knew that wasn't the answer Horan was looking for. "But I say to them, if you were molested, then you know how it feels. You know how powerless a child is under an adult. You know how alone it feels. What happened to you wasn't your choice, and you did not deserve it. So, if you were a victim, why did you, as an adult, choose to do it to someone else?" Myra could feel the sickening gall rise in his throat. "I don't care what their childhoods were like. They were adults when they chose to molest. I charge that adult."

Father Horan pushed his chair back and stood up. Myra did the same thing. "I never molested anyone, Sgt. Myra. I will take a polygraph on that one. I never wanted this."

"I know, Charlie. I have always known that." Myra couldn't

help but ask, “Do you believe God created Wormwood to kill pedophiles and stop the sexual torture of children?”

“Yes, I do,” Horan answered without missing a beat. “At least I hope so, because I prayed for years that He would.”

“Charlie, you need to get some intensive counselling to go on with your life. A good counsellor can help you sort out your feelings. Just because you were a victim does not mean you will become a pedophile.”

“If the thought ever crossed my mind, I would kill myself,” replied Father Horan.

Myra was not expecting that answer.

“Like I said, Charlie, get some help.” As Sgt. Myra walked Father Horan out of the building, he wondered if it was Charles who had started the Wormwood rumours.

22

Presentation Mother House is in the centre of St. John's and part of a larger number of buildings that create a complex of ecclesiastical structures including the Basilica of St. John the Baptist. The cornerstone was laid by Archbishop John Thomas Mullock in 1850, and it was officially opened in 1853. The building remains an active Presentation convent and has been turned into a nursing home for aging nuns. A little-known fact is that the Mother House is home to one of the most perfect gems of religious art in the world—*The Veiled Virgin*, created by internationally acclaimed Italian sculptor Giovanni Strazza from Milan. It is considered a perfect wonder of the sculptor's art.

Father Peter Cooke needed to hide from the world for a little while. He sat quietly in the chapel gazing at *The Veiled Virgin*. The basilica was full day and night with a steady stream of people. He had to bring in extra volunteers just to empty the donation boxes in the back of the church. His office and mobile phones rang constantly. The church's elderly secretary was at her wits' end. Between media requests for interviews and parishioners' requests for blessings, he could not keep up. He was overwhelmed. The archdiocese sent over two additional priests just to have someone in the basilica every day to talk to people. But the public wanted him. He had become a rock-star priest. Something he never thought possible.

"Not words but deeds," said a woman's voice, cutting into his thoughts.

Father Cooke turned quickly to see Sister Pius standing in the doorway of the chapel.

"It's the motto of the Presentation Sisters," she informed him.

Father Cooke looked back toward *The Veiled Virgin*.

"It means we not only talk the talk, but we walk the walk." Father Cooke was deep in thought. "Her facial expression has a holy, ethereal quality, doesn't it?" Sister Pius continued. "Many people say it leaves them with a deeply religious experience, unique and lasting."

The priest sighed heavily.

"Many people believe that if they say the rosary on their knees in front of this statue, the Virgin Mary will answer their prayers." The nun sat in the pew next to Father Cooke. "But your prayers have already been answered. Maybe you are here just to marvel at the beautiful marble and glow of her face. It is quite stunning, isn't it?"

"The church is my happy place," he finally responded. "Growing up, my friends had dreams of being doctors, lawyers, architects. Not me. I wanted to be a priest. My family thought I was nuts. My father threatened to disown me. My mother begged me to reconsider. They thought it was a phase and it would pass. I knew it wouldn't. It was a calling. I could feel the Lord calling me, pulling me into this life."

Sister Pius had known Father Cooke for many years. She had no doubt he was telling the truth. "I felt the same the way," she told him.

"I'd become so disillusioned in the past ten years. I believe in the Lord's work. I couldn't understand why others couldn't."

Sister Pius sat silently, letting him talk.

"I was so frustrated by the Vatican's lack of engagement with their people. They have no idea what it is like to be a priest on the front line. A priest with a big empty church barely able to scrape enough money out of the collection plate to pay the heat bill." He turned to face Sister Pius. "Did I do wrong, Mary? Did I betray those who confessed their deepest sins to me?"

"You certainly got what you prayed for," the nun answered.

"Did I break my vow? These sinners came to my confessional to unburden their souls and confess their sins to me as a priest in the Sacrament of Penance. That's a very sacred trust. Each one of them knows that in the confessional they are not speaking to me, but through me to the Lord."

Sister Pius listened intently. "Sometimes I am glad the Church does not allow women to hear confessions. I don't know if I could hear the sins of a murderer or sexual deviant and not make a call to the police. I don't know if I could put my vows before the protection of people."

"Most days you just hear the same thing," said Father Cooke. "They cheated on a spouse, stole from their workplace, spread gossip. It's so easy to tell them to say ten Hail Marys and do something good for somebody. But then there are the times I struggle." He stood up and began pacing back and forth in front of *The Veiled Virgin*. "When I spoke to the media and the parishioners, I didn't give any names or dates of offences. I spoke in general terms. No one was identified. I know the Code of Canon Law states it is a crime for a confessor in any way to betray a penitent by word or in any other manner or for any reason.

"I asked each penitent to go to the police and confess their sins to truly unburden their souls and give their victims closure. They weren't interested. It left me wondering if they were sitting in my confessional to unburden their souls or to torture me, knowing I could do nothing with the information." He turned to face Sister Pius. "I recognized some of the voices, you know. Having to smile and act normal in front of someone you know just raped a child and intends to do it again is a crucifixion of another kind."

"What are you hearing from the new archbishop?" Sister Pius inquired.

"I am being investigated internally for directly violating the seal of confession. If I am found guilty, it could mean anything from automatic excommunication down to being punished in other ways—like being sent to a monastery for perpetual penance."

"Harsh," she said, already knowing the answer to her question. "So, when a priest molests children, they send him to a monastery for counselling or to another parish to hide him, but they excommunicate a priest who protects children?"

Father Cooke sat in the pew again with his head in his hands. "I don't know what to do. I don't know how to be anything but a priest. I honestly thought I would be buried with my collar on. I never meant any harm."

"I am leaving the church," she said flatly.

"What? Why? I hope this circus I created is not responsible for your decision."

"No, it's something I've thought about for a long time. I think I always knew at some point I would retire from the church. Hang up my habit and live a normal life. I think I would like to own a dog and a cat."

"A dog and a cat." He could see it. "That sounds lovely, doesn't it?"

"Peter," Sister Pius said, taking his hand in hers, "no matter what happens, I want you to know that I support you and I know your heart is pure. I know you had no ill intent."

He could feel tears well up in his eyes and did his best to keep them from rolling down his face. He looked toward *The Veiled Virgin*. "I don't have many friends. Being a priest is a solitary choice for a man, but I have always counted you as a good friend."

She put her arms around him and hugged him tightly. After a few seconds, she let go and stood up. "Not words but deeds, remember. I have some rounds to do on the nursing home floor."

"Thank you, Sister," he said sincerely.

"For what?"

"For hearing the confession of a tormented priest." He grinned.

"Any time, Father Cooke, any time." As she left the chapel, she saw him get down on his knees and begin to pray the rosary. She hoped that *The Veiled Virgin* would answer his prayers as She had done for so many others.

* * * * *

The archdiocese office was busier than it had ever been. The secretary usually took two to three calls a day, and one of them was always from her sister. Lately she was taking over a hundred a day and had gone through stacks of telephone message pads that had been collecting dust in her desk drawer for years. The call that came in that afternoon would be one she would tell everyone about for the rest of her life. Her children, and their children, would talk about this phone call in great detail.

By the time she opened the door to the archbishop's office, she was out of breath and her face was red, even though it was only a twelve-foot walk. "Pick up the phone, Archbishop . . . pick up the phone," she wheezed.

The archbishop was startled when the door to his office flung open so abruptly. His first thought was his secretary was having a stroke. He jumped up from his chair. "Are you okay?"

"Pick up the phone," she yelled. "It's the Vatican . . . the Vatican!"

"The Vatican?" he questioned. "Are you sure it's not another prank call?"

Her hand clasped her chest. "It's not just the Vatican . . . it's the Holy Father! His Holiness is calling you, himself!" she screamed. "Pick up the phone, it's the Vicar of Christ!"

"Oh, good Lord!" He fell back in the chair. "Why didn't you say?" He ran his fingers through his hair and straightened his collar as if the Pope could see him through the phone. He was only on the job two weeks; he had started in the midst of a media storm, and now the Pope was on the phone. His hand shook as it picked up the receiver. "Your Holiness," he bellowed into the phone, then, without realizing it, he blessed himself. "It is such an honour, Your Holiness, it is such an honour."

The conversation lasted almost forty-five minutes. By the time both priests hung up the phone, there was no doubt about what the plan was for Father Peter Cooke.

23

Sgt. Nicholas Myra had meticulously planned every detail in the execution of Operation Wormwood. Thirty marked and unmarked patrol cars sat waiting in the RCMP's hidden garage in the basement of their headquarters. Each contained two police officers, some in plain clothes, some in uniform. At precisely 0900 hours, the garage door would open and the cars would begin to roll. Search warrants had been obtained, affidavits had been sworn to, and charges had been laid.

Myra wanted the takedown to happen after children went to school. He didn't want a child seeing a parent being taken out of the house in handcuffs. Social workers and police officers were waiting in secure rooms in the schools of the children affected. School principals were only notified when the teams showed up that morning. They were told nothing more than it was a police operation and they needed several secure rooms in which to interview children. The police commander in each school informed the principal that at 9:00 a.m. they would be given a list. They would then go to each classroom, ask for the child on the list, and bring them to an assigned room. The investigators and social workers would then interview each child to find out if they were victims of abuse or not. Those victimized would be rescued and sent to secure locations where experts in the child abuse field would be waiting to work with them. Those not abused would be sent to Child Protection Services until their homes were cleared for their return.

At 0800 hours, Myra called out, "Room."

Police officers from both forces lined up in three ranks.

"Attention!"

The shuffle of uniforms was followed by one loud bang as their boots hit the pavement in the garage.

"At ease . . . stand easy."

Myra stood before the rank and file. His six-foot-four stature, broad build, and uniform gave him instant respect. A million thoughts were running around in his head, but he had no trouble keeping them all in order as he made his announcements to the officers.

"At exactly nine hundred hours, the garage doors will open and your cars will leave in single file. We have thirty targets this morning. Each of you has been given a target's file that contains their name, address, work address, photo, and a list of identifying marks such as tattoos and scars. When you leave this building, you will not use lights or sirens. We will not draw any attention to ourselves."

Each officer hung on to his every word. They felt honoured to be part of this operation. They knew this one was for the history books.

"We do not use force unless we are challenged. Some of

the targets have guns in their houses, and they are the files with the red tabs. No one leaves here without their bulletproof vest. You will park as close to the target's home as possible. Each team will go to the front door together, one will knock or ring the doorbell, the other will stand out of sight. When the door opens, if you recognize your target, you ask him to identify himself, then inform him he is under arrest and what the charge is. If someone else answers the door, you ask for your target by name. If he comes to the door, you follow the same procedure. Once the target is in the patrol car, you radio back to the operational command centre. All targets are to be transported to the RNC headquarters for processing." Myra was mentally ticking off boxes in his head from his operational plan.

"If the target is not home, notify the command centre immediately, then began the search pattern outlined in your file starting with the target's workplace, known hangouts, and friends. When arrested, you notify Command. Once the targets are in custody, the search teams will enter the homes."

Myra turned his focus to the second phase of the operation. "Search teams, when you enter the homes, we are looking for computers, cellphones, cameras—even if they are old and don't look used—memory sticks, file folders, photo albums. Take your time searching each home. Look for hidden places like attics, ceilings with tiles that can be pushed up, secret compartments under a computer desk. Everything you find is to be placed in an evidence bag, sealed, then marked with your name, the date, and time." He pulled himself to his full height and looked more menacing than ever before. "I cannot stress the importance of collecting the evidence properly. Read the search warrants and make sure you abide by the law. I want this done properly."

Myra looked into the faces of the police officers in front of him. "Attention!" The room reverberated with the sound of boots on the pavement. "Godspeed and be careful. Dismissed." The police officers fell out and went back to their teams, each one going through exactly what they had to do.

Father Charles Horan's files were a gift from God, Sgt. Myra thought. The archbishop had kept detailed records on everyone in his ring. He had victims' names, dates, where the offence happened, and who was in the room. Myra figured he was using the information to blackmail or control his pedophile ring.

* * * * *

As soon as Father Horan and Sister Pius had left the building, Sgt. Myra went back to his office and spent the rest of the day combing through the files. He called in all members of his team, and they took each file and dissected it according to their specialty. The analysts began the task of putting the information in order and creating a timeline. They began to find links to other pedophile rings operating both inside and outside the province. They outlined links between suspects and tracked past and current charges. The profiler was building a pedophile profile based on everything in the files. He began to analyze the patterns of each suspect, tracking their personality traits and behavioural patterns. The investigators were given a list of victims' names. They were tasked with tracking each one down, explaining the situation, taking statements, and hopefully convincing them to testify.

Myra informed Charles that he may have to testify, even though both of his abusers had died. He could be called as a witness to testify on where all the files came from, Myra explained.

After he finished reading the files, he had called Charles and had a long conversation with him. Myra knew Horan was fragile, and he didn't want to push him.

"I am completely destroyed as a person," Father Horan confessed. "I can never be whole again."

Myra tried to convince him that with intensive counselling he could learn to live with his past.

"The anguish I feel is indescribable," he cried. "My childhood was stolen, and now I fear I may offend myself."

"You're not a pedophile, Charlie," Sgt. Myra reassured him. "You're a victim. You have to keep telling yourself that." He feared Charles would never be able to look in a mirror without seeing a monster in the making.

* * * * *

Nicholas Myra's phone alarm went off at 0850 hours. "To your cars," he shouted. Police officers hurried to their patrol vehicles, anxiously awaiting the order to move. At exactly 0900 hours, the garage door opened. Sgt. Myra, along with his command team, stood next to the open door and watched the cars drive past until the last one left. By 0930 hours, the first target was picked up without incident. By noon, all twenty living pedophiles were in custody and being questioned. The media, who had been tipped off, waited at the side door of RNC headquarters, taking pictures of each handcuffed target as they were taken in for processing by two police officers.

Sgt. Myra and his team were preparing for the news conference that would follow the arrest. They had to ensure that all the targets were formally charged before releasing the names. Once the news release was given the final approval, the notice went out to the media that the news conference would take place in the RNC media relations room.

Sgt. Myra prepared for the conference, reading and rereading the news release to make sure he didn't fumble a word or mispronounce a name. The door to his office opened, and an officer said, "They are ready for you." As he walked toward the media room, his cellphone began to ring. He took it out of his holster and looked at the name on display: CHARLIE HORAN. He put the phone back in the holster and made a mental note to return the call as soon as the media circus died down. He would offer to meet him later for a coffee to make sure he was all right. Myra wanted to thank him in person for all his help. Without Charles, the police would never have been able to take this entire ring down and rescue the victims.

Myra walked into the media room. The bright lights and flashes blinded him. He made his way to the podium and laid down the ground rules. He would first read the news release and then answer questions.

* * * * *

Father Horan got Sgt. Myra's voice mail. He sat in the archbishop's empty office and picked up a framed picture from the archbishop's desk. Charles remembered the day it was taken. He had mixed emotions. He kissed the picture and put it back on the desk. So many bad memories here. So many good memories here. He stood up and looked into the mirror the archbishop kept on the back of his office door. He liked the way he looked in his black cassock with the clerical collar and his freshly pressed black pants.

He looked around the room. Suddenly, he was overwhelmed. It looked like a torture chamber to him, but at the same time it was the only home he had known. He knew he had done the right thing by turning the files over to Myra, but part of him felt like Judas Iscariot. Charles felt like he had betrayed the only father he had ever known. He knew some of his peers would condemn him. The priest would never feel at home inside the church again, but he would never feel at home anywhere else. He thought about the thirty files he had turned over to the police. He thought about the innocent blood of the victims that had been spilled.

In the final act of a man who could not live with himself or with the memory of what he had lived through, he pulled the big leather chair out from behind the archbishop's desk and stood on top of it. He had flung a rope around the heating pipes that ran along the ceiling of the archbishop's office. Charles placed the noose around his neck and bowed his head. He began to whisper the Our Father. "They will bury me in the field of blood. Father forgive me for what I do."

In a matter of seconds, it was over. Father Charles Horan's torment had ended.

* * * * *

Sgt. Myra left the news conference room feeling triumphant. The operation, under his command, had gone off without a hitch. As soon as he got back to his office, he picked up his phone and called his voice mail. Myra heard Charles's voice for the last time.

"Sgt. Myra." Charles Horan's voice cracked with emotion. "I cannot live with my pain anymore. Please forgive me."

24

Dr. Luke Gillespie tapped on the open door to Mrs. Furey's office. She looked up. "Come on in."

"Any word?" Luke asked hopefully.

"Not a thing." She shrugged. "How long does it take a minister to read a report? It was only ten pages long! I sent it over two week ago."

Luke sat in the chair in front of her desk. "It's frustrating. I thought this thing would go like wildfire."

Mrs. Furey leaned back in her chair. "I don't know. I contacted my counterparts across the country. They're having the same issue of not getting any feedback from the Minister of Health. I don't know if he's not getting the reports or if he is just taking his time reading them."

"I hope no one else is vetting my report. I want the minister to know exactly what we're dealing with. Are there any whispers in your world of what's going on?"

"Nothing official," responded Mrs. Furey, "but I'm hearing gossip that the minister has been aware of this issue for more than a year and has been sent several communiqués about it."

"So, if he was aware of it, why hasn't he done anything about it?" Luke asked.

"I guess that's the million-dollar question, isn't it?"

"I thought I would check because I was surprised I haven't heard anything. I've talked to other doctors on the national team. They have all sent in their reports, but no one has heard anything back." As an afterthought, Luke asked, "I don't suppose the government is trying to hide the information for some reason?"

Mrs. Furey replied, "Why would they? What would the purpose be? If some type of epidemic is killing people, it would be in government's best interest to get out in front of it and do something about it."

Luke nodded in agreement. "That's what I was thinking. I researched the way government officials handled the SARS crisis. They spent millions of dollars educating the public and putting money into resources needed by front-line health workers."

"I wonder if it's because the disease seems to only affect a certain group of people? Maybe that's why they're dragging their heels," said Mrs. Furey. "Maybe they're solving their crime issues with a health issue?"

"Do you think politicians are afraid they will get bad publicity by putting public money into curing a disease that is believed to only affect pedophiles?"

Mrs. Furey thought about it for a second. "I don't know. Your guess is as good as mine. But we both seem to have met a bottleneck in the system." She sat up and leaned forward over her desk, resting her arms over the mounds of files that covered it. "I have a friend who is a reporter in Ottawa. I think I'm going to give her a call and see if she has an inside scoop on it. I'll let you know if I hear anything. In the meantime, keep this under your hat. We may have stumbled into a hornet's nest here. I think it's best if we both keep our backs to the wall so we don't get stung."

"Let's keep each other updated on official news and gossip," agreed Luke. He left her office to return to the ICU ward. His report writing and research was keeping him from his patients, and he wanted to get back to the ward to see if anything had changed.

Mrs. Furey closed the door behind Luke. She took her cell-phone out of her purse and typed in the name of her old friend. She pressed the number and waited for her to answer.

"Hello! Greetings from the beautiful island of Newfound-land," Mrs. Furey said happily.

"Well, if this isn't a blast from my past," answered her friend. "It's been a long time. There must be something serious happen-ing for you to call me."

They exchanged a few pleasantries and spent a few seconds catching up on each other's lives. Then Mrs. Furey got to the point. "Have you ever heard of a disease called Wormwood?"

"Yes, everybody has. It's all over the media," the reporter commented.

"Okay. Are you still following the prime minister around these days?"

"Still on the political beat as usual. Why?"

"At your next media scrum, can you question the prime minister on Wormwood?"

"We've been doing that for weeks," her friend explained. "We've been asking him about it daily since the story broke."

"Are you aware the Minister of Health has received reports from all the hospitals across the country over two weeks ago?" Furey teased. "Off the record, we haven't heard a thing back from him. There's rumours that he has known about Wormwood for over a year and has done nothing about it."

"Really," the reporter said, smelling a news story.

"I can't imagine another issue that's more pressing right now than an epidemic that's killing people."

"You mean killing pedophiles?" joked the reporter.

"That hasn't been proven yet," Furey corrected her. "But there are grumblings among the national medical team members. They are wondering why there's no response from the minister. You would think he'd want to get out in front of this."

"Yes, it's weird that a politician has a national soapbox to stand on with guaranteed front-page coverage but isn't using it. That doesn't make sense at all," agreed the reporter. "Let me check into it. Thanks for the scoop."

"Off the record, remember," reminded Mrs. Furey.

"Of course. I built a reputation with 'off the record,'" her friend disclosed.

* * * * *

Dr. Gillespie entered the ICU. The smell and heat were as sickly as ever, but it still smelled like home to him.

"Well, look what the cat dragged in," snorted Nurse Agatha Catania. "We thought the big TV star was too good to do rounds anymore."

Luke sighed. "Please don't start. You know how I feel about the media."

"Well, your patients are all waiting for you. Let's start with Mr. Macy." She was happy to have their team back together.

Luke took the clipboard and started to read through the stats. "Does the fact that people believe this disease is a pedophile disease affect the way you treat them?"

"Do you think this is the first time a nurse had to care for someone they knew was a pedophile?" Agatha asked him. "Or a wife beater? Or a criminal of any kind? Do you know how many times my ass gets grabbed in the run of a day? Or how many times someone grabs my breast? But I take a deep breath, and I give them the best care that I know how to give because I am a professional. That's what nurses do. We swallow our pride and our fear, and we do our job." She stood strong and put her hands on her hips. "Just for the record, how many times has a patient grabbed your penis?"

"None," he confessed.

"That's what I thought," she muttered. "Let's do our rounds."

They entered Mr. Macy's room. "You're the doctor from TV," Macy accused him. "I don't trust you."

"Mr. Macy, I am here to provide care. If you don't want it, I will leave," responded Gillespie.

At that, Macy sat up in the bed and clutched his chest with both hands as pain swept through his body. The blood began to flow from his nose as he began to choke from breathing it in. Luke immediately grabbed his IV drip and opened the valve to release more morphine while Agatha grabbed a towel and tried to keep the blood away from his mouth and nose to improve his breathing.

"Make it stop!" Macy screamed, repeatedly.

"Only you can do that."

Luke and Agatha looked toward the door to see that a solemn-looking Sgt. Myra had entered the room.

"Confessing makes it stop, Kevin. You know that." Myra had an angry look in his eyes.

"Not now, Sergeant," yelled Dr. Gillespie.

"If you say so. You know where I'll be," offered Myra.

Luke and Agatha worked to get their patient under control, and Sgt. Myra sat in the private room near the ICU. By the time the patient was sedated, the doctor and nurse were splattered in blood. They both took off their protective gowns and gloves and threw them in the garbage. "I need to go check my face for blood," said Agatha.

"I'll be talking to Sgt. Myra about hospital policies," declared Dr. Gillespie. "Nick, maybe it's you that sends the patients into convulsions of blood," Gillespie said as he sat across from Myra. "I'm noticing that when you are around, they get worse. Maybe you're poisoning them."

"If it was only my presence, then I would sit in the penitentiary all day," snapped Myra.

"Well, if you came to interview Macy, you've wasted your time," Luke stated. "He is completely out."

"Father Horan is dead."

"What? How? You said he didn't have it!" Luke fell back in his chair. A lump formed in his throat.

"He didn't. He died by suicide." Myra felt a great sense of loss. More than he should have.

Dr. Gillespie looked at the big police sergeant for a long time. "Suicide?"

Myra could feel his body start to shake, and he felt incredibly cold. "He hanged himself in the archbishop's office this morning."

"Oh my God," was all Luke could get out. "Are you okay?"

"I'm fine," Myra lied.

"How does this affect your case?" Luke knew Sgt. Myra was not okay. He couldn't stop staring at his shaking hands.

"Charles gave me the archbishop's files before he died. The archbishop kept incredible details on all his victims and the pedophile ring he operated. We arrested twenty people today, and police forces across the country are still arresting people. Because of Charlie, a lot of victims have been rescued and a lot of criminals will be brought to justice."

"So, does this end your investigation?" Luke asked hopefully.

"No. It's just the beginning. We still have to figure out how people are getting this disease. I'm hoping Macy can give me some details."

"Well, not for the next hour or so. Ms. Power is still here. Are you talking to her?"

"She was next on the list, so I guess she's going to be first, if you don't mind?" Myra was hoping Luke would say no. He really didn't want to interview anyone today. He just wanted to go home. Then he remembered that there was no one home. Just an empty house.

"Is she under investigation?" Luke couldn't remember her being on his list.

"Actually, no. This would only be a courtesy call. I have nothing on her. She is a victim of a crime, if it turns out someone poisoned her."

"Sgt. Myra," said Agatha Catania, a little more loudly than she would've liked. "My two favourite guys in one room. How lucky am I?" She laughed.

Sgt. Myra stood up and walked past the nurse with a slight nod. He took out his notebook as he entered Mary Power's hospital room.

"What was that?" Agatha looked at Luke with a confused look on her face.

"He has a lot on his mind. Father Horan died by suicide today." Luke stood up and rubbed his hands over his eyes to make sure there were no signs of tears.

"Wow. Didn't see that coming." Agatha watched Myra as he entered Ms. Power's room. "He didn't even say hi to me."

"I think Sgt. Myra is married to his job. I don't think he sees anyone." Luke tried to focus on the patient charts in his hands.

"Sometimes he is sweet in that 'I want to save him' kind of way, and sometimes I think he is hollow on the inside." Agatha didn't hide the disappointment on her face.

"The man can't give you what he doesn't have, and today he doesn't have a lot."

Agatha and Luke walked back into the ICU and looked into Ms. Power's room. She caught a glimpse of Sgt. Myra as he sat talking to the school principal.

He looked smaller today, she thought. He looked broken.

25

Father Charles Horan's service would be a private affair and take place in the smaller Marian Chapel located on the right-hand side of the Basilica of St. John the Baptist. Normally a visitor would be fascinated by the hand-carved wooden recessed Stations of the Cross or the four beautiful stained glass windows representing the Immaculate Conception, the Assumption of Our Lady, the Immaculate Heart of Mary, and Our Lady of Fatima. This morning, its lone visitor didn't notice anything but the gold-coloured urn placed on a podium at the front altar.

Sgt. Myra sat in the back of the chapel in a white oak pew, staring at the urn containing the cremated remains of Father Charles Horan. The chapel was empty, as he was the first to arrive at the funeral service. He was glad no one else was there. It gave him a chance to spend some time alone with Charles. Myra felt an overwhelming sense of guilt. He had been so thrilled to receive the files from Father Horan that he got caught up in the excitement and the magnitude of the operation. He had wanted to sit down and talk with Charles, and he made mental notes of the things he wanted to tell him. He'd wanted to tell Charles face to face that he had helped so many victims. But he'd kept putting it off because there was so much happening at once.

The phone call.

He should have answered Charles's phone call. That could have made all the difference. Maybe Charles had called to tell him what he was about to do. Maybe he could have talked him out of it. He could have helped him. Charles could be alive right now if he had just answered the phone. It would have taken a minute or two to save his life. *A damn minute. I didn't have a damn minute to answer the phone for the man who gave me the biggest break of my career.*

The last few days had been like a roller coaster. Tracking down victims and helping them. Tracking down pedophiles and charging them with their crimes. The roller coaster was taking him on high highs and low lows. He needed to get off. He needed his brain to stop over-thinking. He needed the nightmares to stop. On his way to the funeral, Chief DeSilva had called to say Myra would be getting the Chief's Commendation for the good work he and his team had done. How could he accept an award that had cost another man his life? He felt like he had placed the noose around Charles's neck. Sgt. Myra felt like the blood of the lamb was now on his hands.

Someone had set up an easel next to Horan's urn. He guessed it had been Sister Pius. It was covered in pictures of Charles wearing his Roman collar and in plain clothes. In some of the pictures he was very young. Myra thought they must have been taken when he first went to the orphanage. He noted Charles was smiling in the younger pictures, but the smile disappeared as he aged. Myra couldn't help but notice how Charles had started out as a handsome young boy but seemed to age two years for every year he lived. Much like himself.

So much promise lost, thought Myra. The seasoned police officer was relieved that Charles had been cremated. He didn't want to look into his face as he lay in a casket. A Chief's Commendation. The highest honour a police officer could receive. How could he accept it knowing he too was now covered in the blood of the lamb? He would forever see Charles's blood on his hands.

His mind kept going back to the day before. The news conference. The call from Sister Pius. The shock when she screamed into the phone. She was screaming as she told him she was standing in the archbishop's office and Charles had hanged himself. Myra raced to the rectory after alerting other police officers and an ambulance.

Sister Pius had been on her knees, sobbing hysterically. Nick jumped up on the desk and lifted Charles's lifeless body up to take the pressure of the rope off his neck. Two constables arrived at the same time and rushed to his aid. They each held a leg while Nick cut him down. The ambulance attendants arrived seconds later. The three police officers laid Horan's limp body on the stretcher. As the attendants started to wheel him out, Sister Pius grabbed Charles and hugged him, sobbing, rocking him like he had been her own son. Nick had to pull her away. She was hysterical, and it took a while to calm her down. She eventually became very quiet and withdrawn. He had walked her back to the Mother House and left her in the care of her sisters. Then he had sat in his car for a long time, unable to turn the key in the ignition.

Myra couldn't help but wonder who Charles Horan would be now if he had not been put in the orphanage. Where would he be right now? Certainly not in an urn. Maybe married to a nice girl with a family and a career. He may have had a very normal life. A life that was stolen by a very evil man. The archbishop killed Charles, but Myra felt as though he had put the noose around his neck.

* * * * *

Father Cooke stood pacing in the room behind the Marian Chapel, rehearsing his sermon for Father Horan's service. He tried hard to focus, but his hands were shaking. His own future was hanging in the wind. He thought how ironic it was that his last duty as a priest would be to conduct a funeral for another priest. Every time his cellphone rang he jumped, expecting it to be the archbishop's secretary requesting he come to the office.

The news of Father Horan's suicide ran through the religious ranks. Never had anyone in the order heard of a priest dying by suicide. Father Cooke thought back on Horan's relationship with Archbishop Keating. They seemed unusually close. It always gave him a sick feeling in the pit of his stomach. Now rumours were flying about just how unusual that relationship was.

He didn't know Horan that well. The young priest had kept to himself. Father Cooke always got the feeling Father Horan didn't trust him, and he didn't know why. He respected Horan's boundaries and did not pursue a friendship. Still, he was honoured when Sister Pius asked him to do the funeral service. He was worried that other clergy would not respect him now or question his motives after the spectacle he had made of himself in the basilica.

The chapel slowly began to fill to its ninety-seat capacity.

Sister Pius was the second to arrive. She walked in with her head down and didn't notice the police officer sitting alone in the back of the chapel. She sat in the front row and immediately got on her knees and began to pray. Dr. Luke Gillespie and Nurse Agatha Catania came in next. They both nodded to Nick and slid into his pew. After exchanging pleasantries, they sat in silence. Luke was surprised to see Mrs. Furey come in next. She nodded at him and sat in the pew in front of his.

Sgt. Myra kept his eyes on Sister Pius. He stiffened when he noticed her shoulders shaking, indicating that she was crying. He decided to join her in the front row, and as he entered, she looked up at him. He took her hand and held it during the sixty-minute service.

The chapel began to fill with other priests and nuns who were there to show their support and share their pain. Father Horan's death was a death in the family. Whether they knew him or not, they had lost a brother, and they grieved their loss.

Sgt. Myra noticed a uniform out of the corner of his eye. He turned around to see three rows filled with the members of his unit—police officers he had worked with—and Chief DeSilva. As he watched them fill the pews, a lump formed in his throat. Myra remembered he, too, was part of a family, and he was humbled by their attendance. He knew they were there for him. He turned back toward the altar, still wondering how they could award him such an honour while knowing it had cost the life of this priest.

Father Cooke donned his holy vestment, took a deep breath, and stood at the back of the chapel. As the organist played "Be Not Afraid," he walked in behind the few altar boys still volunteering at the church. He took his place at the altar and observed the small crowd in front of him. The funeral service was the same as every other he had conducted throughout his career, but his sermon was different.

He wished he had listened to his gut about Father Horan. Maybe if he tried harder, he could have helped him. Maybe Charles didn't trust him because he thought Father Cooke was a pedophile, too. It made him sick to his stomach. He felt the same as every clergy in the room. Like he should have done more. Like he should have investigated the whispers about Charles's relationship with the archbishop.

There was a lot of guilt to go around in this small chapel.

Father Cooke tried to explain during his sermon why Father Horan had taken his own life. He told the story of a friend who boarded a plane with his young child. During the flight, they experienced severe turbulence. The child became very frightened and started to cry. The father comforted the child until the turbulence stopped, and then the child went back to playing. On the flight back from their vacation, the child became very anxious when he had to board the plane and began to cry. People around them rolled their eyes in disgust at this unruly child. There were comments of, "What a spoiled child!" "Why can't you get him under control?" And, of course, the angry stares and judgment. The father sat there with the child and rocked him, comforting him.

Father Cooke said, "The child's father knew how he'd gotten that way. The father knew it was his experience with turbulence that created the anxiety and made the child cry. He knew the best thing he could do for his son was ignore everyone around them and sit and comfort his child until he stopped crying." He then said, "God the Father knew why Father Horan had such anxiety. He knew how he'd gotten that way. And he is now in his Father's arms being comforted without judgment."

Sister Pius began to weep even more, and Sgt. Myra put his strong arms around her, offering her comfort. He knew she was thinking of yesterday, holding Charles's lifeless body on the stretcher. He knew the image would never leave her mind . . . or his.

After the service, everyone sadly walked out of the chapel. The sisters at the Mother House had arranged for a tea and cookie reception. The clergy all attended. The police officers went back to work. Dr. Gillespie, Nurse Catania, and Mrs. Furey walked out together and headed back to the hospital. Sister Pius and Sgt. Myra stayed in the chapel.

"I thought he was ready to move on with his life," she confessed.

"He may have had this planned all along," replied Myra.

"Do you think so?" the nun asked, while her mind went over every conversation she'd had with him over the past week. "I didn't see this coming. I missed something."

"You didn't miss anything," he reassured her. "I think Charlie was on a mission. I think when he turned the files over to me his mind was made up."

"Why?" she sobbed. "Why? I had offered him a safe place. He could have gone on with his life."

"He was broken. He didn't know how to fix himself." Myra's guilt only grew with each word.

"I am broken now, too," said Sister Pius, leaning heavily on Myra's arm. "Help me back to the Mother House, please. I need to lie down."

Along the walk, Sgt. Myra lamented on a past belief. "Sister, my mother used to say everything happens for a reason. Do you believe that?"

"No, I don't. I believe good things happen to bad people, and bad things happen to good people. There's no rhyme or reason to it. The universe is a random place, but I do believe you get back what you put out." She let out a heavy sigh. "Sgt. Myra, you of all people should know the difference on that one."

"Yes, I guess I suppose I should."

As he left the Mother House, the grey sky that had been threatening rain all morning opened and began to pour. He walked past the statue of the Virgin Mary in the front yard. The rain looked like tears streaming down Her face. Even She was disappointed in him today. Even She judged his selfishness.

26

Father Peter Cooke left the Marian Chapel and returned to the room behind it. He removed his holy vestment. Just as he returned the garment to his closet, the new archbishop's assistant appeared in the doorway. "The archbishop would like to see you as soon as possible."

He nodded. "I will be there shortly."

After she walked away, he closed the door to get a few minutes to himself. His heart was racing, and his hands where shaking. He got down on his knees in the middle of the room and began to pray the Lord's Prayer. "Our Father, who art in Heaven, hallowed be Thy name; Thy kingdom come, Thy will be done, on earth as it is in Heaven; Give us this day our daily bread and forgive us our trespasses, as we forgive those who trespass against us; And lead us not into temptation, but deliver us from evil."

His hands were clasped tightly in front of his heart and his head bowed with his eyes closed as he asked the Lord to be with him. Protect him. Forgive him. With each request, he prayed the Lord's Prayer repeatedly. Finally, he opened his eyes and stood up. He took a deep breath and released it, trying to slow his heart rate. He opened the door and walked from the basilica to the office of the archbishop at the Pastoral Centre on Military Road, minutes from the church. It was lightly raining as he passed the town clock in the East Tower. The clock struck noon, and the sweet sounds of the great Joy Bells ringing could be heard for miles around.

The Archdiocese of St. John's had a Catholic population of 111,000 in thirty-six parishes. The total population of the geographic area was 213,000, meaning 52.1% of the population of the area self-reported as Roman Catholic. Since Father Cooke's news conference, that number had grown well beyond the last census. Churches within the thirty-six parishes were full of people day and night. The basilica now had volunteers and paid staff on hand every day doing crowd control. This was an excellent example of "Be careful what you pray for."

Father Cooke was shaking, wet, and cold when he entered the archbishop's office. A chill had entered his bones and ran through his spine. He could hear his teeth chattering as he greeted the archbishop with "Your Excellency." The archbishop pointed toward a chair in front of his desk, and Father Cooke sat down.

"Do you know that the word 'news' is actually an acronym?" he quizzed Father Cooke.

"No, Your Grace. I did not."

"It stands for north, east, west, and south. Father, I had an interesting phone call this morning."

Father Cooke shifted his weight in the chair. His throat was too dry to respond. The archbishop continued.

"The Most Holy Father called me himself. Can you imagine

picking up the phone and hearing the voice of His Holiness calling from the Vatican?" The archbishop himself was now visibly shaken.

"No, Your Grace, I could not." The impact of being fired by the Pope felt like a million-pound weight on Cooke's shoulders. "His Holiness is firing me?"

"Firing you?" The archbishop was surprised. "He is not firing you. He is hiring you. The Most Holy Father himself called with strict orders to promote you to the position of media relations spokesperson for the archdiocese. You will now be given the title Very Reverend Peter Cooke."

Cooke sat stunned in the chair, trying to grasp what the archbishop was saying. His heart was beating so rapidly he was sure the archbishop could hear it.

"Do you understand what I am saying?" The archbishop was trying to wrap his own mind around this new way of doing things. "The Holy Father wants you to continue what you are doing."

"He is not firing me?" Father Cooke asked in shock.

"No, not at all. The Holy Father reports that, since your news conference, people throughout the world have been rushing to churches and filling the pews to capacity. My fellow, you have brought people back to the church in droves!"

"I didn't think about the impact outside of my own parish," Father Cooke sputtered.

"North, east, west, and south!" laughed the archbishop. "Your little media coup was broadcast worldwide. News stations throughout the world are playing and replaying your news conference and impromptu Mass. The Pope himself has called you 'The Rock-Star Priest.'"

Father Cooke could not control his shaking. He stood up and began pacing the room. "What do I do now? I didn't think beyond the news conference. I really didn't think the media would be that interested in what I had to say. I hoped they would, but I never imagined this would happen."

"Well, I have been instructed to hire you a digital media communications strategist to handle your media needs, and an assistant to handle your phone calls. My assistant has a message from a persistent fellow who wants to be your agent. You should call him." The archbishop handed him a pink message slip with a name and number on it.

"So, you want me to continue?" Father Cooke asked the archbishop. "Because I don't know what my next move should be."

"No, I want to fire you for going behind my back and causing this circus, which I am sure will implode at some point, but the Holy Father sees value in what you are doing, and he wants you to continue. Surely you had a plan from the beginning?"

"My only plan was to bring people back to the church. To apologize for the atrocities that some priests have committed against children."

"Well, you'd better have an Act II," the archbishop warned him. "Your audience is waiting for you."

Father Cooke was lost. This was not what he was expecting. "What would Jesus do?" he asked himself out loud. "Speak to me, dear Jesus. Guide me through this."

"I am told to have your staff in place immediately, so we are not going through the normal hiring procedures. I have engaged a headhunting firm to get people in place by next week. The Vatican has already put the money into our budget to cover all your costs. You will be on a separate financial code than the rest of us. You are now working directly for the Vatican. An office has been cleaned out for you down the hall from mine."

"When should I move there?" Father Cooke felt like his questions were almost childish at this point.

"Today," sighed the archbishop. "Do me the professional courtesy of keeping me informed, please. You now report to a public relations cardinal in Rome. He will be calling you soon."

"I am not reporting to you?"

"No. You're Rome's problem now."

"I never meant to be a problem. I meant to be the solution."

"Well, get yourself together. You have a lot of phone calls to return. Please shut the door on your way out."

Father Cooke opened the door to the archbishop's office and looked back at him. "Can I consult with you from time to time, Your Grace?"

"Keep me informed of everything you are doing, as I asked, but your reporting line is now to the Vatican. You are blessed, my son. The Most Holy Father himself has reached out and appointed you. That does not happen every day."

"I don't know where to start. What about my duties as a priest at the basilica? Can I still say Mass?"

"No, you won't have time for those duties anymore now. You're a rock star! I have already put another priest in charge of Mass." Cooke wasn't sure if the archbishop was being sarcastic or helpful.

"Mass was the best part of my job." Cooke turned to leave the office.

"It's not a job, Father Cooke. It is a way of life." The archbishop leaned back in his big wooden chair. "Heavy is the head that wears the crown, Father. That's why Jesus's head is always bowed down on the Crucifix."

"Yes, Your Excellency." Father Cooke's head was heavy as he left the room and met the assistant who led him to his new office.

The archbishop sat in his office remembering a Bible quote from his youth. *For the lamb who is in the midst of the throne shall feed them and shall lead them unto living fountains of waters; and God shall wipe away all tears from their eyes.*

He prayed this lamb was not being led to the slaughter.

27

If eyes could burn a hole into someone, Mary Power would have an entry wound just above her temple, into her brain.

This tiny woman was sleeping peacefully with her two hands neatly resting on her chest as if she were lying in a coffin. Sgt. Myra sat in the chair across from her bed, glaring at her. *You rotten bitch*, he thought. *You molested your students, and I'll prove it if it's the last thing I do.*

His team had come up short. Mary Power was clean. Not even a traffic ticket. They heard some rumours, but nothing concrete. Myra instructed them to start again. He thought up another investigative approach. Now his team was pouring through school yearbooks from the junior and senior high schools where she had taught or had served as principal. They were instructed to compare each class picture to the class picture from the next year. They were looking for any student who was missing from the next year's class pictures. If they could find girls who were missing from those pictures, they were to cross-reference the names with criminal records. He was sure he would find her victims that way. His experience as a seasoned child exploitation investigator taught him that young victims of abuse, especially sexual abuse, tended to lash out by running away from home, quitting school, and committing criminal acts. It seemed to be the only way to get someone to listen to them.

Mary Power woke with the feeling someone was watching her. She looked toward the police officer sitting next to her bed. “I wasn’t expecting company. How nice of you, Sgt. Myra, to watch over me.” Her voice was soft and sweet like a dear grandmother speaking to her favourite grandson. Her face was thin and grey from loss of blood. She pulled the wool blanket up around her chest with her long, skinny fingers as if to show her modesty. But Nick knew she was more a wicked witch than a loving grandmother.

“You’re going to hell, Miss Power, and I am here to drive you.” Nick was out of character today. Normally he wouldn’t talk to a suspect like that. But today he wanted to grab her by the throat and pull the information out of her. He was having a hard time keeping himself in check.

“Really? How can that be, Sgt. Myra? You have nothing on me, and you won’t get anything on me,” she answered smugly.

“Oh, I will get something on you,” he snarled back at her. “I won’t stop until you’re in prison.”

“What? A little old lady like me?” She sat up in the bed, put her hands together, and cracked her knuckles, sending a shiver down Myra’s spine. “I taught discipline, morals, and manners. I turned my girls into ladies.”

Myra knew she was evil to the core, and he needed to find a way to bring it out into the open. His gut told him Mary Power tortured her students without any sense of regret. He hated when people had that "I am above the law" look to them.

Their conversation was interrupted by a hospital worker who brought in her lunch tray and put it on the table across the foot of her bed. "Lunch is here." The young worker greeted the patient with a friendly smile as she did with every other patient.

"Shouldn't you ask for permission before you come into a room?" asked Ms. Power. "Do you really need to tell me it's a lunch tray? Do you think I don't know what this tray is for? There's no need to talk to me every time you enter this room. Do your job and leave." Myra noticed how Ms. Power seemed to delight in using tone of voice to belittle those she considered below her. The worker turned and left, giving Myra a sideways glance and a nervous smile.

Mary Power pulled the table closer to her. She laced her fingers together in front of her and bent them so every knuckle cracked. She took a tea bag from a small bowl, shook it, and placed it in the silver teapot full of hot water. "Why can't they put the tea bag in the pot and then pour the hot water over it as it is supposed to be done!" she complained. She lifted the small tub of orange juice from the left side and placed it on the right. Then she rolled the silverware out of its napkin and placed it beside the plate in the proper order. Myra took note of her quirks. She lifted the cover off her plate and used the fork to push the green peas away from the mashed potatoes and the meat away from the vegetables so they didn't touch. Myra noticed the small, pink bow in her hair. It looked like something a child would wear, he thought. She looked at him again, timid now that she knew he was watching her. He was amazed by how quickly she changed character from evil to innocent—a true psychopath.

"Funny no one visits you."

Myra had barely finished his sentence when Ms. Power put up her bony hand, ordering him to stop talking. "I am eating. I do not like conversation while I am enjoying my food. You may leave." She dismissed him without looking at him. She cracked her knuckles once again and began to eat, as if oblivious of Myra's hate and frustration directed at her. Ms. Power was an expert at detecting those emotions, and she truly enjoyed making people feel them.

He stood up, feeling the anger rising in his chest, and headed for the nearest exit. While walking toward the car, his phone rang. His team had found someone at the correctional centre for women in Clarenville, a two-hour road trip away. Myra asked his team to notify the prison he was on the way to speak to this prisoner, and he hit the highway.

* * * * *

Rosemary Penashue was from Sheshatshiu, forty kilometres southwest of Happy Valley–Goose Bay. She sat in the small interview room staring at the top of the table in front of her. She had no idea what she had done wrong, but she knew enough to keep her mouth shut and say nothing. When the tall policeman opened the door, she did not lift her eyes to meet his. As he was pulling a chair out from the table to sit across from her, she snuck a peek and realized that he was twice her height.

"Rosemary, my name is Sgt. Nicholas Myra. I am with the Royal Newfoundland Constabulary." He reached his hand out to shake hers. She looked at him from under her eyes and stretched her hand toward his for a weak handshake, then quickly drew it back. The woman nervously sat on both hands, still wondering why she was there.

"I am hoping you can help me," he continued. "Do you know a schoolteacher by the name of Mary Power?" He observed her reaction to the name. Her chest caved in as her shoulders came forward, and her head lowered almost to the tabletop.

"Rosemary, do you remember Miss Power? She was your teacher in grade five."

Rosemary lifted her left hand and begin to chew on her thumbnail. "I don't remember her," she whispered. Her thick Innueimun accent and low tone made it hard to understand what she was saying.

"Are you sure, Rosemary? She was your teacher in grade five. I have your class picture. Let me show you." Myra took out his phone and opened the picture one of his team members had sent him. "This is you in the front row." He then pointed to the prim and proper teacher sitting three students to the right of her. "And this is Mary Power. Do you remember her now?"

The young woman looked at the screen on his phone. Her hand moved to her forehead, and she began to rub it in a circular motion. "No, I don't remember her. Why, is she dead?" She looked directly into Myra's eyes.

Sgt. Myra put his phone back in its holster and paid careful attention to her face. She was pretty, with deep brown eyes and golden skin. Her file said she was forty-five years old, but he was expecting a much older-looking woman after reading her long history in the corrections file room. Her record contained mostly drunk in public charges and petty theft, and she had been the victim of domestic violence several times. His team pulled her juvenile record, which showed her run-ins with the law started when she was around ten years old. Approximately the same time this picture was taken.

"No, she is not dead. She's in hospital and very sick."

"Nothing to do with me," she muttered.

"Well, that's what I am trying to find out." He decided to cut to the chase. "Do you know what Wormwood is?"

She looked at him and shrugged her shoulders. "Is that a plant or something?"

"No, it's a disease that some believe only affects pedophiles." He watched her face for a response.

Rosemary shrugged her shoulders again. "Nope, never heard of it."

He could tell from her body language that she was telling the truth.

"What has that got to do with me? I never touched nobody!"

"No. That's not what I am saying." He tried again. "Are you sure you don't know Miss Power?"

She looked down at the table again. "No."

He knew she was lying. He intertwined his fingers and cracked his knuckles. Rosemary jumped, putting her two arms over her head as if someone was about to hit her. Her reaction startled Myra.

She looked at him from the space between her two forearms as her hands stayed over her head.

"She beat you, didn't she?" Myra knew his gut was right.

She shook her head but kept her arms and hands firmly in place.

"Rosemary, you ran away at ten years old, and you haven't stop running. I can help you stop running. If you help me, we can put this monster in jail for good."

She slowly lowered her arms and wrapped them around her body, hugging herself as she rocked back and forth. With her eyes still looking at the tabletop, she began. "One day a girl in my class told Miss Power someone stole her lunch from the coatroom. Miss Power told the class she wanted the lunch returned. She made every girl get up, one by one, and go into the room. She said that after the last girl went in, she would check, and if the lunch was not returned, she would strap the thief in front of the class. The lunch was not returned.

"She came out of the coatroom with her long, wooden ruler in her hands. I knew when I heard her knuckles crack, someone was getting it. She grabbed me by the hair and dragged me out of my desk to the front of the class. She bent me across the teacher's desk and lifted my uniform, then started whipping me with the ruler. She kept screaming 'This is what happens to bad girls who steal!'"

Rosemary rocked faster now and lifted her head to face Sgt. Myra. "I didn't steal the lunch. I was poor, and I was hungry, but I didn't steal the lunch." Myra did his best to hold his anger in. "Later that morning," she continued, "the girl whose mother had made the lunch came to the school, bringing the lunch. The mother had forgotten to put it in the girl's bookbag. And so, the girl had thought the lunch was stolen."

She looked at the table again. "You never knew when you were going to get a beating or how brutal it would be. Sometimes she would leave welts all over your body. Sometimes she would leave you unconscious."

"Were there other incidents?" Every muscle in Myra's body was pulled tight in anger as he listened to her story.

"There were lots of incidents. The beatings were a daily

thing. Anything would set her off. Like, if we tried to speak Innueimun or said we wanted to go hunting with our families. She would not allow us to continue with our native traditions. She called us 'savages.' You knew you were going to get a beating when she cracked her knuckles. To this day, I can't take the sound of it."

Sgt. Myra wasn't going to be happy with a simple assault charge. He needed more. "Can you tell me if she was ever sexually inappropriate with you or any of the other girls?"

"She liked girls. She hated men, she would say that all the time. She had a secret room behind her office that had no windows. It used to be a storage room. She had a small bed put in there for 'sick kids.' No one could hear you when you screamed in there. At least no one came when I did."

"When you say she liked girls, do you mean children?" He needed her to say it without putting the words in her mouth.

"I know what you're trying to do, Sgt. Myra. The Mounties tried to do the same thing. We all gave our statement years ago to the RCMP, and it never went anywhere."

It felt like someone had come up behind him and driven an ice pick through the centre of Myra's skull. He was nauseated from the pain. His breath stuck in his throat, and his voice grew louder than he planned. "When? When did you give statements to the Mounties?" He tried not to show his anger, but his whole body was shaking.

"About twenty-five years ago. I think I was twenty." She looked at him like he should have known this. "Sure, about thirty of us went to the detachment in Goose Bay that month and gave our statements. Nothing ever came from it because they said we weren't credible."

He pushed the chair back and jumped to his feet. "You're kidding me, right? Are you pulling my leg?" He had to put his hands in his pants pockets to hide their trembling.

"Why would I do that? I'm already in jail! Go talk to Inspector Michaels. He had them all in a white box. I saw them in his office. I thought he really believed me. He wanted to put her in jail, too."

Myra wanted to punch something. He tried not to show how angry he was. "I will find him, and he will be held accountable."

"Sgt. Myra." Rosemary's voice was low. "She's heartless and cruel." She shook her head back and forth, not understanding why her life had turned out like this. "When you put her in jail, please put her in *this* jail."

He was taken back by her request. "Why would you want her here, near you?"

"I have to look her in the eye. I have to see her face when you bring her down." His heart broke as he watched her eyes fill up.

"Rosemary, it's not going to help you heal. Have you been thinking about your abuse a lot lately?"

"I usually drink to forget it, but in here there's no booze. When I am sober, it's all I think about." It made sense to him now. That's why Mary Power was in hospital—Rosemary was dry and thinking about her abuse all the time.

"I want to hurt her. Sometimes I want to kill her. But it won't change anything. It won't give me back my childhood."

"Rosemary, you may be able to help me answer another question." There was something sticking in his brain about Mary Power.

"Sure, if I can."

"She wears a pink bow in her hair. It looks like something a child would wear. Do you know the significance of it?"

"That belongs to Suzie Rich. She died when she was in grade two. Everyone was told she fell off the swing set on the playground, but I know Miss Power beat her in the room that morning and she fainted. Miss Power walked her out to the playground, sat her on a swing, and walked away. That's where another teacher found her. On the ground, under the swing."

"Are you saying Mary Power killed a child while she was a teacher at your school?" Myra's heart was beating wildly.

"I believe she did. I know Miss Power took her out of class and brought her to her office, because I was the prefect on duty that morning and saw it. Miss Power was also the principal of the school. So, no one would question her on that."

"Are you sure she walked her to the playground?" Myra realized he now had a whole new investigation.

"My sister was sitting in class and could see the playground from her window. She watched Miss Power walk Suzie to the swing and sit her on it. Then walk away. She was wondering why Suzie was allowed to go to the playground during class. Then the bell rang, and she changed classes. Suzie was found during the lunch break."

"Was there an investigation?"

"I know the police came to the school, because I saw them in the front office. They didn't talk to any kids, just Miss Power and the teachers."

Really?" Myra was stunned by this new information. "What about the bow?"

"Suzie wore that bow all the time. After she died, I noticed

Miss Power had it in her hair. It was like a warning to the rest of us what could happen if we didn't do as she said."

"For helping me out, I am going to talk to the warden about getting you the help you need. You have to talk to someone who is a child abuse specialist. You need to be closer to your family and your Innu culture. Would you like to be transferred to the women's facility in Goose Bay?"

"Yes!" Rosemary let out a loud, piercing cry. "I want to go home." She began to sob.

He sat back down, reached across the table, and took her hand. "Rosemary, the more you talk about your abuse, the more you will heal." Myra knew that was true, but he also knew the more she talked and thought about it, the more pain Mary Power would endure, if Father Cooke's theory was right.

"You're a good man, Sgt. Myra."

He waved at the guard watching through the protective window, indicating he was finished. He watched her being led away. As soon as the door closed behind her, all the spite, rage, and frustration came to the surface as his fist hit the steel door. Blood spattered over the dull grey paint, and the pain ran through his arm to his shoulder. The guard fell back against the wall, scared out of his wits. "What was that for?" he yelled.

"For assholes who spend money keeping people in prison when they should be in facilities getting the care they need!"

Myra walked past him holding his hand. The guard waited for him to leave before going over to look at the dent in the steel door. "Glad that wasn't my face," he muttered.

Myra's first stop was the warden's office. He told him Rosemary was part of an undercover investigation that he was conducting, and he needed her moved to the Goose Bay facility immediately. He also requested that due to the stress this investigation could cause, he wanted her to see a psychologist weekly.

By the next morning, Rosemary was moved, and the help she desperately needed was made available to her. The psychologist gave her a diary and told her to write down her feelings every day and they would discuss them at their weekly meetings.

* * * * *

Myra hit the highway in a fury. He asked his team to track down RCMP Inspector Michaels who oversaw Labrador twenty-five years ago. His team started making calls, and by the time Sgt. Myra got back to his office, they had tracked down Inspector Boyd Michaels, who was now retired and living just outside of St. John's.

He sat at his desk and picked up the phone. His hand was swollen and bruised. The blood had dried around the cuts, and his knuckles felt like they were broken. His fingers were still shaking when he dialled the number.

"Hello," answered an authoritative voice.

"I am looking for retired RCMP Inspector Boyd Michaels," Sgt. Myra responded.

"This is Inspector Boyd Michaels speaking."

"Inspector, my name is Sgt. Nicholas Myra with the RNC. Do you have a few minutes to talk with me?

"Yes, of course. What is this about?"

"When you were the district commander in Labrador, you investigated the physical and sexual abuse of girls in Sheshatshiu." Then he added, "And a death which could have been a murder of a young girl at the school."

There was a pause, and Myra could hear him taking a deep breath. "I have been waiting for twenty-five years for this phone call, Sergeant. When can we get together?"

"When is good for you?"

"I can be at your office within an hour."

"It's late and I have had a long day. Why don't we meet tomorrow morning?" Myra was tired and sore from the long drive to Clarenville and back.

"Okay. I have waited so long to get this off my chest. It haunts me every time I close my eyes. I suffer from severe PTSD from carrying the guilt of this file. I thought I would die with this on my conscience. I can't tell you how happy I am to receive your call." Michaels's voice shook with emotion.

"How about nine a.m. tomorrow morning at RNC headquarters?" Myra offered.

"Yes. I will be there with bells on."

28

Sgt. Myra arrived at the side employee door of the Royal Newfoundland Constabulary at 8:00 a.m. As soon as he unlocked his office door, the phone was ringing. The sergeant on the front desk informed him there was a guest in the front lobby who had been waiting for him since 7:00 a.m. He immediately went to see who it was and looked out through the small glass in the lobby door. There stood Inspector Boyd Michaels, pacing back and forth. He was approximately seventy years old, with short white hair, stocky but trim, about six feet tall with neatly pressed pants and shirt. *Your typical Mountie*, Myra thought. He opened the door and extended his hand. "Inspector Michaels. You're early. Thank you for coming in."

"Early bird gets the worm, as they say." They exchanged a firm handshake. "Quite the pair of mitts you have on you, Sgt. Myra. Looks like you taught someone their manners recently." He pointed to Myra's knuckles.

Nick rubbed his sore hand. "I took my frustrations out on a steel door. Doors don't make complaints." He laughed.

"Been there, done that, and have arthritis in my hands to prove it." The inspector laughed.

They made their way to Sgt. Myra's office. He closed the door, and the two police officers sat across from each other.

"Sgt. Myra, I want you to know up front that I did everything I could for those girls. I threatened to quit my job and go to the media. I couldn't get anywhere." The frustration showed in his face.

"Start from the beginning. Tell me what happened."

"One of the parents came to the detachment in Goose Bay with her daughter. She showed me the whip marks on the child's back and behind. The child was only six years old!" Michaels let out a heavy sigh. "I was outraged. I had kids that age, myself. I asked her what happened, and the mother told me all about Principal Mary Power." He leaned forward and put his hands on his knees with a slap. "I took a statement from the mother and the child. I took pictures, and I got in my patrol car and drove to Sheshatshiu. I walked right in her office and said, 'Principal, we are going to have a chat.'" Michaels was spitting with anger.

"She was so smug. Sitting there all prim and proper. I could have pulled her over the desk and pounded her for whipping that child." He sat back in his chair. "She said she didn't know anything about it. She tried to convince me the mother did it. I knew she was lying."

He ran a shaking hand over his white hair. "The mother called me later that afternoon and withdrew the statement. She said it was a lie, that Miss Power hadn't hit her. She blamed the marks on her son, who was a year older than the daughter. I called the Crown prosecutor's office and was told to drop it. I didn't have enough evidence for a charge."

Myra leaned forward in his chair. "I met with Rosemary Penashue at the correctional centre for women. She said she also gave you a statement."

"Yes, I know Rosemary. I met her when she was a toddler and watched her grow up. She was a good kid, but she changed around the time she turned ten. It broke my heart when I saw her in the jail cell one morning," Michaels remembered. "I didn't give up on that first file. I kept digging, but I wasn't finding anything. Then, one night we busted a couple of young girls who were sniffing gasoline behind a bar. They were only thirteen or fourteen years old. While they were in the police car, they were going on about Miss Power and how she raped and beat them and how I should arrest her. I brought them to the hospital for monitoring, and in the morning I went back and asked them about what they had said the night before. At first they denied it, but after a few questions they started to spill the beans."

Myra had taken a notebook out of his desk and was writing as fast as he could.

"I told them I wanted to speak to any girl who had been abused at that school, and they spread the word. By the end of that month, I had thirty statements from girls of all ages. Their abuse was horrific. It ranged from sexual to physical torture." Inspector Michaels was disgusted with the memory.

"What happened once you had all the statements?"

"I notified the RCMP's criminal operations officer of what I had, and he notified the Department of Justice and the Department of Child Welfare. I was ready to take the top off it. I notified my staff to be ready for this huge takedown, where we would arrest Power and a lineup of social workers would be there to help those girls get the help they needed."

Michaels folded his arms in frustration. "I waited for days, then weeks. I didn't want to rattle the chain of command. Labrador is already an underserved area when it comes to headquarters. You know, out of sight out of mind. I got tired of waiting, so I picked up the phone and called the second-in-command. I asked him what was taking so long. These children were being abused daily, and we needed to move." His eyes narrowed. "I was told the Department of Justice would not be proceeding with any charges against Miss Power because the girls were not credible. I was flabbergasted." He slammed his hands down on his knees again.

"I was ready to rip the head off someone! I knew I had enough to charge her, so I started to dig again. I found out that the ministers of Justice and Social Services spent quite a bit of time in Goose Bay, and rumour had it they liked young girls. Miss Power had an ample supply. I also found out that the families of every one of the thirty girls who gave a statement got a call from social services saying their welfare allotment was now under review. Apparently, the Minister of Social Services himself made the call."

"That's unusual," remarked Myra.

"That's damn unusual!" Michaels sputtered. "I found out from a maid who worked at the hotel in Goose Bay that a few of the government ministers were running a sex-for-welfare scheme. Some big names were showing up in Goose Bay and not making any government announcements but spending a night or two at the hotel, and young girls—very young girls," he emphasized, "were being brought in to spend time with them." Inspector Michaels seemed equally happy to get this off his chest but sick to relive it.

"Did you charge them?" Myra asked.

"You have to remember the time. It was the early eighties, and government ministers were above the law. One of the politicians involved went on to federal politics, another one died. The rest retired but stayed involved with their parties in different ways. A lot of favours were called in. I tried to investigate it but kept hitting brick walls. I even ran an undercover operation, but I couldn't get the girls to admit to anything. Everyone was getting kickbacks. Better welfare benefits, jobs, and apartments or housing." Michaels threw his hands up in the air out of frustration. "The investigation was shut down from the highest level. I was warned repeatedly to leave it alone. I wrote strongly worded memo after memo. To no avail. Then I came into the office one morning and was informed I was transferred to Corner Brook. Corner Brook!" he yelled. "Nothing against the west coast, but I was happy where I was.

"A week later, my house was packed up and we were on our way. Fastest transfer you have ever seen. I was frustrated beyond belief. I became very bitter after that, and Sgt. Myra, I was never a bitter man. I loved my job. I loved putting on the uniform. But after Labrador, I struggled for a lot of years."

"I understand your frustration. Believe me, I do. Inspector, you mentioned thirty statements. Where are they now? Would they be in records?"

"Nick . . . you don't mind if I call you Nick, do you, son? You can call me Boyd."

"Not at all."

"Nick, the funniest thing. I was told to send all the statements to the Department of Justice so the Crown prosecutors could decide if we had enough to go to trial. I told you I waited a long time and then called our criminal operations people?"

Myra nodded. "Yes, that's right."

"Well, after they said there wasn't enough to go to trial, I asked for the box of statements back. You see, I put them all in a white banker's box with hanging file organizers. I am meticulous when it comes to note taking and being organized."

Myra felt like he was talking to an older version of himself.

"Each of the thirty files contained the victim's handwritten statement, my typed copy of their statement, a photo of each victim, and an information sheet giving their age, address, etc."

Myra recognized and appreciated his old-fashioned way of doing good police work. "So, where is it?"

"They lost it!" Michaels snarled. "They said the box was lost in the mail after they sent it back to me! I asked for the courier's receipt, so we could track it, and I was told it was shipped through the general mail!" He huffed in disgust. "Now, have you ever sent a statement through the general mail?"

"What do you think happened to it?"

"Well, you know what happened to it. It may be my dirty mind, but the politicians involved in the sex-for-welfare scam had it destroyed."

"So, they are all gone?" Myra was sick of these dead ends.

"Now, Nick, we may wear different uniforms, but we have the same beliefs. You wouldn't trust a politician any more than I would. You also know that a good police officer keeps two sets of notes. A set he turns in, and a set he keeps in a safe place. Politicians have a way of making things disappear." He slapped his hands on his knees. "I had a feeling that was going to happen. I made a copy of everything in the files. I shipped it to my parents' house in New Brunswick. It stayed there until they passed away, and then I stored it in a safe place in my basement, hoping to God that someone would call me someday and ask about it."

Myra felt a warm feeling coming over him and thought, *This must be what happiness feels like.* "So, you have the files?"

"Yes, they're in the trunk of my car. I wasn't bringing them in until my gut told me you were going to do something with them."

"What does your gut tell you now?"

"That you're a good cop. Maybe a better cop than me, because you're going to do something with this that I couldn't," responded Michaels.

"Only because the timing is right and two good cops collaborated on this file," agreed Sgt. Myra. "What about the death of the young girl, Suzie Rich? What were the details around her death?"

"That was tragic," the older man said with a sigh. "We got the call early in the afternoon. I was in St. John's for meetings, and two junior officers responded. Miss Power had moved her body into the school nurse's office. She had an obvious red mark on her forehead, but Miss Power told the officers the girl fell off a swing and she had put her there to rest. Then when she came back to check on the girl, she was dead." He looked down at his feet as the feeling of dread came back over him.

"The ambulance came shortly after the officers arrived and took her to the hospital. The doctor said the head wound was the cause of death and the fall from the swing was consistent with the injury. The doctor also said there were other marks and bruises but nothing out of the norm for a child of her age. Her parents buried her shortly after that." Michaels was obviously distressed. "I went over that file. The body had been moved, and they let the kids out to play shortly after the police arrived. So, the scene has been contaminated. We had to go on the doctor's report."

"What did you think?" pondered Myra.

"I was flying back from St. John's to Goose Bay. The planes they used for that run were small, two-seater models. Probably about ten to twelve people would fit in one. I made the trip quite frequently. When I got on the plane in St. John's Airport, who should get on with me but the Minister of Justice and the Minister of Social Services. I said hello, and they just nodded and took their seats. They weren't in a talkative mood. I figured they were pissed with me and my investigation."

Myra had almost filled out his notebook.

"So, when we got to Goose Bay, I had an unmarked car, you see, that I had left at the airport. So, I got in my car and waited. Then I followed them. Sure enough, the two ministers went straight to the hospital, then to the home of the deceased child. They were there about an hour. Then they drove straight back to the airport and flew back to St. John's." He looked Myra in the eyes. "Now," he paused, "what do you think happened?"

"I think Mary Power got away with murder by calling in a few of her own favours." Myra's blood was beginning to boil again.

"Can I ask why you are calling me now? Are there more complaints?" Inspector Michaels asked.

"Have you been following the media stories on Wormwood, the disease that is allegedly killing pedophiles?"

"Yes, of course. It's the talk of the town."

"Well, Mary Power is in hospital with what seems like this disease, but her record is clean. I am digging, trying to find something, and I happened to find Rosemary, who told me about you."

"You're a good cop, Sgt. Myra. I know what it's like to forget that about yourself, but you are a good cop." Michaels reached over and patted Myra on the shoulder.

"I forget that a lot, lately," declared Myra. "Boyd, I have to ask you one last question. As a police officer who has been around the block a time or two, do you buy into the theory that God created this disease?"

Inspector Michaels could tell from the look on Sgt. Myra's face that he was serious. "Well, my son, if it is, it would be the first time God answered my prayers," he responded with a very serious smile.

29

The fallout from the media coverage was severe. Dr. Luke Gillespie sat across from Mrs. Furey at the small meeting table in her office with the door closed.

"We have to be very careful about what we say and who we say it to," Mrs. Furey whispered as she pointed to the door. "My entire day is now spent chasing down, squashing, and trying to find out who is spreading rumours." She was usually well put together, but today she looked out of sorts. "Maintenance has just finished putting together the special ward for these patients," she said, looking tormented. "Other patients are refusing to share rooms with anyone with blood on their gown! How silly is that? This is a damn hospital!" she declared. "Everyone has blood on them!"

Gillespie sat back and let her talk.

"I am sorry to burden you with my problems. I am just so friggin' frustrated!"

"That's okay," he reassured her. "I know how it feels. I went to a grocery store last night, and the clerk at the checkout told me to *let those bastards suffer.* Can you believe that?"

Mrs. Furey shook her head in disgust. "So, I wanted to meet with you to discuss the national scene," she said, taking her notes out of a file folder. "Did you attend the doctor's national teleconference this morning?"

"Yes, I did." Luke took his own notes out of a folder.

"Good, then we will be on the same page," she continued. "The big thing right now is, we are not referring to the disease as 'Wormwood,' because that is what the alleged pedophiles call it."

Luke jumped in. "Yes, we discussed that, also. Although the disease showed first as a bleeding disorder, we have to be very careful not to associate it with hemophilia."

Mrs. Furey looked up from her notes. "My God, the poor hemophiliacs are devastated. I have heard from the president of the Hemophiliac Association. He has members who won't even go to work or school because they are afraid." She shook her head again. "Can you imagine? They have men and women who are scared to death they may bleed in front of someone and be accused of being a child molester."

"I know. I'm hearing it from patients, too."

"For Jesus' sakes, I have von Willebrand's disease!" Mrs. Furey confessed.

"I didn't know that. It's quite common," Luke said.

"We were told the doctors would come up with a name for it. Have they decided yet?"

"We agreed it is to be considered a rare disease, because so far it affects fewer than 200,000 people in Canada. The official medical name will be PPXI," Gillespie informed her.

"Okay, that sounds very medical. What does it mean?"

"Well, for blood to clot, your body needs blood proteins called clotting factors and blood cells called platelets. So, we took the P from proteins and the P from platelets. The XI means it occurs in about one out of 100,000 people."

"PPXI, kind of rolls of the tongue," Mrs. Furey joked. "We were told that once the name was decided on, there would be a federal rollout of PR material to all hospitals, media, and public announcing the name. All medical staff will then refer to it by the medical name to take away the stigma of Wormwood."

"I would like to meet the PR team who is going to take the stigma of Wormwood away from this disease," Luke said, and laughed. "Speaking of federal, any word back from the Minister of Health?"

"Not really. I am getting a trickle of information, but no big response like I thought."

"What about your reporter friend? Did she find anything?"

"She has heard a few rumours. Apparently, the federal minister has some skeletons in his closet."

"Oh, really? Do tell."

"She heard from a cop, off the record, of course, that the minister was once investigated for a sexual assault against a young boy when he was in his early twenties."

Luke leaned back in his chair and gave her a hard look. "What happened?"

"No charges were laid. The complaint was dropped. My friend believes the complainant was paid off."

"Interesting. That may explain the blockage at the top."

"That's what I was thinking," she confessed.

"I wonder would Sgt. Myra be able to track down that info?"

"Might be worth asking him."

"I'll be seeing him shortly," Luke said. "He called this morning to say he was coming over to officially charge Mary Power, one of the PPXI patients in ICU."

She shrugged. "Nothing surprises me anymore."

"Well, that was the plan, anyway. She took a turn for the worse last night. I don't know what happened. She was stable, then yesterday afternoon, the floodgates literally opened."

"Any idea what happened?" There was concern in Mrs. Furey's voice.

"I don't know. She's being tortured, that's for sure. I bet she has lost most of the blood in her body. We have given her transfusion after transfusion." He stood up and looked out the big window overlooking the parkway. "I can't give her any more morphine—it would overdose her—but she is screaming with pain."

"Do you think she's going to make it?"

"I don't think Sgt. Myra will be able to charge her. I don't think she'll live to see tomorrow."

30

By the time Dr. Gillespie made it back to the ICU, Sgt. Myra was already sitting in the private room reserved for families of the palliative care patients. "I was hoping to find you here," he greeted the police sergeant. "You're just the guy I'm looking for."

"And they say miracles don't happen anymore." Myra grinned under his thick moustache.

Dr. Gillespie closed the door and sat across from Sgt. Myra. "Can you find out some information on the federal Minister of Health for me?"

Myra's ears perked up. "Are you doing investigations now? Should I scrub up for surgery?"

"No, thanks. I wouldn't want your job for all the money in the world," Gillespie answered. "I'd rather be up to my elbows in blood and guts than have to put on a uniform and do what you do."

"It does weigh you down at times. Although I can't imagine being up to your elbows in blood and guts makes for a restful night's sleep either."

“I guess we all have our crosses to bear.” Luke sighed. “Can you use your investigative skills to find out some information about the minister?”

“You mean you want me to snoop around?” Myra cocked his head to the side. “That requires fewer skills.”

Gillespie filled him in. “We’re having trouble getting any information from the minister’s office. I thought it was just my office, but I’ve had several conference calls with our national medical group, and we can’t seem to get any help from his office.”

“Maybe he’s busy. You know politicians have staff to do all the work. They’re just figureheads. Bureaucrats run the country.”

“At the beginning I was thinking it was caught somewhere in the system, too, but the national chair for our group has sent correspondence directly to Minister McKenzie, and he doesn’t get any response.”

“So, you want me to snoop around and gather information on the federal Minister of Health because he doesn’t respond to his email? Should I investigate the prime minister while I’m at it?” Nicholas Myra knew how hard political investigations were to conduct, especially on the down-low.

“No,” Gillespie said. “But there is a rumour he sexually assaulted a young boy years ago and it was swept under the rug.”

“People make accusations about famous people all the time. Ninety-nine per cent of the time it comes from jealousy or hateful people who just don’t like to see anyone else get ahead.” Myra had seen this happen many times before. “I once had a call from a lady who demanded I make arrangements to have Elvis’s body exhumed and a DNA test done because she was convinced he was her father. There are lots of nutbars out there.”

“The rumour is the minister paid off the accuser,” Gillespie continued. "But where there's smoke, there's fire, as you would say."

"Okay, you have to stop hanging out with me, or maybe you're watching too many TV crime shows."

"Come on, I know your spidey senses are tingling." Gillespie could see the wheels turning in Myra's brain.

"Well, normally when one victim of sexual abuse comes forward, I believe there are ten who are afraid to speak up," Myra said. "Do you know where the victim made the accusation? Canada is a big country."

"I'm not sure, but I would try his political riding. He's from Nova Scotia." Luke knew Myra couldn't resist.

"I'll make some calls." Myra's gut told him there was more to this. "By the way, did you run any tests on the blood of the Wormwood patients?"

"It's called PPXI now, and yes I did," Gillespie informed him. "No poison or any foreign substance showed up in their bloodwork. They didn't even test positive for illegal drugs. The most I found was cold medication."

"I don't like medical terms. I am calling it Wormwood." Myra knew the name scared child molesters. "That's interesting. So, that proves no one is poisoning them. Now I have to look at other ways this could be happening."

"So, you're still not buying the God theory?"

"Atheists like us are going to have a hard time swallowing that one." With the poison theory off the table, Myra didn't know what he believed anymore.

Gillespie agreed. "It would be professional suicide if I announced I even remotely considered the God theory."

"What about past patients? Are you finding out anything

in that area?" Myra knew he would have to get a warrant to officially get the records.

"I have a research team going through emergency's records in Newfoundland and Labrador. We found ten patients who may meet the criteria for PPXI, but they were not admitted. Some of their charts said it was pneumonia or a stomach flu. One patient was a hemophiliac, so that would explain his bleeding. All ten talked about pain in their joints, nosebleeds, thirst, weight loss, etc." Gillespie shrugged his shoulders. "Nothing screamed 'new disease' to any of the attending doctors or nurses."

"Any of them die?"

"My team is in the process of following up with phone calls to the patients." Gillespie stopped, realizing past patient information couldn't be shared. "You're going to have to get a warrant if you want the results of that research. I can't share it with you."

"I understand," said Myra. "It's different circumstances when you're investigating a past investigation as opposed to a current investigation."

"I'm okay with the professional courtesy of sharing information among professionals, but the results of the search and the names of past patients are something that you would be better off going through the proper channels on."

"In the meantime, I am here on official police business. I am formally charging Mary Power with sexual assault on a minor in her care."

"You're going to have a hard time doing that. She's in rough shape," Dr. Gillespie confided.

"Really? She was fine when I left here yesterday. What happened?"

"I don't know. Last night she took a violent turn for the

worse. Her body has been drained of blood." Gillespie noticed the look on Myra's face. "Why are you smirking? You never smirk."

"I assure you, Doctor, I do not smirk," Myra said. "I interviewed one of her victims last night. We had a long talk. I am sure her victim thought about the abuse all night."

"Oh my God!" Luke stood up. "You're testing Father Cooke's theory! You made a victim relive the abuse to torture her perpetrator!"

"You don't believe in God," Myra answered. "You're a man of science. So, Father Cooke's theory should be bullshit to you."

"Is that what you did?" The doctor wasn't sure what he believed anymore.

"I was investigating a historical crime. I questioned a victim about her abuse, and we talked for a long time about a lot of allegations against Ms. Power. If she took a turn for the worse while one of her victims was reliving her abuse . . ." He paused. "That's mere coincidence."

Dr. Gillespie opened the door. "We can look in on her, but if I feel she is not coherent enough to understand what you're saying, you will be escorted out." He pointed toward her room. "Do you understand?"

"I do." Sgt. Myra followed him toward Mary Power's room. Suddenly, the ICU was on full alert. Dr. Gillespie was running toward Mary Power's room, and nurses were following. "She's started again!" he heard Nurse Agatha yell.

Sgt. Myra stood outside the hospital room and watched through the viewing window as a full team of medical specialists frantically worked to keep Mary Power alive. Her hospital gown and blankets were covered in her blood.

"That's not her blood. It's the blood of all her victims," Myra said under his breath. He played back the recording in his head of Rosemary telling him about Suzie Rich. He imagined the small child being overpowered and beaten by this woman who had all the control. Mary Power still wore the tiny pink bow in her hair.

For a brief second, he caught Mary Power staring directly at him. He put his left hand over the sore knuckles on his right hand and cracked them, making a sound that rose above the commotion in the room. The last thing she saw was Sgt. Nicholas Myra mouthing the words, *Your ride is here.*

31

Sister Pius sat on her double bed looking around at the pale yellow walls. The nun had lived in this bedroom for the past thirty years. She looked up at the large crack that ran across the white plastered ceiling. It was there when she first moved in. The room was only painted once to her recollection. The walls were bare except for a gold-coloured crucifix that hung above the head of her bed and a calendar pinned to the wall over a small brown desk. She took her vow of poverty to heart.

She had very little to pack. Her navy blue tunics, white blouses, and veils were neatly folded at the foot of her bed. Sister Pius suspected they would be recycled and given to whoever needed them. She had a small brown worn leather suitcase with two brass locks on the front, which she had last used when moving into the room. Standing up, she lifted the case off her bed. She looked out the bedroom window for the last time, peering down into the garden at the front of the Mother House. There stood a white statue of Our Lady of Fatima surrounded by three little children. The statues were grey when she first moved in. A couple of years ago, the groundskeeper had painted them white to give them new life. She decided, like Our Lady of Fatima, she too needed a good coat of white paint to give her new life.

The tenants who rented her mother's house had moved out. Her paperwork was filed with the church, and soon she would no longer be a nun. With the help of some of the Sisters, she was able to modestly furnish the house and turn it into a comfortable home for herself. She was looking forward to her first night in her own home. The home she had grown up in, and now the home that she would most likely die in.

Sister Pius knew before she went home there was one stop she had to make. She picked up the plastic bag containing the flower arrangement she had bought earlier in the week and drove to the graveyard.

Holy Sepulchre Cemetery is in Mount Pearl, the adjacent city west of St. John's. The cemetery is a sacred place to a lot of people, and at Holy Sepulchre, great care goes into the maintenance of the resting places for the faithful departed.

Father Charles Horan's grave was in a plot reserved for Catholic priests. At first she thought there would be some pushback on burying him there. She remembered a time when a person who died by suicide would be denied funeral rites and even access for burial in a church cemetery. Many Catholics believed suicide victims were destined to go to hell, but she knew Charlie had already been to hell. No one in the Church so much as batted an eye when she planned his funeral. She, much like the other nuns and priests, no longer worried about the stigma of granting a funeral to a victim of suicide. As she put it to the archbishop, "They all knew Charlie was still subject to God's love and mercy and therefore entitled to a proper funeral."

She parked her car and walked the short trail to Charles's gravesite. The earth was still brown below his headstone. She took the flower arrangement and carefully put it in front of the stone. Sister Pius sat down on the dirt and begin to cry.

"I'm so sorry your life turned out like this," she sobbed. "I'm so sorry I could not stop this. I'm sorry you thought this was your only way out." The sorrow overtook her tiny frame, and her body shook. The sun shone in the sky, but an airy chill ran through her body.

* * * * *

Kathie Fagan had big dreams for her future. She wanted to be a teacher, to get married, and have children. At sixteen she already had her first boyfriend, whom she was sure she would marry. Six months into the "carefully monitored" relationship, Kathie had missed her period. Then the next month she missed another one. Before she knew it, her little belly was beginning to swell. She confided in her mother, who knew exactly what to do.

She told her friends she was gaining weight due to poor eating habits. When she reached her seventh month of pregnancy, Kathie was sent to live with her mother's friend, a spinster who lived in central Newfoundland. It was June, and her school year had finished. In August, she quietly gave birth to a beautiful, healthy baby boy. He was taken from the delivery room and given to a good Catholic couple who would raise him as their own. Kathie was sent back to St. John's. No one would know the difference. She never saw his face. She returned to school. It was never spoken of again.

For years she wondered what he looked like. On his birthday she would spend the day in bed, crying. She gave up her dream of getting married and having children. Instead, she felt a calling to do God's work. In her heart she felt she should be punished for her sins. What she didn't know was the spinster had kept the baby and raise him until she died. The boy, who was then twelve years old, was placed in an orphanage in St. John's to ensure his good Catholic education.

When Kathie first saw him, she recognized his face. There was no mistaking his deep blue eyes. They were the same colour as her own. In the beginning, she thought it was her imagination. She had often seen her son's face in every child she taught. Then one day she watched him walk down the corridor of the school. It was like seeing the ghost of her father. He walked with the same gait. He had a sadness about him. She thought it had come from being given away at birth. Kathie longed to tell him how much she loved him and how she would regret that decision for the rest of her life.

But she had never planned to tell him. She never thought she could be part of his life. Then, through what she thought was divine intervention, the moment had presented itself. She would leave the convent and move into the house her mother had left her. She would finally take her baby home and put him in his bed.

* * * * *

Sister Pius stood up, wiped the dirt off her pants, and dried her tears. She began the walk back to her car. At the bottom of the short hill next to Charles's grave, she stopped and looked back. The sun was shining brightly on her flower arrangement.

The plastic blue flowers spelled one word: SON.

32

Sgt. Nicholas Myra sat in the ICU quiet room contemplating the past few days. It had been an hour since Mary Power passed away. Her file was now closed. Rosemary Penashue would never get to look into the eyes of her molester and see justice. He wondered if Power's death would still give her closure. He had called the penitentiary in Goose Bay and spoken with her for about twenty minutes. Rosemary was glad she didn't have to testify, but she was quiet. There was no screaming or crying. She stayed very calm. Myra figured she was in shock. When he finished talking to her, he called the warden and requested Rosemary see her counsellor immediately.

"Penny for your thoughts." Myra snapped to and looked up see Agatha Catania standing in the doorway.

"You look more tired than I do," he said with a grin.

"Is that a smile? I thought I saw a smile there!" she teased.

"How are you feeling?" His voice had a genuine sincerity in it. "These deaths are traumatizing. I know what you're feeling. I have PTSD, and I'm here if you need someone to talk to." It was the first time he had openly admitted to having post-traumatic stress to anyone other than his psychologist.

Agatha felt a lump in her throat, and tears filled her eyes. She wiped them away. "No one understands what this is like. You know, my sister says, 'Time to put on your big-girl pants and put the past behind you'. She is a computer programmer!" She laughed through her tears. "She doesn't understand that my past is my every day. The trauma never ends. The death never ends."

Her tears disarmed Myra, and he didn't know what to do. Seeing someone else's weakness reminded him of his own. "I understand what you're going through."

"I know you do." She smiled. "I need a coffee to snap me back to life. Would you like one?"

"I would love a coffee. Just black, please." Myra always did his best to reach out to others when he recognized symptoms of PTSD, but he always maintained a safe distance so he didn't trigger his own stressors.

Agatha returned with a coffee in each hand, followed by Dr. Gillespie, who was carrying his hot tea. She sat next to Sgt. Myra. Even in this traumatic state, she still marvelled at his good looks. His eyes were kind but sad. He had a persona that made her want to cuddle into his chest and encourage him to let his guard down. She didn't know how to get through to him.

Luke was spent. Every patient he had in ICU, except for Kevin Macy, had died. He took each death personally. The three of them talked for a long time about their workplace stress and how trauma had become their norm. They took turns giving examples of trauma from their past.

"This job is not for everyone," Nick confessed. "People often think they could be a cop or a nurse. Little do they know the pressure and stress that our jobs entail."

Luke nodded in agreement. "You're preaching to the choir, brother." He threw his paper cup in the garbage bucket and sighed heavily. "We have one last PPXI patient left in ICU. That's the psychiatrist. Macy. Anyone else coming in with those symptoms will be put in the new isolation ward."

"I'm not calling it that," Myra muttered.

Luke shrugged. "We can't call it Wormwood anymore. The medical community worldwide is to start referring to it by its medical name."

"Really? I am still calling it Wormwood," Myra hissed. "So, only the psychiatrist is in your care? Has he been bleeding lately?"

"No, not at all," Agatha informed him. "We are only monitoring him. It looks like he'll be going home soon." She would be happy to see him leave. She'd had enough of this disease. "Strangest fellow, though."

"Why is that?" Myra asked.

"He shaves his whole body!" She laughed. "Every day, he gets in the shower and shaves. Not just his head and face, either. He shaves his legs, his privates, under his arms. Everywhere." She found it creepy when she had to take his vitals. "I've never seen a man do that."

"That is strange." Sgt. Myra made a mental note to let his profiler know this information to see what he would make of it.

"Well, this guy blows Father Cooke's theory out of the water," Luke added.

"How's that?" Myra was intrigued.

"Macy has no victims except for a rubber doll who can't think about abuse. Father Cooke says PPXI patients display the symptoms when their victims relive the abuse. So, Macy proves his theory wrong."

Sgt. Myra didn't believe in Father Cooke's theory any more than Luke did, but he liked how it sent a ripple of fear through the pedophile community. "Maybe I just haven't found his victims yet."

"Either way, I hope to release him today or tomorrow. He is out of the woods, as far as I am concerned." Dr. Gillespie was happy to see him go, too.

"Not as far as I am concerned," Sgt. Myra reminded him. "He still has to face charges on child pornography. Luke, can I have a word?" He pointed toward the door. "It's a personal matter," he said as he looked at Agatha.

The two men found a private corner a few feet away. "I called a friend in the RCMP in Nova Scotia who did a search for me, and sure enough, Minister McKenzie did have a complaint against him, but it was withdrawn after the victim recanted."

"What happened after that?" Luke's gut told him how that story ended.

"Nothing. No victim, no crime." But Myra knew there was more to it. "My friend also told me there were rumours, nothing that could be confirmed. But without a complaint, he can't investigate."

Luke headed back to the ICU, and Sgt. Myra went back to see Agatha. As he walked back into the room, she stood up and walked toward the door. "Well, it's been nice talking to you. Some of us have to work for a living."

"Remember, any time you need to talk, call my cell. I never sleep." Myra wished he could get his own PTSD symptoms under control.

For a second, she thought he had let his guard down, but he turned and left the ward.

A million thoughts swirled around in his brain as Sgt. Myra waited for the elevator door to open. Only the psychiatrist was left from the original four, but he still couldn't find any real victims. His team was granted a warrant that allowed them to contact his patients, and he personally went to visit the ones he thought had potential to be victims. He was clean. Other than the child pornography on his computer and the sex doll, they had nothing on him.

The elevator door opened as Agatha's information kept running through his mind. *He shaves his whole body. Why would he shave his whole body every day?* Myra knew there was something to that piece of information.

Then it hit him.

"No victims have come forward," he concluded, "because they don't know he is the perpetrator!"

He hit the elevator button for the main floor, hoping there would be no stops in between. He had to get back to the office as soon as possible.

Why hadn't he seen it before? "Macy shaves his whole body, so he doesn't leave DNA at a scene." He ran to his car and called his office. A detective answered the call.

"We need a warrant for Kevin Macy's car!" Sgt. Myra yelled in to the phone.

"Why?" asked the confused detective. "What are we looking for?"

"A rape kit," Sgt. Myra answered.

33

The heat inside the television studio was stifling. The bright lights were blinding him and creating big white spots every time he blinked. After his news conference on the steps of the Basilica of St. John the Baptist, Father Peter Cooke had done a few stand-up interviews with the local media, and then the church put a halt to it. That was until he met with the new archbishop, who had unveiled Rome's plan for him.

Over the past week he was quickly educated on the church's new strategy. It was a two-part plan: to bring people back to the church and keep them there; and use social and traditional media to their advantage.

Ever since he announced God had created a disease that killed pedophiles, churches throughout the world were filled during worship times and bustling with people during regular hours. The collection plates were overflowing. It was like manna from heaven. There had even been reports of statues of the Virgin Mary crying in a European country and a statue of Jesus blinking in New York. Miracles, it seemed, were everywhere, and Father Cooke had become the ringmaster to the whole circus.

This was his first national interview, and it was nerve-wracking. He had spoken to the producer a week ago, who was doing the initial background research. She warned him the deadline was extremely tight. The interview would be only a couple minutes long. Then it would be edited to include some visually compelling footage from his original news conference and footage from stories about churches around the country. The whole thing would air that night during the evening newscast.

Father Cooke came prepared with his key messages passed down from Rome's public affairs agency like the Ten Commandments:

1. The Roman Catholic Church is a welcoming, inclusive, open, and family-oriented church that is sorry for the abuses of the past.
2. The church is a place where people who are hurting and struggling can find meaning in their lives.
3. The church is a safe place to seek answers to complex questions about religion, life, and personal identity.

He sat down with his assistant before the interview and rehearsed his answers to the anticipated questions. Father Cooke thought the interview would be positive, because he truly believed God had come back to earth and washed it in the blood of the lamb, but he knew there would be some difficult questions about the Church's lack of support for abuse victims. He knew he would have the home team advantage when it came to research on the Church. Father Cooke had been a priest for a long time, and he had an honours degree in theology. A reporter given a Google search paragraph on the Catholic Church was not going to stump him.

He took great care with his appearance, and he'd had a haircut that morning. Father Cooke had even splurged on a professional shave from his new hairstylist. He wore his white Roman collar with a freshly pressed black shirt and pants, and he'd sat down the night before and polished his shoes for a full hour. To get into the mindset of the image he wanted, he even watched the old black-and-white classic *The Bells of St. Mary's* so he could imitate the Bing Crosby–Father Chuck O'Malley style. He did voice exercises while getting dressed to ensure he wouldn't sound monotonous. The priest was glad the interview would be done sitting down. He told himself to focus on his key messages and remember not to swivel in the chair, as the public affairs person at the Vatican had told him.

Father Cooke tried to keep his thoughts together and his mind calm as producers and studio people pinned a small microphone to his lapel. They had two chairs set up directly across from one another, and he was told there would be a camera over each of their shoulders to tape them separately. He was warned to look directly at the reporter and never to look at the camera. He'd just finished his mic check when the reporter came in and sat in the other chair. She was a young woman, probably in her late twenties. She had short brown hair that stylishly framed her beautiful face, and she wore a smart navy blue pantsuit. He wondered if she was Catholic.

The young woman immediately reached out her hand to him as she sat. "So nice to meet the real Jesus Christ Superstar!"

Father Cooke blushed. "Oh . . . no," he stuttered. "Just a poor, simple priest trying to do God's work." He was trying to focus on his breathing and get back his Father O'Malley persona.

As the producer clipped the mic to her lapel, a makeup person dabbed powder on her face. She kept smiling, singing the lyrics to the rock opera *Jesus Christ Superstar* to herself.

"Okay, we are going live in sixty seconds," the producer informed them.

"Live? You mean you're taping this to edit for the news? Is that what you mean by live?" Father Cooke felt a flash of panic.

"Sorry, didn't they tell you?" the interviewer asked him, pushing the makeup person aside. "We decided to go live on the national feed, then I suppose they will edit it for tonight's news." She took out a small mirror and checked her hair and makeup. "Did you want a touch of powder? It takes a way the glare of the lights on your face."

"No, no, no." His forehead was already shiny from the beads of sweat coming down from his hairline.

"No powder?" She looked at him.

"No, I don't want to go live." He tried to stand up, but the wire from the mic pulled at his collar. "Your producer said this was taped."

She reached over and tapped his knee. "Don't worry. It's the same story. You know your stuff. Just take a deep breath and relax."

"I don't know if I want to do this." He suddenly felt like he was going to pass out.

"Well, we are going live in fifteen seconds, so your choice is a shot of you walking off set or a shot of you sitting down talking with me." She smiled sweetly at him. "What's it going to be?"

Just then he could hear the producer saying, "In three . . . two . . ."

The reporter looked directly into the camera over Father Cooke's shoulder. "Today I am speaking with Father Peter Cooke, parish priest at the Basilica of St. John the Baptist and the priest at the centre of the Wormwood storm. Father Cooke held a news conference a few days ago announcing that God was unleashing His plague upon the world and going after pedophiles." She then turned her eyes toward Father Cooke. "Father Cooke, it's a pleasure to speak to you."

He could feel his whole body shaking, and he stared directly into the camera lens, only managing to let out an awkward smile and a "thank you." A producer standing just off camera waved his arm, motioning him to look at the reporter, and he jolted his eyes back toward her.

"Thank you," he repeated. "It's a pleasure to be here," he lied.

To his surprise, the reporter went for the jugular. "So, God is killing pedophiles. Can you explain that?"

"Well," he began, "I believe Wormwood was created by God as a punishment for people who sexually abuse children."

"You believe," she shot back. "Is it that *you* believe or the *Church* believes? Which one is it?" Her eyes had daggers in them.

"Well, we both believe," he stammered. "I mean to say that everyone in the Church community thought that Wormwood was a natural disaster that would devastate the earth and kill millions. But now we believe it is a disease. A disease that affects only pedophiles!"

"So, the Church hierarchy is changing the belief they had for thousands of years because of a few bloody noses in Newfoundland?" She showed no sign of stopping, and Father Cooke began to wonder how long this minutes-long interview was really going to last.

"That's not true," he said, leaving his Father O'Malley image back at the beginning of the interview. "I have documented dozens of cases here, and they have also been documented around the world."

"Is this a miracle?" She sat back in her chair, looking smug.

"What?" He was lost.

"Father, I am asking you if this is a miracle. You know, like from God. There have been lots of reports of miracles throughout your religion. Burning bushes and such. So, I am asking you if this is a miracle."

The reporter knew he was flustered and kind of felt sorry for him. She almost regretted not letting the producer call this morning to tell him the interview would now be live. This interview would be a defining moment in both of their careers.

"I guess you can call it that." Then he remembered his three talking points. "The Roman Catholic Church is a welcoming, inclusive, open, and family-oriented church that is sorry for the abuses of the past." He almost shouted it at her.

"Really?" She smirked. "When will women be able to say Mass? Why is it the Roman Catholic Church puts such importance on the Virgin Mary, yet you give no importance to women in your ranks?"

"That's not true . . ." He looked like a deer in the headlights. "Women play a very important and active role in the church. It has to do with sacred tradition and has nothing to do with the subject of this interview."

"If you are sorry for the abuses of the past, why is the Church still protecting pedophile priests?"

"We believe that even those who are guilty of heinous crimes are entitled to our mercy. I understand that victims may find this hard to believe, but we have zero tolerance on abusive priests." His mouth was extremely dry, and he was now infuriated.

"Doesn't your Pope sentence pedophile priests to penalties like a lifetime of penance and prayer? That's a far cry from bleeding to death, don't you think?"

When will this end? he thought to himself. "Priests who are pedophiles also get Wormwood and die an agonizing death."

"Which priests?" She smelled blood in the water. "Are you talking about Archbishop Keating? Are you confirming that he was a pedophile?"

Father Cooke froze in the chair and couldn't get enough air into his lungs to form a word. He sounded like he had just run a ten-mile race. "I am not confirming anything!"

"But you're not denying it, either. Are you?" She wasn't letting go.

"How did this happen? I came here to talk about how the Church is a place where people who are hurting and struggling can find meaning in their lives."

"How about a place where people can find justice for pedophile priests ruining their lives?" The producer was giving her the "finish up" sign, but the young reporter kept going.

"We invite people, all people, to come to the church," Father Cooke said. "To seek answers to complex questions about religion, life, and personal identity." He was losing this fight, and he knew it.

"All people except for women who want to say Mass, gays and lesbians who want to marry, and victims of pedophile priests who want justice." The producer now gave her the throat-slash cue to stop.

He was confused and couldn't get his thoughts in order. "Jesus tells us He forgives the wrongs we have done, as we forgive the wrongs that others have done to us."

"Father Peter Cooke. The Roman Catholic rock-star priest. Thank you for joining me."

The lights came up, and Father Cooke sank down in the chair. The producer unhooked the mic from his lapel, and the reporter stood up to check her face in the mirror.

"Did you get my facial expressions, or should I do them again?" she asked the producer.

"Yes, we got it all. Our switchboard is already lit up."

"Goody." The young woman was thrilled. She looked at her guest, who was still sitting in his chair in disbelief. "Thanks for coming in." She walked off the staging area and disappeared down a hallway.

Father Cooke stood up, still confused. The producer was showing him to the exit. "Your reporter was confusing the teachings of Jesus in the Bible with the musical by Andrew Lloyd Webber. They're not the same thing." He was now standing on the front step of the TV studio. "Can we redo that? I need to clarify that for her."

"I'm sorry, Father. She is on to her next story, and the interview has already aired." She didn't make eye contact with him as she closed the door.

A deflated Father Cooke staggered toward his car, asking himself what had just happened.

A line sung by Pontius Pilate in *Jesus Christ Superstar* kept running through his mind, something about a misguided martyr.

34

Sgt. Myra had to work fast to get another warrant to search Kevin Macy's vehicle. He decided to fill out the form himself. The sergeant knew the judge would consider his long history and excellent reputation as an investigator when he assessed whether Myra's subjective belief was objectively reasonable.

He needed the search warrant to legally enter Macy's vehicle and seize any specified evidence that would be relevant and material to a sex offence. Myra knew that Macy would never give him consent to search the car, and if he was being released from the hospital, he would have an opportunity to dispose of any evidence that could incriminate him.

Myra was very specific and assured the judge that he required the warrant to "locate, examine, and preserve all the evidence relevant to a suspected sex crime." Considering the charges that Macy already faced, Myra knew he had reasonable and probable grounds to believe that other offences had been committed. He needed to find evidence that would prove Macy had human victims, too.

It took two hours for Sgt. Myra to be granted the search warrant, and forty-five minutes later he and two detectives were in Kevin Macy's driveway. He looked at the detective with the lock kit. "Pop the trunk, then the doors," he ordered. Each put on their rubber gloves. One detective searched the front of the car, while the other searched the back seat. Myra searched the trunk.

Macy's BMW was meticulously kept. Not so much as loose change in the cupholder. His trunk was equally as empty. The car looked like it had just come out of the showroom even though it was two years old. Myra lifted the trunk floor covering the spare tire. It was in showroom condition. Then he saw it. The corner of a shiny black box sticking out from underneath the spare tire. He lifted the tire out of the car and grinned. He'd hit the jackpot. Hidden behind was a box of condoms, a roll of duct tape, black leather gloves, and a black balaclava. What police officers refer to as a rape kit.

He carefully lifted out each item and placed it in a clear plastic evidence bag. Labelling each one. By the time they were bagged, the tow truck was on site and ready to take the car into evidence, where it would be dusted for prints, hair samples, bodily fluid, or anything else that could be used as evidence against Macy. Now all Sgt. Myra had to do was wait.

* * * * *

Two days later, Sgt. Myra sat in Chief DeSilva's office in a very foul mood.

"Do you know why no one wants to be your partner?" the chief asked, not waiting for an answer. "You're broody!"

"That's not even a word," Myra groaned.

"It means you're brooding and moody," said DeSilva. He threw his hands up in the air. "All the time!"

"That's not true. I am pleasant sometimes." Myra was trying to recall when.

"Name one time," the chief snapped. "Just one, over the last, say, twenty years?"

"I'm pissed off!" Myra interrupted. "I'm more than pissed off. I'm sick of it."

"Sick of what?" The chief's voice softened. "The job?"

"The job! People! The weather! You name it. I am just sick of it." Myra knew he had passed burnt out months ago.

"You need some time off, Nick?" Chief DeSilva was concerned. Nick Myra was one of his best friends as well as one of his best cops.

"I thought I had him." Myra stood up and faced the big window looking toward St. John's harbour. "I can't believe they found nothing."

"Nick, you know as well as I do that this was a fishing expedition. The car was clean. I even ordered them to go through it again. There are no victims, and there's no DNA besides Macy's on the items you seized." DeSilva felt for Sgt. Myra. He knew he took the losses too personally.

"He left the hospital this morning," Myra informed him.

"You didn't confront him, did you?" The chief was hoping he hadn't done something stupid.

"No, you know I didn't. I stayed in my car and watched him from a safe distance."

"Jesus, Nick." The chief jumped up. "We have him on other charges. A careless move like that could get them thrown out. He didn't see you, did he?"

"No. He was grinning ear to ear getting into a taxi. He knew I was going to search that car. He knew what I would find." Sgt. Myra felt defeated. "He set me up."

The chief tried to reassure him. "Maybe you're reading too much into this. For God's sake, Nick, I have duct tape in my car! What guy doesn't? It doesn't mean I am a predator!"

Nick smirked. "Do you also have condoms and a balaclava in your trunk?"

"I use a balaclava when I'm on my Ski-doo. It doesn't make me a criminal!" The chief knew he was grasping at straws now to make Nick feel better.

"You know he shaves his body hair and uses condoms so he doesn't leave DNA. You know he covers his face and hands so he can't be identified." Nick was pissed that he had been outsmarted.

"Yet we do not have one sexual assault complaint with that MO in the whole province. Not one!" the chief emphasized. "Let this one go. It will eat at your gut. Maybe you should take a couple of weeks off after the award ceremony. Maybe it's time to leave the unit." He knew Myra wouldn't take this well. "You know, I could use someone with your credentials up here to keep me out of trouble."

"You want me to come here and read your files for you?" Disgust was written all over Myra's face. "You think I'm ready to come to the third floor and say, 'Yes, sir, no, sir,' all day?"

"It's not a demotion. I'm giving you the Chief's Commendation. It's the highest honour." Chief DeSilva knew he wasn't buying it. "You'll be my right-hand man."

"I'll be your lackey. No thanks." Nick was having none of this.

DeSilva puffed out his chest. "It's an honour to work directly for the chief!"

"It's where you put those who have been promoted beyond their level of competence. You and I both agreed on that many years ago."

"I know you don't see it this way, but I am offering you an amazing opportunity." Chief DeSilva became very serious. "I'm not planning on spending more than another year or two in this chair. With your education and policing track record, you could easily become a front-runner for the top job."

Nick looked at his friend. "I never aspired to be chief."

"That's the best kind of chief. You know that." DeSilva sat behind the desk and pulled his chair in. A sign that it was time for his visitors to leave.

"I'm not a politician, Chief. If I can't do the job, I will leave on my own terms." Myra took the hint and opened the chief's door.

"Nick, you did great work here. I will see you at the award ceremony tomorrow. Think about my offer."

Sgt. Nicholas Myra left the chief's office with a heavy heart. He knew as soon as he left the room the chief would be on the phone to Health Services asking them to "drop by" and do a mental health assessment without letting on what they were doing.

He was having a hard time controlling the night terrors lately, and it showed on his face. He knew he was taking his files way too personally. Watching Kevin Macy walk out of the hospital earlier that day was like a kick in the guts to him. Myra knew his anger was becoming harder to control, and he wondered if the chief knew that he had punched the door at the corrections centre. He thought about calling Agatha Catania and asking her out for coffee just to talk to someone, then decided against it when he realized she may not like this side of him.

Sgt. Myra didn't know how to get close to anyone anymore. He thought about calling his psychologist, but she would only tell him what he already knew: he was suffering from severe PTSD symptoms. He was struggling every day. He couldn't live with the job, but he couldn't live without it. It was a struggle to get out of bed each morning and go to work.

I will leave on my own terms, he thought to himself. He just didn't know what those terms were yet.

35

The kitchen was quaint and lovely. The tea pot and cups were antique and lovely. Even the date crumbles and homemade chocolate chip cookies on the plate were sweet and lovely. Father Cooke thought everything in Sister Pius's house was just lovely.

She poured the tea and sat at the table next to him. "Sister, I didn't know where else to go." His big hands were still shaking.

"It's Kathie," she reminded him, and he looked at her like he didn't know what she was saying. "My name is Kathie." She sipped her hot tea. "That's my real name, and it's what I go by now, not Sister Pius."

"Of course. I'm sorry. I'm just not thinking. He didn't realize that he had put on his fisherman's cap backwards until he arrived at her house and took it off.

"Are you cold?" Kathie was concerned about him. She had watched the interview but wasn't going to bring it up until he did.

"No. I am fine. It's nerves." He used two hands to steady his cup. "The house looks great. It feels like a home." He looked around the kitchen. "A really good home."

She looked around, taking note of all the renovations she wanted to make. "I need to update the cupboards. They were built with the house over a hundred years ago. I'm scared to death when I think about what I am going to find behind those old plaster walls," she laughed. "Could be hundred-year-old copper pipes or the corpse of an old pirate. I think I would prefer the pirate." They both gave a small chuckle, knowing they were just stalling before the real conversation took place.

"Did you watch my interview?" Father Cooke laid the porcelain cup on the table.

"Yes, I did." She felt so sorry for him.

"What did you think?" He valued her opinion on everything.

"You were ambushed. Simply put. Ambushed. That reporter was trying to make a name for herself at your expense." She was angry that someone would treat such a kind, decent man that way.

"I was inexperienced. I should have been more prepared." His hands began to shake again.

"There's no one more knowledgeable on Wormwood, or the church, or even God, for that matter, than you. She took advantage of your kind heart." Kathie was disgusted with the way the reporter had spoken down to him.

"I watched *The Bells of St. Mary's* last night. I thought I could be Father O'Malley, saving the church while singing a fine tune." He still had a boyish charm about him.

"Does that make me Sister Mary Benedict? I always thought I looked like Ingrid Bergman," she said, touching a hand to her cheek and striking a movie-star pose.

Father Cooke joined his hands together on the table as if in prayer. "I didn't see it coming. I'm afraid to go back to the rectory. There will be quite a few people waiting to make fun of me." He was embarrassed and sad.

"Then make fun of them back," she scoffed. "Ask them what they have done throughout their careers that gave people back their hope, their dignity . . . their church?"

"I didn't think this through. I didn't see beyond the news conference. I know that's hard to believe, but I honestly thought I would bring this disease to light, tell people God was not only listening but responding to their prayers, and they would come back to the church and we would start over." He sighed. "That would be the end of it."

"I believe you, Peter. I know you don't have a bad bone in your body." She was sincere and had always had a soft spot for him. "You walked into a hornet's nest, and you got stung."

They both sipped their tea, deep in thought.

"So, what's your next move?" She poured him another cup.

"Some remote cove in Labrador after the Holy Father sees that interview." His future seemed more uncertain now than ever.

She laid down her cup. "Peter, that's not what I meant. What is *your* next move. You have to do something to fix this mess."

"Like what? I'm a laughingstock now."

"You're an excellent priest, probably the best I have ever known. You believed when you held that news conference that God had a plan for you, right?"

He nodded.

"Do you think God has changed His mind? Do you think He has given up on you?"

"Then maybe God should have sent me on a media course before He put me in front of a live camera."

"Well, that's where you start." Kathie stood up and took a notepad and pen out of a drawer. "Let's make your list of demands."

"Am I the hostage, or are they?" She was beginning to see a glimpse of her old friend in his eyes.

"Right now, you're both. You need to go back to the rectory with a list of things you need to do your job. If you want to solve a problem, you must find a solution you can live with, otherwise they will give you a solution that you can't live with." She knew the archbishop's staff would be scrambling just as Father Peter was. "Well, first they need to send you away for media training. And not some one-day course. It should be one that is in-depth and deals with issues specific to the church."

Father Cooke wrote down every word.

"Then you need a communications assistant who will help you. One that will work with reporters and build a relationship. They should go to all interviews with you to keep you on track and take notes."

"Are you interested in the job?" he asked seriously.

"Maybe. I do have an honours degree in English and a master's in communications."

"Are you kidding me?"

"I'm a teacher. I did go to university to learn to teach," she scoffed. "When I was finished my degree, I realized how much

I liked learning, so I kept going. Doing courses here and there. Pretty soon I had my master's."

He shook his head. "You never cease to amaze me."

"I will help you put together a proper communications strategy, and you go back to present it to the archbishop."

"I answer to Rome now, not the archbishop, and that's what I'm afraid of." He felt like a fool. "They must think I'm a buffoon! Just some local hack who bit off more than he could chew."

"Rome has made their own mistakes, don't worry. Let's go with a 'those without sin throw the first stone' on that one," she teased. "Peter, before we spend the next two hours writing this up, tell me up front—what do you want?"

"I want this to go away. I want to do it over and be more prepared." The anger was evident in his eyes.

"You can't make it go away. You'll just have to roll with this one. Promise yourself that you'll be more prepared next time." Kathie put her cup down and asked again, "In the beginning, what did you want?"

"I wanted the Church to say they were sorry for the hurt they caused. I wanted them to expel pedophile priests. I wanted people to come back to the Church and let God in their lives again." Tears were stinging the corners of his eyes. "I never wanted fame or to be a celebrity. I wanted to have a full Church on a Sunday morning."

She pitied him. She knew he was telling the truth. They rolled up their sleeves, and a few hours later he had a communications strategy and an action plan he could live with. He hated to leave Kathie's kitchen. He felt safe there. But he knew he had to face the music. He put on his coat and hugged her goodbye.

"Hey, Father O'Malley!" She tossed his hat at him. "Don't forget your cap."

* * * * *

Father Cooke felt much better going into the archbishop's office with a plan. The look on the archbishop's face told him he was still angry and not in a very forgiving mood.

"What happened? Were you daydreaming? Did you have a stroke?"

Father Cooke sat back and waited for the tirade to end.

"I'm hoping it was a stroke. We could all just pray for you and find you a nice little convalescent home where you can live out your years." The archbishop was grinding his teeth at this point. "Because I have to come up with a good reason why you lost your bloody mind on national television!"

"I was ambushed," Father Cooke tried to explain. "I was told it would be pre-taped and edited for a later newscast. Things were changed at the last minute. I was given a choice of walking off and the camera following me, or staying and doing an interview. So, I stayed. Then she kept changing the subject and I got off course. I will do better next time, I promise."

"You think there's a next time? Why did you have to start this in the first place?" The archbishop was so angry and frustrated he couldn't contain it.

Father Cooke very calmly began. "I started this because I was sick of getting up Sunday morning to preach to less than a dozen people. I was tired of children crossing the streets rather than walk next to me because they have been warned to 'stay away from priests.'" An internal anger rose in his heart, and it hurt. “I started this because I wanted to be a priest, and I still do. I still believe in this Church.” He leaned forward and pointed his finger at the archbishop. “Isn’t that what you want? Don’t we want the same thing?”

The archbishop sat back, joining his fingers over his belly. After a few seconds he said, “Peter we have something in common.”

“We do?”

“We both started at the same place. We both started as young men in seminary school with dreams of serving God in whatever capacity He asked. We both walked away from having a wife and a family so we could serve the Lord. We both know how lonely that can be.” He rubbed his temples with his fingers to try and push away the pain. “Peter, we both want the same thing. Don’t look at me like I am the enemy.”

Father Cooke bowed his head and thought for a few minutes. He reached into his coat pocket and pulled out the communications strategy and action plan that Sister Pius, or Kathie, had helped him write. “Read this, please.”

The archbishop picked it up and started speed-reading through the material. A trick he had mastered in university. It seemed like an eternity before he laid it back on his desk and looked at Father Cooke.

“This is brilliant!” he shouted. “This is what you should have done from the beginning. You needed a plan.”

Father Cooke was happy he had stopped by to see Kathie before the archbishop. The other way around could have proved detrimental to his career.

“Let me make some calls. The first thing we need to do is get you on a plane to the Vatican, where you can work with their public affairs department and get you the training and experience you need."

"Won't that take months?"

"I don't care how long it takes. If we are going to do this, we're going to do it right. This debacle . . ." He pointed toward the TV. ". . . will never happen again."

Father Cooke felt a whole lot better coming out of the archbishop's office than he had going in. As he passed lay staff and other priests in the halls on the way back to his room, he received only words of encouragement and praise.

He realized that if he wanted to get his point across, he needed to turn to a higher power—the Vatican spin doctors. The next morning, he was packed and on an early-morning flight to Rome, where he would learn to tell an old story a new way.

36

Sgt. Nicholas Myra was meticulous.

The cup on his desk held seven sharpened HB wooden pencils and seven uni-ball, fine black ink pens, caps down. The blinds on his office window were twenty-one inches from the ledge. Not approximately twenty-one inches—they were twenty-one inches.

When his mind was stressed, he counted in sevens or derivatives of seven. He took seven steps, or fourteen, or twenty-one, or twenty-eight. Never eight, twenty, or thirty. If there were only four windows in a house, he had to count three windows in the next house to keep his mind steady.

For the past two years he had been seeing a psychologist every two weeks. It wasn't easy to get him there. A few months ago, his mother mentioned he was keeping to himself too much. Shortly after, his father offered to have a chat when he was ready. Friends would run into him and ask where he'd been.

Two years ago, after a debriefing that involved a particularly brutal investigation into the sexual assault on a three-month-old boy, the force's health services coordinator made it mandatory that every police officer involved in that file was required to attend a psychological debriefing before returning to duty.

Myra had no intention of talking to the psychologist; he was going only to get his clearance and get back to work. There were so many files waiting for him. Every day there would be a new one. Another complaint. Another victim. One day he was standing in the break room talking to the police services dog trainer, who was commiserating about his never-ending stack of files. He said in the past three months alone he had been told to stand down a hundred and ten times. Myra realized that he had not been told to stand down in three years. He went from investigation to investigation.

He sat in the psychologist's office counting the books on her shelf. There were seven standing up on the shelf and seven piled up on their sides on top of each other. She had seven framed educational documents hung on her wall, and her blinds were pulled up twenty-one inches from the ledge of the window.

She was a petite woman with friendly eyes, and she greeted Sgt. Myra like she knew him. He had no intention of talking. She started talking about the weather, how the winter felt like it was ten months long. She asked if he wanted a coffee. He politely said no. She asked how long he had been on the force, and he started to cry.

At first he choked back the tears, clenching his jaw to stop the sound of pain from coming out of his mouth. The tears welled up in his eyes and spilled down his cheeks, filling the deep crevices on his face and falling from his cheeks. He couldn't stop it. He leaned forward and put his face in his hands to hide the pain, and his big body shook uncontrollably. The psychologist pulled some tissues from the box next to her chair and handed them to him without judgment. It took a good few minutes for Sgt. Myra to compose himself. He dried his face with the tissues and took a few big gulps of air.

He apologized. The psychologist said it wasn't necessary. He poured out his heart to her. Giving her details of the nightmares that felt so real he was afraid to sleep. He confessed he isolated himself because he didn't feel "normal" anymore and was unable to talk about anything other than policing. Sgt. Myra had no hobbies or interests since his divorce. He wanted to be alone, but he was afraid to be by himself.

He trusted her after that session and made appointments every two weeks. Never missing one. Over their many sessions she introduced him to coping techniques to deal with psychological stress. She introduced him to meditation and encouraged him to take up walking or running. He took her advice to heart and taught himself to meditate. He ran seven miles every day. She encouraged him to use humour and try to make light of stressful situations, as many police officers did. He could never master that one.

The one thing she could not do was stop the night terrors, the flashbacks, and the paranoia. She could not help him un-see the things that he had seen. She could not help him un-hear the sounds of children crying while being sexually tortured.

Sgt. Myra stood staring out his office window. It was evening now; the city was dark. At night, the windows at police headquarters became reflective so no one could see in. They became a mirror when you looked out if the lights were on.

Tonight, his blinds were pulled up as far as they could go. Way past twenty-one inches. He stood in front of his office window looking at himself. Earlier that afternoon he had been presented with the Chief's Commendation. The highest honour a police officer can receive. The investigation into Wormwood had been long and exhausting. There was no sick serial killer hunting down pedophiles. There were too many victims across the country and around the world to make that theory stick. No poison showed up in any blood test. The medical community still hotly debated the God theory, while the religious community promoted it every chance they could.

His dedication to the file, the numerous arrests and the hard work of his task force, had earned accolades from the public, politicians, media, and his own chief. But he only focused on the one that got away. Macy had walked.

Sgt. Myra had never really believed in God until now. He had not even thought about religion until this morning, when he had taken his dress uniform out of the storage bag and put it on. His pith helmet made him look another seven inches taller, and his parade boots were polished to perfection. He could not remember the last time he had worn his dress uniform—or his regular uniform, for that matter. Myra had been in plainclothes units for so long he forgot where he had stored them after his divorce. He was surprised it still fit. All the running his psychologist suggested had paid off.

He had been thinking about God all day. God had managed to do what he could not. God had come up with a way to stop predators from preying on children.

Sgt. Myra had decided to thank Him in person.

He took a deep, long breath in through his nose and let it out through his mouth just like his meditation had taught him. He looked at his reflection in the window. He thought about Father Charles Horan and what his last minutes must have been like.

He looked deep into his own eyes. He took his service handgun out of the holster.

A cold breeze blew through Royal Newfoundland Constabulary headquarters. Everyone working that night felt a cold shiver down their spine.

Sgt. Nicholas Myra, named after the patron saint of protecting children, made a life-altering decision.

He would leave on his own terms.

37

I never thought I would see the day when we had to create a special ward like this, Mrs. Furey thought to herself as she stood in the hallway looking around at the small PPXI isolation ward. She had been able to pull together a ten-room section on the top floor away from the other patients. It was an overflow area used when the hospital was at capacity but more recently had become a graveyard for broken beds and other equipment.

She was pleased the province had reallocated funds to help with the set-up. She would have been given a hard time by other hospital administrators if she took funds from already overburdened wards to set up what the gossips called the "Pedo Palace." It was the first time she had to hire around-the-clock security guards to stand at the doors of a unit 24/7 checking hospital workers' credentials and visitors' IDs. She realized it would be big news to the gossip circuit whenever someone entered the unit. It was also incredibly hard to staff. From the nurses to the cleaners, they all claimed, "I have children; I don't want to be near them."

Dr. Luke Gillespie and Nurse Agatha Catania were standing at the double doors to the unit getting their hospital IDs checked by a big, husky guard when Mrs. Furey spotted them. Waving them in, she yelled, "They're with me." The guard passed back their IDs and closed the doors behind them.

"I feel like I have just been granted access to some swinging nightclub," Luke joked.

"Can you believe this?" Mrs. Furey shook her head. "A ward dedicated to sick people—not to contain their disease, but rather to protect the victims from other patients, media, and prying eyes?"

"Just when you thought you'd seen it all." Agatha was looking around at the set-up of the reception area. "I guess I better get started organizing this." She had agreed to manage the unit. Luke had agreed to share his duties between the PPXI unit and the emergency ward.

There were already two patients admitted, and more were on the way. The provincial Department of Health decided that hospitals in the rural areas did not have the resources to dedicate to PPXI. All patients with those symptoms would be transferred to St. John's to the Health Sciences Centre and kept on the dedicated PPXI ward. This would ensure their safety while allowing doctors to figure out a treatment plan. Two more patients were already on the way in, one from Corner Brook and one from Gander.

Dr. Gillespie, with the help of several other infectious disease doctors, had already organized the ward into a medical experimental control group. They had put in a strict isolation policy for patients, health care workers, and visitors. There was still no way of knowing how the disease was being spread. They implemented several safety measures. Doctors originally thought it couldn't be spread by bodily fluids, but now they were not so sure. Anyone entering the ward was required to wear hospital gowns, masks, and gloves.

"What's the latest from your group?" Mrs. Furey asked Luke.

"There's no medical evidence stating PPXI is being spread through human touch of any kind. But we must be careful. Better safe than sorry." Luke walked into a vacant room and noticed the dark shades covering the windows. Pointing to them, he asked, "What's this about?"

Mrs. Furey pulled the shades all the way down, shutting out the sunlight and turning the room dark. "This is a security measure in case media or vigilante justice groups try to use a drone to take pictures of patients through the window. It was a recommendation from my national committee. Some hospitals are already having to deal with that, believe it or not."

"Really?" Luke had a feeling of dread. He knew this was going to get worse before it got better. "We know this is not a sexually transmitted disease and has no relation to hemophilia."

"So, is this God punishing pedophiles?" Agatha just wanted an answer.

"My scientific mind wants to laugh at you for asking that question," Luke continued. "But there's a nagging in the back of my brain that tells me it is possible."

"You can't be serious!" bellowed Mrs. Furey.

"My group has had in-depth discussions with some of the most brilliant medical minds in the world. This group has someone from just about every religion. Some are atheist. None of us are taking the act-of-God factor off the table."

"You know," Agatha chimed in, "last year, a huge oak tree fell across my father's car when we had that big storm. When he called his insurance company, they called it an act of God and wouldn't covered it."

"And . . ." Mrs. Furey waved her hand, encouraging her to continue.

"Insurance companies are notorious for nickel-and-diming you when you put in a claim, but even they recognize natural catastrophes as acts of God. So, if PPXI is a natural catastrophe, shouldn't the medical community recognize it as an act of God?"

"My head hurts." Mrs. Furey sat down behind the front desk. "That kind of makes sense to me."

"Just think about it," Luke explained. "Where did cancer come from? Every person on this earth has up to a hundred million cells in their body. When just one of those cells begins to grow and multiply, they can turn into cancer. Why does one person get cancer, and someone who has smoked cigarettes for fifty years doesn't? Some medical minds believe cancer is a man-made disease caused by environmental factors such as pollution and diet."

Luke paused to get his thoughts together. "Which seems credible when you track the disease from the Industrial Revolution to today. But where did it really come from? If you believe God created man, then you must also believe that God created cancer cells. Did God create cancer to deal with overpopulation? Some theorists believe that!" He looked at Agatha and Mrs. Furey. "Aren't all diseases God's way of dealing with overpopulation? Without disease, the only way a human could die is by accident, murder, or old age. How would we feed a population like that? There are already people dying of starvation in areas of the world."

"I don't believe that," stated Agatha. "I don't believe God wants anyone to suffer. As much as I want to believe He is making pedophiles suffer, I don't believe He wants little children to go through chemo. I believe in God, and I am a spiritual person. I even believe God created disease, but I can't believe he created it to make little children suffer. If you believe Wormwood is created by God to protect children, why wouldn't He create a cancer that can't kill children?" As an afterthought, she added, "Why hasn't cancer been cured yet? With all the money being raised, where is the cure?"

"Well, if people refer to PPXI as Wormwood, the disease created by God to kill pedophiles, and this unit as 'Pedo Palace,' then I don't think we will have to worry about fundraising efforts from the public," offered Mrs. Furey.

"As a doctor, I know some of the money goes into research, and the proof is in the new medications and equipment that keep people alive for longer and sometimes keeps them cancer-free for years." Luke wondered himself sometimes. "I do question the large salaries of the management of these fundraising groups and why so much of the money leaves the province instead of staying here. I don't understand why most of the money doesn't go to help families with living expenses and other financial burdens cancer brings. It's incredibly frustrating to me when I see someone fighting for their life who should be focused on healing. Instead, they're fighting with banks to stop foreclosure on their homes, losing their cars, and going to food banks because they can't work and run out of benefits."

"Sometimes I wonder," added Agatha, "what would happen if people stopped giving to cancer groups that fund research? Pharmaceutical companies make billions off cancer. Why would they release a cure? I often wonder, if a pharmaceutical company can create a drug to maintain your life throughout a disease, why can't they create a drug to cure the disease?"

"There's no money in curing diseases," huffed Mrs. Furey. "So, seriously, this doesn't leave the room. What are your personal thoughts on PPXI, or Wormwood, or whatever you want to call it?"

Agatha went first. "I want to believe that God is washing pedophiles in the blood of the lamb. I want to believe He is protecting children. But as a nurse, I don't like to see anyone suffer. If these people abused children, then I think the law should deal with them. If God created this disease, then I am going to need more proof."

Mrs. Furey stood up. "I am on the fence. I know people are saying if it's only affecting pedophiles, who cares? Let them die! But I agree, we have a justice system to deal with that. Our job is to offer the best health care possible to everyone who comes through that door. I am going to need more proof to believe God is killing pedophiles."

Luke sighed. "I am tired of watching people die. My job is to save lives and not judge. But sometimes I see little children come in, some just babies." The gall from his stomach came up in his throat as he remembered the case of the baby girl he had treated years earlier. "I don't know if God created this disease to kill pedophiles. I don't know if you get it some other way."

Luke felt his pager go off. He tilted it up toward his face. "It's emergency."

Agatha felt a sudden chill go down her spine. Luke picked up the phone to call the emergency unit.

While it rang, he finished with, "All I can say is, after watching the way the last three patients died, and the torture they went through, pedophiles had better watch their backs. Someone is coming for them."

The emergency nurse answered on the second ring. "What's up?" asked Dr. Gillespie.

"Paramedics just called in a trauma," the nurse him. "A gunshot wound."

Luke hung up the phone and looked at Agatha. "We're needed in emergency."

They ran toward the elevator. Once inside, Luke hit the button for the main floor.

"Luke," Agatha asked. "Straight up. Would you tell a pedophile that Wormwood is created by God to punish them and protect children?"

Luke thought for a moment. "My question is, are they willing to take that chance?"

The elevator door opened to a scene of chaos. Police in their dress blue uniforms were everywhere. Agatha felt her knees give out and fell back against the elevator wall.

"Please, God, no!" she cried.

acknowledgements

As a writer, I tend to work in a bubble and live in a fantasy world. Sometimes for long periods of time. It's the only way I can see a chapter through until I reach the right ending. That state of mind can only exist with the support of others.

No writer is an island.

I would like to thank the many dedicated and hard-working police officers I have had the honour of working with throughout my career in the Royal Canadian Mounted Police. My Sgt. Myra is a combination of every one of you.

Many times I have lost my Christian faith, and many times Rev. Robert Cooke and Father Mark Nichols at St. Mark's Anglican Church have found it for me. They have become friends of my family, and I love the way they teach that God loves everyone. There are no exclusions.

I spent ten years writing this book and finally had a rough draft in October 2017. I decided to take an advanced writing class with Matthew LeDrew. He helped me bring my writing and this book to a new level. His enthusiasm about writing is infectious. He brought me from a novice to a professional. I can't thank him enough for turning my spark into a flame.

My dream was to have Flanker Press publish this book. I admired the way they promoted their artists and supported the local writing community. The day Jerry Cranford called to tell me Flanker wanted to publish this book was one of the most exciting days of my life. It really was a dream come true. I am so honoured to become a member of the Flanker Press family, and I hope it is a relationship that will flourish for years. Thank you, Jerry, and everyone else at Flanker for making my dream come true.

For ten years my husband, Robert, kept saying, "You have to write that book." Every time I ran another idea for *Operation Wormwood* by him, he was extremely supportive and helpful. He believed this day would come long before I ever did. Having someone who believes in you is the most amazing gift a person can have.

I wrote this book to give some comfort to victims and to create paranoia among pedophiles. No book can erase the horrific pain of being a victim of child abuse. I only hope that each survivor can somehow heal and learn to love themselves. What happened to you is not your fault, but most importantly: I believe you.

PHOTO BY GREG LOCKE

Helen C. Escott is a retired civilian member of the world-renowned Royal Canadian Mounted Police (RCMP). She served as the senior communications strategist for Newfoundland and Labrador and was the communications lead on high-profile cases, including the RCMP's response on September 11 after terrorists attacked the World Trade Center in New York City. During her service, Escott wrote and implemented the Atlantic Region Communication Strategies to combat organized crime and outlaw biker gangs. She created the media relations course and guidebook used by the RCMP, and she taught the media relations course for senior management at the Canadian Police College in Ottawa.

Before joining the RCMP, she worked in the media for thirteen years in various capacities, including reporter, on-air personality, and marketing and promotions representative.

Helen C. Escott is the author of the widely read humour blog-turned-book *I am Funny Like That*. In her first crime novel, *Operation Wormwood*, she taps into her darker side and takes readers on a thrill ride through the historic city of St. John's.

Helen C. Escott h.escott@hotmail.com
https://www.instagram.com/helencescott
https://www.facebook.com/helen.c.escott
https://twitter.com/hescott

Visit Flanker Press at:

www.flankerpress.com

https://www.facebook.com/flankerpress

https://twitter.com/FlankerPress

http://www.youtube.com
/user/FlankerPress